ANN GRANGER

A MATTER of MURDER

HEADLINE

First published in Great Britain in 2020 by
HEADLINE PUBLISHING GROUP

1

Cataloguing in Publication Data is available from the British Library

ISBN 978 1 4722 7059 7

Typeset in Adobe Garamond by Palimpsest Book Production Limited, Falkirk, Stirlingshire

Printed and bound in Great Britain by Clays Ltd, Elcograf S.p.A.

HEADLINE PUBLISHING GROUP
An Hachette UK Company
Carmelite House
50 Victoria Embankment
London EC4Y 0DZ

www.headline.co.uk
www.hachette.co.uk

This book is for my grandson, William. Good luck in your studies, Will, and in everything you undertake in the future.

Depend upon it, Sir, when a man knows he is to be hanged in a fortnight, it concentrates his mind wonderfully.

Dr Samuel Johnson

Chapter 1

Miff Ferguson had been living rough for two years now. He had managed pretty well, in his own judgement, but still each day seemed to present another hurdle to clear in the obstacle course called survival.

Today he was contemplating the coming winter, a little way off yet, but it never hurt to plan ahead. Winter could be a real Becher's Brook of a hurdle if you were without a permanent roof over your head. It had been raining a lot recently. His small tent, just big enough to let him crawl into a sleeping bag and curl up like snail, was rainproof up to a point; but wet trickles found their way in, if the deluge was persistent. It certainly wouldn't protect him in snow and ice, should either arrive. When that happened, he'd need some form of more solid shelter. Nothing fancy, he told himself as he padded along the pavement at first light, gripping a cardboard cup of hot coffee from an early-opening garage. The staff there knew him. If the manager was around, he had to pay for his coffee. The girls never charged him. An empty warehouse, the upper floor of a vacant house, anything bricks and mortar, that's what he sought. There were several empty shop premises in the area, but they tended to be well protected by an alarm system.

Early though it was, there were already quite a few people about. Some were going to work, some returning home from night shifts. Shopkeepers, newsagents in particular, were opening up their businesses. One old dear was clearly on her way to some early church service. It was surprising how many people there were out and about as soon as it was light. The great thing about them all, as far as Miff was concerned, was that they generally ignored one another. That was why it was a good time for someone like Miff to suss out the possibilities.

If you prowled around during the hours of darkness, there was a good chance some busybody would pick up a phone and call the cops. A lot of people stayed up late in their own homes. Miff sometimes speculated on what they were doing that kept them from warm, comfortable and dry beds. They were at their computers, perhaps, playing games, watching porn, using gambling sites. Or they had been summoned by a fretful child, a hungry baby, or they couldn't get off to sleep and thought a cup of tea might help. Whatever they were doing – and frankly, Miff didn't care what it was – there was always the possibility one of them might decide to go to the window and stare down into the shadowy streets. A lone figure ambling along and studying the buildings made them nervous.

It was not that he envied the householders in any way. Miff had no desire to join them permanently in a desirable residence with double glazing, and perhaps a former garden, now concreted over to provide off-street parking. Most of all, he didn't want to be part of a fixed community. He'd tried that and had hated it. Neighbours meant other people knew more about you than they had any right to do. They marked your comings and goings. They wondered what you did for a living. They invited you to little supper parties that turned out akin to being invited to appear before the Grand Inquisition. The less they knew, the more suspicious they grew. It stoked the fire of their Great Fear: falling property prices. All of this Miff had experienced. All of it had finally become unbearable. That was when Miff decided to walk away. So far, he hadn't regretted it. Although, to be honest, last winter had been tough. This coming winter he'd make better plans.

If Miff felt kinship with any kind of living creature it was with the foxes that came out under cover of darkness to scavenge. Or with cats. Miff liked cats and felt he had a lot in common with them.

At night, cats stopped pretending to be domesticated moggies – part of an ordered world – and turned feral. They popped out through flaps kindly owners had installed in their back doors, leaving the home as well-groomed, well-fed affectionate family members. They were transformed, before they reached the nearest flower bed, into predatory hunters, small but quick and ruthless. They were alert to every tiny sound or movement, catching the most elusive of scents, and endowed with that other, nameless sense that warned of danger. Then they were off, consummate athletes, scrambling easily up a wall, fence or tree, and slithering through narrow apertures that a human male could just slip a hand through.

When any cat and Miff passed in the gloom, they ignored one another, each going about his own business. But once their wild instincts were satisfied, most cats turned back into domestic moggies and trotted off to comfortable homes to snooze the day away, unlike Miff. Yet he didn't envy them. He sometimes thought that, by accepting even a part-time domesticity, the cats had sold out.

By day, he was always cheerful and chatty with passers-by who stopped to commiserate with him on his misfortune at being homeless, occasionally to offer a little money or a sandwich, or sometimes to berate him for being work-shy.

'You try it, mate!' he would always advise these last. 'You try and survive on the streets.' Mostly they would mumble and walk off when he told them this.

The only time he'd tucked in his head and pretended to be asleep was the day he'd spotted a guy he'd been at school with, marching towards him with all the confidence of the successful. The old schoolfellow had marched on by, oblivious, and Miff had breathed a sigh of relief.

After that, he'd left London and found himself a refuge in this Cotswold town of Bamford, where surely he'd avoid meeting anyone he knew. If word got back to his former work colleagues that he was living rough, that would be bad enough. But if it made news at the next school reunion, the governors would probably erase his name from the list of alumni. His parents would be mortified, because they'd told everyone he was volunteering in a refugee camp in some unvisitable spot on the globe. They'd also taken the precaution of moving to Portugal.

In truth, he was really happiest at night. At night, there was no need for pretence. You could be yourself. He avoided drunks – always unpredictable, you never knew with them. Sometimes they were lurching homeward, reliving the evening, and more concerned with fellow revellers than with rough sleepers. Sometimes they fell out of the pub or club in a tangled mass, and immediately set about those nearest to them for reasons they wouldn't remember in the morning. Sometimes the drink released a cruel humour and a sleeping body became a target. Miff hated the drunks the most.

You saw all sorts of things at night, of course. But you kept your mouth shut. That was understood. He was on nodding terms with quite a few professional burglars. He didn't bother them and they didn't worry about him.

He had reached a neglected area of the town. Once there had been a busy estate of small manufacturing businesses here. They had long ceased to operate. While the planners argued over what to do with the site, and its deteriorating buildings, it sank slowly into dereliction. Rain entered through damaged roofs; the windows were broken and patchily boarded up. At ground level the weeds crept in, together with wildlife. There was also the human kind from time to time: those who wished to avoid authority and awkward questions; and people like Miff. Or not exactly like Miff, who did not want to share his spot with those who could be a danger, whether druggies stoned out of their skulls, or schizophrenics abandoned to non-existent 'care in the community'.

Miff was not on the streets because of drug abuse, or fleeing justice, or suffering from a mental illness. He was here because, one day, he had simply opted out, out of the rat race, of other people's expectations, of responsibilities to other entities. He hadn't suffered what doctors called a 'mental breakdown'; only a complete mental change of viewpoint. He'd simply, as he explained to himself, woken up, as from a long, disturbing dream, and set out to find an escape.

To return to present practical objectives, he had been sussing out this area for a week or more. So far, it had seemed reasonably deserted and as safe as could be expected. If a few drifters like him moved in over the coming winter, that didn't matter. There was a kind of safety in numbers, provided they stayed small. If the residents grew too many for chance visitors or passers-by to ignore, some busybody would inform the authorities, and they'd be turned out. But he had marked this place down as a distinct possibility.

Nevertheless, he discovered to his annoyance that he wasn't the first visitor that early morning. Not that the first arrival on the scene was there for the same reason as himself. No, the other visitor – whoever he was – had arrived in a clean, shiny black BMW, with new registration plates, looking as if it had just been driven away from a dealership. The sight of it in these surroundings was incongruous, its presence inexplicable.

He should, of course, have turned round and left the scene with all haste. Unfortunately, for once, he didn't trust his instincts. He stayed. Miff sometimes wondered later why he didn't just take to his heels. Human curiosity? Or because he found the car's presence somehow offensive? It had no business here: that was for sure.

The driver had parked up by an opened side door into the building. Miff knew that, normally, the door appeared to be shut fast. He also knew that the solidity of the obstacle was an illusion. The lock was broken. He hadn't broken it – someone else had done that, a little while ago. If you wanted to gain entry, you just had to put a shoulder to the door and push hard. Then it would scrape open enough to allow you to squeeze through. It didn't open all the way because there was a heap of junk stacked up behind it. But it was enough to let you in. Simple trespass, as Miff understood it from wet afternoons spent in the local library reading about such things, was a civil offence. Wonderful thing, the public library system. You could sit there with book and, with luck, no one would bother you. Trespassing was also what the driver of the BMW was doing, or so Miff deduced.

How he (the driver) knew about the door Miff couldn't say. But the unknown visitor was inside the warehouse: that much Miff was pretty sure about. But what was he doing in there? Not looking for a winter bolt-hole. Not someone driving a car like that. But why sneak around the place, taking advantage of previous vandalism to get in?

'Bloody developer!' muttered Miff. Someone was making a private dawn recce to weigh up the possibilities before making a business proposition to the site's owners. That was Miff's guess. This was someone who wanted to tear down the whole rickety edifice and build a mini estate of starter homes, or a block of retirement flats, a gym and recreational facility with indoor bowling and squash courts . . . Well, it could be any of those options, or something else entirely.

Curiosity drew him closer. He edged past the gleaming body of the BMW. 'Capitalist!' muttered Miff to its empty driver's seat. 'Bread from the mouths of the starving poor! Enemy of the homeless!' For good measure he added, 'Burning up fossil fuels! Polluting the atmosphere and pumping out greenhouse gases!' That seemed to be enough to be going on with.

He had reached the partly opened door, where he stopped and listened. At first, he could hear nothing within and wondered whether whoever it was had already left, and was wandering around the general site. Miff had as much right to be there as him. In reality, probably neither of them had any right to be there. Either way, as Miff judged it, they were equal. He edged nearer and put an ear to the gap. He couldn't hear any movement. He decided to take a risk and slipped silently through the opening and into the dark interior.

It stank inside. Funny, thought Miff, the smell hadn't bothered him the last time he'd been here. Now it seemed overpowering, with the reek of damp, rat urine and decay – as well as a foul miasma formed from everything rotting. Old graveyards sometimes gave off a similar odour after heavy rain, as earth turned to mud and began to sink down to what lay beneath, and the gases started to rise. Someone *should* pull the whole place down, he thought. Maybe the BMW owner had the right idea, if he was indeed a developer on the prowl for a project. Bulldoze the rickety dead thing that was the warehouse until it was just a pile of rubble, then clear it out and throw up a block of flats. Why not?

But where was he, the driver of the flash car? Miff withdrew into the darkest corner and waited, listening, watching for a movement. And it came: the slightest ripple in the shadows ahead of him; the faintest sigh that he knew was a human breath. BMW man was in here, and Miff – who must have been crazy to give way to curiosity – was in here with him. Instinct kicked in at last and he knew that this was a bad place.

Had he reached this decision too late? Did the man know that Miff had joined him? You bet he knew. He might have seen the outline of the newcomer as he slipped through the doorway. He might have heard a step, a creak, something so slight that it was hardly there and yet, just as Miff knew BMW man was there, so the man knew of Miff's presence.

What now? wondered Miff. Just go back the way he'd come and get away from here altogether? The shadows rippled again like a silk curtain in the breeze. BMW man was moving. Miff's eyesight was adjusting to the darkness. The form had been bulky, hunched, but, as Miff watched, that shape changed. It grew taller, narrower and its breath made more noise, a low rasping sound. The man had been crouched and now he had risen to his full height, about the same as Miff, who was a little less than six feet tall. He'd been engaged in something requiring effort and, despite his best attempts to control his breathing, the man could no longer silence the ragged gasps of lungs drawing in extra air. Whatever had been the object of his efforts lay at his feet: another shape, not moving. Had the man disposed of something unwanted by leaving it in here? A sort of concealed fly-tipping? One thing was confirmed in Miff's mind: BMW man was indeed a trespasser. Otherwise, he'd have been in Miff's face by now, telling him bluntly to clear off.

A thought suddenly occurred to Miff. Perhaps the man was afraid of him, of Miff. The man could not have expected to find anyone else here at this early hour. Did he think Miff was a caretaker or watchman? Did he see Miff as a threat or challenge?

Miff made a decision. It must be his day for making bad decisions, he later thought. He called out, 'It's all right, mate, I'm not here to make any trouble. Just passing through, as you might say!'

What on earth possessed him to attempt a feeble joke? Miff wondered. Because he was scared, that was why.

Suddenly, the man was moving, and very fast, moving towards Miff. His form was growing ever larger, becoming distinctly human, with arms swinging, breath hoarse and desperate. One outstretched hand held a weapon of some sort, stick shaped, but whether made of wood or metal, Miff couldn't tell.

He didn't wait to find out. He turned and ran to the opened door behind him. But he couldn't dart through its narrow gap. He had to negotiate it. He was two-thirds out into the open air and freedom – escape – when the man reached him and the weapon struck him a painful blow on the shoulder.

Miff threw himself forward, stumbling and, in a moment of panic, finding himself falling. He was scrabbling in the dirt when the man reached him again. Another blow struck him but he was able, just, to throw up his arm and deflect its full force.

Miff scuttled on all fours across the ground, and then managed to get to his feet and turn. For a split second, the two of them faced each other. Miff saw the features, white, twisted, filled with a terrible rage and resolve. He thought: *he wants to kill me. He bloody wants to kill me . . .*

For a moment the blood in his veins turned to ice. He was frozen in terror. Then Miff ran. He ran as he'd never done before. He'd been in a few tight corners, living on the streets. But never before had he feared for his very life. He must either outrun or outmanoeuvre the attacker: or else he, Miff, was a dead man.

Out here in the open he had the advantage. He was familiar with this urban wilderness, knew its odd corners, blind alleys and gaps between buildings, and he scurried through them like a fleeing cat. He was making for the area beyond the abandoned site, heading for the back gardens of houses in the sizeable estate next door. Miff knew he had to avoid the roads, because his pursuer could go back and get into his car and then just drive round until he saw Miff and run him down. But on foot, *no chance, mate!* Miff told his pursuer silently. He scrambled over fences, knocked garden ornaments flying, crashed into a barbecue stand with a clang and clatter, and splashed through a fishpond.

His noisy progress had been heard in at least two houses. Upper windows were thrown open and angry shouts followed him. But the presence of witnesses was enough finally to deter the pursuer. Miff was thankful to stop in the shelter of a garden shed, gasping for breath, with aching lungs and ribs, and know he had won the race.

* * *

It had been a bad experience and he couldn't put it out of his mind for the rest of the day. What the devil had the other man been doing there? He hadn't been the likely developer scouting for a new project, as Miff had first thought. What had that other shape been, the one huddled at the man's feet in the shadows of the warehouse? There was a corner of Miff's curiosity that made him want to return and investigate. But caution was stronger. Now he had time to think, he realised that not only could he identify BMW man – as he still called him in his mind, for want of a better name – but BMW man could identify Miff, too.

He glanced round the bar room of the pub he was in. It was a small, ordinary sort of place. The people who drank here of an evening weren't the sort who drove expensive cars and did property deals. But Miff found himself searching faces.

'A girl, then, was it?' asked a voice nearby. 'This body they found?'

'Yeah, don't know who she is, don't think the police know yet. Someone said she'd been strangled!' came the reply.

'And dumped out in the old warehouse?' The questioner was a doubting Thomas.

'I told you! It was early this morning and there was some ruckus, a couple of fellows chasing across the back gardens beyond. Several people heard them, saw them, even. One of them is a friend of mine. He was just about to go down and put the kettle on, when he heard the commotion, and looked out in time to see some joker kick over his stone Venus.'

'His stone what?' came the incredulous response.

'Venus, you know, one of them goddesses wearing a bit of drapery and nothing else. He's pretty furious. He paid two hundred quid for that Venus. Not marble or anything, just some sort of substitute mix.'

'Two hundred quid for a fake stone Venus? Not even marble! He's nuts, your mate.'

'Well, his wife wanted it. And she's very upset because its head broke off. Anyway, he called the cops and reported it all. He wasn't the only one. The cops went out there and searched around. They thought it might be dossers in the warehouse and checked it out. That's when they found the body.'

'Well, you never know what's going to happen, do you?' replied Thomas, convinced at last. 'Listen, tell your mate he wants to get on to his house insurance! Has he got cover for garden contents?'

Miff decided it was time for him to make an unobtrusive departure. Once outside on the pavement, he felt horribly vulnerable. The police were looking for a murderer. Miff had witnessed the murderer in the act of disposing of the body. The murderer would be looking for Miff. There was a cruel and inescapable logic to this. However you shuffled the cards, the deal was the same. The murderer had seen Miff as he scrabbled on the ground. And Miff had seen him. The image of that white face, distorted in rage, was printed on his memory. Miff's bearded countenance, and long hair braided into a plait, would be stored in his attacker's memory banks. The killer had no option but to find Miff and silence him.

He had to get away from here. Where could he go? Get across to Europe and thumb his way down to the Algarve, arriving on his parents' doorstep looking like Van Gogh on a bad day? Out of the question.

So, where? Somewhere no one else would think of looking for

him. That was when he had his brilliant idea. He'd go into the country. That's what people did years ago, when they wanted to get away from things. They rattled off in their carriages to their country estates. So Miff would do the same.

BMW man would never think to look for him outside of any urban area; the homeless were a feature of towns and city centres.

Miff had no country estate. But he had family members rusticating away in retirement. He was long out of touch, but they were both, as far as he knew, still alive. He would go and stay with old Uncle Henry and Auntie Prue in that sleepy neck of the woods called – what was it? – Weston St Ambrose. It was in another county, Gloucestershire, and well away from his present location. Yes, that's what he'd do. It would give Henry and Prue a bit of a shock when he turned up. But they were kindly souls and they wouldn't shut the door in his face. Or so he hoped. They'd always been decent to him when he was a kid, after all: less demanding and critical than his parents, and always good for pocket money.

Throwing himself on their mercy for sanctuary would mean giving up, at least temporarily, the independence he had won by learning to survive on the streets. He'd have to invent some reason for turning up out of the blue. He couldn't tell them the truth. They would advise him to go to the police, insist on it. But Miff had been on the streets long enough to be wary of the constabulary. He'd make up some other reason. He was a hunted man, prepared to do anything to save his skin.

Chapter 2

Miff spent a restless night in the local park. He'd waited until the park keeper had made his final patrol, because although he might have hidden from the man himself, the dog would've scented or heard him. The park keeper's dog, Miff knew from previous encounters, was large, muscular, provided with a fearsome set of teeth – and it really didn't like people like Miff. But once the keeper had locked up and taken himself off, with his canine sidekick, Miff climbed over the boundary wall and kipped in the area behind the tennis courts. There was a rickety shelter there, much like a bike shed – only, these days, the tennis players didn't arrive by bike but by car.

Early the following morning, before there was any chance of being awakened to find a fanged hairy face growling at him, Miff hopped back over the wall. He headed first to the nearby garage forecourt where he cadged another coffee from the girl on the till. He then bought a bacon sandwich from an early-opening roadside van. The public toilets had been unlocked now and he could spruce up. Then, as soon as it was open, he made his way, yet again, to the local library.

This time, Miff chose a book of quotations for his purposes. He'd grown rather tired of the law, and the medical books were disturbing. He settled down near a window now and began to leaf through it idly, eyes on the page, mind elsewhere. He had to organise his flight carefully. Be well organised: he'd learned that in his brief stint in a merchant bank in the City of London. He'd done his best to erase that term of imprisonment, as he viewed it, from his mind, but the discipline it had instilled in him came to the fore now.

He had to change his appearance. That was a priority because it would throw the murderer off, at least temporarily. But chiefly because he couldn't turn up at Uncle Henry's door with his plait of hair and bushy beard. Henry and Prue were an old-fashioned pair. True, they had a slightly unconventional side to them, in that on Henry's retirement, both he and Prue had decided they would each write a novel. Miff wondered whether either of them had ever finished the project.

The other thing Miff needed to do, before making for Weston St Ambrose, was think up a reason for being there. The Blackwoods would have been told, by Miff's parents, that he was digging toilets in some wild spot where the locals had managed for generations by simply wandering into the forests when need arose. So he had to explain why he wasn't still doing that, how long he'd been back in England, and why he'd not informed his parents of his change of location. It was always best, when laying a false trail, to include as much genuine detail as possible. A fellow street dweller had once told him that. 'Tell 'em something they can check out,' had been the advice. 'If they find one thing is true, they won't bother checking the rest.'

Living rough was an education in lots of ways, thought Miff. You did meet some really interesting people. Perhaps he should write a book about them, and his own experiences on the street.

Yes! Miff almost dropped the book of quotations in his excitement. Eureka! As the old Greek guy had said when taking a bath; and thought of the answer to some puzzle or other. The thing Miff did know about aspiring authors was that they tended to congregate in groups. They tracked one another down and needed no introduction to other members except the revelation that they, too, were writing a book. Henry and Prue were probably still working on their books. So, tell them he was writing a book about homelessness and alienation from society. Tell them he'd been researching for a couple of years by joining the rough sleepers. (After he'd returned from digging latrines in the jungle, of course, mustn't forget to work that bit in.) Henry and Prue would accept that explanation without a moment's hesitation. He, Miff, might even write the book – one day.

The librarian had twice drifted casually past his chair and was heading his way again with more determination in her aspect. She knew him of old and her tolerance of his presence got shorter every time he visited. Miff got to his feet, brandished the book of quotations at her enthusiastically, and told her, 'This is a really good reference book!'

She removed it firmly from his hands. 'Yes,' she said. 'It is. Shall I replace it for you?'

'How sweet of you,' Miff told her with his most charming smile, probably lost in his facial hair.

Ah, yes, the beard . . . and the long plait. Next port of call, a barber's shop. And not any old barber's shop. Miff knew exactly the one to make for. It was a razor barber's shop run by a Turk. He had a passing street door acquaintance with the barber, who had occasionally given him a cup of very sweet, thick black coffee, while eyeing Miff's hair and beard with an air of frustrated ambition. 'You want to lose all that? You come to me.'

So Mick went to him; and was received like a prince.

'Why now?' asked the barber.

'Family . . .' Miff told him in a confidential tone. 'Family reunion, got to be there. Grandfather's birthday. Ninety-five years old. But very traditional, you understand.'

The barber understood absolutely. 'Family . . .' he said. 'Ah, yes. Don't worry, I fix you up so they will be delighted to see you.'

Well, thought Miff, they might not be delighted, but at least he hoped they wouldn't have hysterics.

The Turk was a creative artist. Miff had to admit he was genuinely impressed. He had to answer some questions about the ninety-five-year-old grandpa, of course. Miff became very creative over that, giving the old fellow a terrific backstory, so full of daring exploits that the barber was entranced. 'Ah, what a wonderful old gentleman!'

'Yes, he is,' agreed Miff, himself quite sorry he wasn't ever going to meet the ancient hero.

There were only a couple of moments when artist and customer disagreed. One was when the barber lit a match and waved it around Miff's ears. The other concerned Miff's refusal to consider a moustache. 'I could create a beautiful moustache,' said the barber wistfully, eyeing Miff's upper lip and the growth of hair adorning it.

'No moustache,' said Miff firmly. 'The family would argue about it. They argue about everything, you know.'

'Ah, families . . .' said the barber.

Miff inspected his newly revealed face in the mirror. It was a lot thinner than he remembered it the last time he'd viewed it, before the beard. Where features had been exposed to the elements, his skin had a weather-beaten look, tanned and a bit leathery. Where the hair had been shaved off, the skin resembled that of an oven-ready chicken, pale and naked. With luck, his complexion would even out in a few days. Right now, his face was rather disconcerting, like looking at a stranger, or someone he used to know and had lost touch with. But would it be enough to throw the man who hunted him off the scent? Could they pass in the street in safety? Miff could not be sure about that. Anyone could see he'd recently lost a beard. The murderer would notice that. The shave alone would not be enough to ensure his safety.

He was well aware he would be a stranger to Henry and Prue when he knocked at their door. They might recognise him, just. They'd have no idea why he was there. He wondered how suspicious they would be. He felt mildly sorry for them, but not enough to change his resolve. In Weston St Ambrose, he would be safe.

'Your family will be pleased to see you,' the barber said, with a beaming smile, as he graciously accepted the handful of assorted coins Miff handed over as payment.

'Yeah . . .' mumbled Miff. Initially, yes, they might be. Once they realised he meant to hang around, they might prove less keen.

Family reunions were in the air, including in Gloucestershire where Jess Campbell was visiting her mother, Leonie, accompanied by Mike Foley. For some time, Mike had been working alongside Jess's twin brother, Simon, for a medical charity in Africa. But

Mike had fallen ill there, seriously so. He'd been sent back to the UK. Although he'd now been given a clean bill of health, he was still obviously a man who had got through a spell of illness. The weight he'd lost was slow to return. He looked much better than he had when he'd arrived home and Jess had seen him for the first time in years. She wouldn't forget the sight of him waiting outside her flat, leaning on a car borrowed from his uncle. Simon had warned her that his old friend had been ill. He hadn't told her to expect a walking scarecrow, his clothes hanging loose, his joints angular, his features drawn.

Mike had now recovered sufficiently for Jess to judge it safe to take him to see her mother so that he could update her on Simon's situation. They were both unsure of what kind of reception they would get.

To describe Leonie Campbell as a worrier didn't do the situation justice. She had carried worrying to a fine art. She worried about Jess because her daughter had chosen a career in the police; and Leonie couldn't understand why. 'It seems such a – strange thing to do, dear,' she'd said, on originally being informed of her daughter's decision. Jess had tried to explain but her mother had simply looked more bewildered.

Leonie worried even more about Simon's medical work, 'Out there in such danger!' She was desperately anxious to hear first-hand from Mike that all was well.

'Dad was in the army,' Jess had pointed out to her. 'The army isn't a safe career – not your idea of risk free, anyway.'

'It was different for your father,' retorted Leonie.

Because of this, they had put off visiting her until Mike was reasonably fit again. Even so, things were not going well.

Ann Granger

If Jess had needed one word to describe her mother, the word she would have chosen would have been 'tidy'. She'd always been neat in appearance. Jess couldn't remember her mother with tousled hair, or starting the day without carefully applied make-up, or clean clothes. As an army family, they had lived in a variety of accommodation, when Jess and Simon had been young. But any house or flat, wherever it was, had been marked by Leonie's obsession with tidiness.

She and her brother had once discussed this, after Jess had joined the police. 'You know what it is that attracts you to a police career?' Simon told her. 'It's because the cops deal with people whose lives are untidy. They're people who've got into a mess, either deliberately or accidentally, but in any case, their lives are out of sync with society.'

'Hey! You're not a shrink!' Jess had protested.

'Don't need to be a shrink. Just observant.'

'Okay, then, what if I said you had gone into medicine for the same reason. People get sick. You want to make them whole. You want to tidy them up.'

This had led to a lively argument but had ended amicably.

She and Mike sat now in Leonie Campbell's cottage, where not a thing was out of place, ate cake and made stilted conversation.

'You are quite sure, Mike dear,' Leonie Campbell said for the umpteenth time, 'that Simon isn't ill?' She leaned forward and scrutinised him. 'You caught something awful, didn't you? Anyone can see you've been terribly ill. When I think of what it must be like, out there with all those diseases; and no proper sanitation or anything. Besides, there are all those men with guns, as well. There was a bit on the news about it recently. They said fighting had flared up there again.' She shuddered. 'Simon must be in the same awful danger.'

'He was as sound as a bell when I last saw him,' Mike told her – again.

'Only I worry about him, you understand.'

'Oh, yes, I quite understand, Mrs Campbell.'

'You could so easily have died,' went on Leonie, meaning well but being, thought Jess, tactless, to say the least.

'I'm altogether recovered,' Mike assured her.

'You won't be going back there again, though, will you?' asked Leonie anxiously. 'Do have another piece of the sponge cake.'

'No, really, oh, thank you . . .' The cake had appeared on his plate.

Jess closed her eyes briefly. She did not visit her mother often enough. She acknowledged this freely. But being force-fed cake, and discussing every possible disaster likely to befall either Simon or herself, was discouraging. Now Leonie had Mike to worry about, as well. New material.

Mike had a look on his face that told Jess he was gearing up to defending his determination to return to his work overseas. This wouldn't be something Leonie would understand, just as she couldn't reconcile herself to her son's dedication to his chosen career. There was a further complication, too, in Mike's case. Put simply, the charity had doubts about sending him back into the field. His battle with disease had left him vulnerable. They didn't want to fly him back out there, only to have to evacuate him in a rush later. They'd offered him a job at their London headquarters. He'd turned that down. 'I'm not a deskman. I'm a doctor!'

Yes, and a dedicated one, which meant, in turn, there was a brake on their relationship, his and Jess's. How and when could it develop beyond the point it had reached now? And what was that, exactly? Jess wondered. They didn't talk about the future. They were both thinking about it. But neither of them could find a way to talk about the subject.

Leonie had turned her attention to her daughter. 'I'm sorry, darling; I should be asking you how you are getting along. Still determined to stay in the police force?'

From the corner of her eye, Jess saw that Mike looked relieved, now he had been spared Leonie's cross-examination. Her mother was looking at her with a forlorn sort of hope. Jess steeled herself to reply cheerfully.

'Absolutely, Mum. I am in CID, you remember. It is interesting.'

'Is it?' asked Leonie, with disappointment echoing in her voice and showing in her body language. She sighed. 'Well, I hope you have pleasant people to work with. I mean, not the criminals, they must be awful. I meant, your colleagues.'

'They're great, all of them.'

'Inspector Carter still there?' A note of hope entered her mother's voice.

'Yes, he's still there.' Time to deflect another line of conversation. Really, any conversation with her mother was an obstacle course. 'Unfortunately, I've just lost Phil Morton, Sergeant Morton. I shall miss him. Not that all the others aren't completely reliable, but Phil was exceptionally good at his job.'

'So what happened to him?' asked Leonie anxiously.

'Nothing bad!' Jess tried not to sound exasperated. 'He got promoted and sent to a new posting.'

Her mother relaxed. 'Oh, yes, well, I suppose it is like the army!'

'In that way, yes. His replacement has arrived. His name is Ben Paget. I think he'll fit into the team As a matter of fact, he's come to us from Bamford. You remember, where I used to be part of the team back in Alan Markby's day.'

Leonie brightened. 'I remember Superintendent Markby. You were working with him again recently, weren't you?'

'Well, Ian Carter was, not me. He's retired now, Markby, but he was able to help out the local force in Bamford. It was a cold case and it tied in with an old case in Gloucestershire, on which Ian Carter had worked years ago. A coincidence, really. But it's how I got some up-to-date news about Alan Markby, and saw him again, very briefly.'

She saw her mother was looking confused, as she always did when the conversation turned to police work. Jess went on briskly, 'You know, Mum, I'm really sorry, but Mike and I are going to have to leave in about ten minutes. I don't want to get stuck in the traffic.'

'Could have been worse,' said Mike, as they drove homeward. 'You can't blame her for worrying.'

'I don't blame her. The fault is mine, I suppose. I don't cope with it very well. It's hard not to get impatient. It's wrong of me, but there it is.'

'She's lonely,' said Mike simply.

There was a silence.

'Yes,' Jess said eventually. 'I know she is. It makes me feel guilty.'

'I wasn't suggesting you should feel guilty. You can't solve other people's problems for them. Just try and understand, that's all.'

'I don't understand,' Jess muttered resentfully, 'is that what you mean?'

'I think you do. I think that, like your mother, but in your own way, you're worried.'

The rest of the drive home was spent in an edgy silence.

In Weston St Ambrose, whither Miff was making his way courtesy of a friendly lorry driver, yet another sort of reunion was already on the cards. Totally unaware of the impending arrival of the family black sheep, Henry and Prue Blackwood were being entertained by Peter Posset. He had invited them round for a glass of wine and some 'nibbles'. The wine was all right but the nibbles consisted of an avocado dip (home-made, chiefly out of mayonnaise and mashed avocado, but referred to grandly by Peter as 'guacamole'), plus some nuts, crisps and cheese straws purchased at the small supermarket opened in the village just under two years earlier. There was also a small loaf of Peter's home-made bread. He was proud of his bread-making skills. Others were less complimentary. With the bread came a tub of goat's cheese.

'The Mediterranean diet,' Peter liked to tell people, 'is well known for being very healthy.'

At the moment, Prue Blackwood was wondering whether guacamole was technically Mediterranean. Wasn't it Mexican?

Peter was a retired bank manager. He'd also lived in Weston St Ambrose for several years and he wrote plays. (He liked to say he was a dramatist.) Until some unfortunate happenings locally a little while ago, Peter had been the convener of the Weston St Ambrose Writers' Group. The group had fallen to pieces, due to events so dramatic even Peter hadn't considered his pen adequate to the task of making a stage version. But memories of the 'unfortunate time', as Peter liked to call it, were fading.

'And I do believe,' he said enthusiastically, 'that it's time to think about re-forming our little group.'

There was a silence.

Henry, feeling obliged to fill it and make some kind of an answer, said, 'Oh, well, Peter, of course, it would be . . . very nice, but so few of the original group are still around here and . . .'

Posset sat with his hands folded on his generous stomach, which meant on his latest pullover. Peter liked to knit his own pullovers, having been instructed in the art by his grandmother, when he was a boy. The sweaters were all the same in pattern, only differing in the strip of design across the chest. This one showed a line of anchors linked by something vaguely like a rope.

Henry had been sitting looking at it while Peter pontificated about how jolly everything had been before the, um, unfortunate time. Why the nautical theme? Henry wondered. They weren't on the coast. He'd never heard that old Posset had any interest in boats. Really, the fellow was a terrible bore and the thought of re-forming the group . . .

While Henry floundered for a reply to Posset's suggestion, his wife spoke up. 'I don't know, Peter,' she said. 'It seems sort of, well, tasteless. People remember . . .'

'People,' declared Posset, 'remember all sorts of things because things happen, don't they? It doesn't mean creative art stops. In fact, to the contrary, we should all be inspired! If things didn't happen, we'd have nothing to write about!'

He beamed at them, defying them to find fault with his logic.

'Now, look here, Peter old chap,' began Henry. 'You are not suggesting we all write about – about *that*?'

'No, of course not!' retorted Posset testily. 'But we all still write, don't we? I know I do. How about you – and Prue?'

The Blackwoods both looked guilty.

'You see,' said Prue at last, 'I know that I – and Henry – both felt a bit awkward writing anything after – after the reality. I mean, I write romantic fiction; and nasty happenings in real life sort of put a damper on that. And Henry, well . . .' She turned to her spouse.

'Absolutely,' supported Henry. 'I write thrillers and, well, after everything that happened, it seemed . . .'

'Tasteless, as I said,' finished Prue.

'What you mean,' Posset told her, 'is that you have "writer's block"!'

'Oh, is that it?' murmured Prue weakly.

'Yes! And the way to get over it is to start something new! You don't mean to tell me that neither of you has written anything lately?'

'I did try, Peter . . .'

'I have reread my earlier work,' Henry declared, because he didn't want Posset to think he, Henry, lacked strength of character. 'I have been revising.'

'There you are, then,' said Posset. 'I'll pin up a notice on that board they have at the supermarket; local events are often advertised on it. I'll arrange a meeting and say all are welcome. I suggest the first Wednesday of this coming month, and fortnightly Wednesdays thereafter. That will allow time for the word to get around!' Posset paused and when there was no response, added testily, 'That was a little joke! The *word* to get around.'

'Oh, right, Peter,' said Prue dutifully. 'Very good.'

'Oh, good grief . . .' murmured Henry sotto voce.

'I also thought we might rename ourselves the "Writers' Circle", just to, um, distance ourselves a little from the, er, unfortunate events you mentioned, Prue.'

Prue felt she had been reprimanded, and for two pins . . . But Peter was oblivious to the reactions of others. For a dramatist, that must be a drawback. And when he was a bank manager, approaching him for a loan must have been a near impossibility.

'And it will give any potential members time to put something together, by way of work. So, agreed?' He beamed at them.

'Yes, I suppose so,' the Blackwoods muttered, this time together.

'I have phoned Jenny Porter and she's interested in coming along if we start up again. She would have been here tonight, but she's had to cycle over to the Meadowlea Manor retirement home, to visit an old friend. She asked me to keep her informed.'

Neither of his visitors spoke, but they did exchange looks.

'Honestly, Henry,' said his wife, as they started to walk homewards. 'I'm not altogether sure it's a good idea. I suppose, if we get some new members, it might be all right, but if it's going to be just us, with Peter Posset, and Jenny Porter . . .'

'Pity he phoned her,' agreed Henry. 'Nothing against her, of course, but just tends to be a bit critical of everyone else's work. Constructive criticism, of course, is fine, but Mrs Porter—'

'Henry!' his wife interrupted him. 'There's someone sitting outside our front door, on the step! He's got a very big bag beside him. Could it be a burglar?'

'Not if he's sitting on the step in full view, Prue. By Jove, so there is! We'll ask him. Perhaps it's a lost hiker.'

Henry made an effort to sound unworried because he wanted to reassure Prue. But he felt far from confident himself. It was getting dark. The shrubs in the garden had started to take on strange shapes. They had left a lamp lit in the sitting room behind drawn curtains to suggest someone was at home. But if the visitor on the step had knocked or rung the bell, he would know that wasn't the case. Perhaps, leaving a single lamp like that, was giving the game away.

'Hello there!' hailed Henry in hearty fashion. 'Looking for someone?'

'Oh, there you are, Uncle Henry!' replied the stranger. 'I thought you might be away. But as you'd left a light on, I decided you must be coming back tonight.'

(Definitely, thought Henry, leaving a single lamp lit was not a good idea.)

Then it sank in that he'd been hailed as 'uncle'. The only nephew he had was his sister's boy, and wasn't he doing voluntary work overseas somewhere?

'I expect you're surprised to see me,' said the newcomer.

Henry peered at him in the dusk. 'Good grief!' he exclaimed. 'It's Matthew!'

There was a silence. Henry couldn't know it, but it had been such a long time since anyone had addressed Miff by his given name, that Miff almost didn't recognise it.

'Yes,' Miff said at last. 'Sorry I couldn't let you know I was coming.'

'We thought you were in Central Africa, or somewhere like that . . .' objected Prue doubtfully.

'Oh, I got back ages ago. I've been doing other things since then.'

'Your parents didn't tell us . . .'

'They don't know I'm back, either. I've dropped in to see you, because I know you both write a bit, or you used to. I've been researching a book about homelessness and now I mean to write it.'

Henry was about to exclaim, 'What? Write it *here,* you mean?'

But his wife prodded him in the ribs and muttered, 'Everyone will be wondering what's going on!'

So Henry hastily changed his words to, 'Well, you'd better come in.'

The new arrival stooped and picked up the bag. They could now see that it was a bulging rucksack. He hitched it over his shoulder. Prue found her key and unlocked the door. They all trooped inside.

'I can probably make you a sandwich, Matthew,' said Prue. 'I'm afraid Henry and I have eaten.' (If you could call Peter Posset's guacamole and crisps a meal.)

'No probs, Auntie,' said Miff, beaming at her. 'A sandwich would be great!'

Prue set off for the kitchen, wondering what she had in the fridge to use as sandwich filler. Surely it was a little late in the day to be eating cheese?

Henry wondered whether he ought to offer his nephew a drink. He very much felt like a drink himself. He was happy for his wife to feed the new arrival, but he hoped Prue wasn't going to come back with a plate of sandwiches sufficient for them all. Peter's bread was already sitting in his stomach like a lead weight. Now he had to cope with something as unexpected as a nephew who must have been about fifteen or sixteen when he'd last seen him.

And just when he felt like sinking into an armchair in front of the telly for half an hour before bed, catching up on the news. Not that he wasn't pleased to see the boy, of course! Actually, he ought to say 'man', not 'boy'.

Henry made renewed efforts to recall the last time he'd actually spoken to Matthew. Let's see . . . Good grief, years ago! And hadn't his nephew done rather well since then? According to long emails from Henry's sister, Ginny, her son had been carving out a brilliant career in the financial world. You wouldn't think so, looking at him now. He looked as if he'd been sleeping in a ditch. Ah, but then, he'd given up the world of finance to take up some kind of voluntary work, in Africa. All to his credit, of course, although he might have been more sensible stay in the job in London and donate some of his generous salary to projects run by others. But that would account for his, well, weather-beaten look.

Another thought struck him. How had Matthew known where to find them? Ginny must have told him they were now living in Weston St Ambrose. It was a pity, thought Henry, that Ginny and her husband had decamped to Portugal. If they hadn't, Matthew might have gone home, instead of turning up, completely unexpectedly, here!

'Sandwiches?' enquired Prue brightly, entering carrying a heaped plate.

Doorsteps! Henry thought with a sinking heart. What was she thinking of, after that bread of Peter Posset's?

'Oh, great, Auntie Prue!' exclaimed the visitor.

Miff might be a night person, but the Blackwoods certainly weren't. They retired early – rather to Miff's relief, because they didn't ask him too many questions. They were probably keeping those for the following day. Miff had little option but to retire to bed at the same time, even though it seemed unnatural to him. He now lay awake in the spare room and considered his new situation. It couldn't be permanent, that much was already obvious. Henry and Prue would get restless after a week. He had been wrong in thinking that no one would take any notice of him in the country. On the contrary, everyone in this fairly small community would be fascinated by any new arrival. Miff had been well aware, while sitting on the front doorstep earlier in the evening, that he'd been under observation from behind the curtains of every dwelling from which the Blackwoods' home could be seen.

Probably, thought Miff, nothing happened in Weston St Ambrose from one month's end to another. (He was wrong in this, had he but known it.) Poor old Auntie Prue would be besieged when she went shopping the next day. Miff supposed Weston had a shop somewhere. Prue had mentioned something about a super-market when she'd brought in the tinned salmon sandwiches. Henry had seemed quite annoyed about being fed tinned salmon before he went to bed. Miff had already overheard part of the dispute, apparently taking place in the bathroom, as a result of Henry being unable to locate some cure for indigestion.

'Not my fault!' Miff heard Prue declare. 'It's always the same when you've eaten at Peter Posset's!'

'Then it's that damn awful bread he makes. And what was that green stuff?'

Now all was eerily quiet again. Miff was used to noise throughout the night. There was always the sound of traffic some-where in town, or revellers heading home. The rumble of lorries making overnight journeys down the nearby motorway made a distant but constant hum.

The deep quiet of the countryside was unnatural to him. Yes, there were occasional noises, and some of them were quite spooky. The air outside his window was disturbed by the passage of wings. Surely all the birds had gone to roost? An owl, yes, must be an owl. Trees rustled. Quite a stiff wind had got up and it would probably bring rain. Something made an unearthly squeal, causing Miff to sit up and strain his ears. There was a bark but not a dog's bark. Miff recognised that of a fox. These days, you met them in town after dark, scavenging around rubbish bins. Something with claws rattled its way across the roof above his head. Rats? Mice? Cats? Miff shifted awkwardly. His body was unaccustomed to resting on a soft surface and his joints didn't know quite what to do about it. The mattress offered no solid support, unlike asphalt or paving stones. His spine was already forced into an 'S' shape. He'd creep downstairs at breakfast time looking like the Hunchback of Notre Dame.

Then there was the changed quality of the light. As a town was never quite silent, so it was never quite dark. Street lamps bathed the pavements in a familiar and comforting orange glow. Shop premises were wrapped in a muted apricot security blanket. Neon-lit advertisements assaulted the darkness until the early hours.

In the country, it was as if some controlling force had decreed that it was 'lights out'. It had thrown a switch, plunging the world into a velvet darkness in which the moon hung like a silvery bauble.

When Miff had switched off the bedside lamp, he'd initially

panicked because it was as if he'd been struck blind. Now his eyes had adjusted. The moonlight seeped through the thin curtains, and bathed the room in a cold metallic sheen. He had left his rucksack on a chair over there by the wall, and in the pale unearthly light it looked like a crouched form, watching him. It reminded him too much of that dark figure in the gloom of the warehouse, slowly swelling in size, coming nearer . . .

Unable to bear it, he slid out of bed and padded to the window. Yes, there was the Blackwoods' back garden, bleached by moonlight and dominated by the black and sinister twisted limbs of an oak tree, stark against the moonscape. Miff, during those hours spent in the public library on rainy days, had spent a whole week reading about Norse and other legends. Now his memory threw up a name: Yggdrasil! The great tree that held the worlds together in Norse legend was real. It was out there . . .

Miff retreated to sit on the bed. It sank beneath his weight disconcertingly. This place gave him the creeps. He knew he had to revise his plans. It was still advantageous to stay in Weston St Ambrose for a while because it was so remote, far, far away from the threat of encountering that white face with fury in its eyes and, clearly, murder on the owner's mind. BMW man (Miff still called him that) had killed once. He'd kill again.

It helped to have family here. The locals would understand that and be more likely to accept his presence, once they all knew about it. It sort of, well, legitimised him.

But he needed to find somewhere else to live: because he couldn't live rough here, and he'd been crazy to think he could spin out his stay with the Blackwoods indefinitely. And he had to earn some extra money, somehow. Get a job. It was all so bloody unfair!

He'd envisaged sleeping in a comfortable bed, in a peaceful village retreat. The reality was that the oak tree would give him nightmares, the soft mattress meant he'd wake up all aches and pains, and his free existence had gone for who knew how long? He was back with family, clean-shaven, committed to writing a book, and to finding some sort of employment. He had fled one nightmare to find himself trapped in another.

Ben Paget's transfer to Gloucestershire had come up during another discussion some distance away – back in Bamford, to be precise.

Inspector Trevor Barker stood in the warehouse, with his hands in the pockets of his heavy jacket, and a look of despondency on his face. The desolate interior, in which Miff had encountered BMW man at his sinister work disposing of a body, looked even more of a rubbish tip than when Miff had left it so hurriedly. Not that the police yet knew anything about Miff. But, as Miff had overheard in the pub, complaints from nearby residents that yobs had invaded their gardens, leaving a trail of wreckage, had led local police to check out the building and so to the discovery of the body.

The identity of the dead woman was not yet known, but Barker clung to an optimistic belief that it soon would be. He was similarly optimistic about finding the killer.

'Whoever it was left her here,' he declared now, and not for the first time, 'he knew about this place and thought it would be the spot to leave the victim. There's no regular caretaker and, if it hadn't been for all those householders making a fuss about their broken garden statues and busted barbecues, no one would have looked in here for – well, possibly a couple of weeks at least.'

34

'No, sir,' said Sergeant Emma Johnson dutifully, trying not to sound as if she hadn't already heard her boss say this at least three times before. 'Real old mess,' she added, by way of a contribution of her own.

It was truly a real old mess. Following the discovery of the body, the abandoned warehouse had seen much activity. Trained crime-scene investigators had been all over it, involving a thorough search, dragging out heaps of mouldering rubbish that lay strewn around. During this, a member of the team had chanced upon a well-hidden litter of kittens, and had been attacked by the ferociously defensive mother.

Outside, the surrounding area had also been combed, but the fresh tyre tracks of a car had been the only real evidence to come to light so far. They were not the only tracks in the area, however. Joyriders in stolen vehicles were known to visit the site from time to time. But they were the freshest. All were recorded. Otherwise, the mud was churned up by a confusion of footprints. Among them were the marks of strong footwear that showed the wearers had been running. It was safe to assume this was where the chase through the nearby gardens had started.

The drinkers in the pub, as well as the police, had not been the only ones to learn about it. One enterprising local resident had picked up his phone and contacted the press. Reporters from local papers and regional television had descended on the site as soon as the police would let them anywhere near. So far, the news cameramen had only been allowed to take photographs outside the warehouse. Their journalist colleagues were combing the area, interviewing the owner of the headless Venus, and anyone else they could find who might possibly be able to tell them anything.

They'd not had much luck so far. One broken garden ornament doth not a news story make.

That didn't mean there wasn't a lively local interest. An army of sightseers had gathered, largely composed of the pupils of a nearby secondary school. To their frustration, they were being kept at bay behind fluttering police tape and barriers, under the watchful eyes of a couple of uniformed officers in a squad car. They made up for being denied access, and refused answers to their many questions, by filming everything on their mobiles.

'This would happen now,' Barker continued to grumble, 'just when we've lost Ben Paget. He deserved promotion, because he's a good officer. But it would happen *now*.'

'Ben, I mean Paget, always hankered after a move to Gloucestershire,' observed Emma with a touch of regret.

'What on earth for?' muttered Barker.

'Spent his school holidays there, he told me once. Still, it's a bit of a coincidence that he's joined Superintendent Carter's team!' Emma decided to deflect the discussion.

Barker, hands still in pockets, turned slowly and fixed his junior with a jaundiced eye. 'Coincidences, Emma, I can do without . . .' He paused and frowned. 'I wonder if Carter would let me have Paget back for a few weeks? No, I suppose not.'

'We can manage here,' Emma said, rather more sharply than she'd intended. 'Sir!' she added quickly.

'Yes, I suppose so,' muttered Barker.

'I meant, he's been gone a month.' Emma made the mistake of trying to explain. 'And it's only now that, well, anyone has suggested he's needed back here. I mean, he was a nice bloke and did his job. We all miss him, of course we do. But workwise, we can cope. Even with this.' She gestured at the surrounding scene. 'And someone is coming to replace him at the end of this month.'

'We're getting an officer with minimal experience,' Barker reminded her, 'and have lost one with an excellent record and plenty of experience. It's hardly like for like! Well, it never rains but it pours!'

'Yes, it has just started to rain, sir,' said Emma, not without a touch of malice. She'd had enough of this. She had personally been sorry to see Paget leave because she'd, well, to be honest, rather fancied him. Not that he'd ever shown any particular interest in her, not in that way. 'It's going to pour in through this rickety old roof!' she concluded.

'Very witty, Sergeant Johnson,' she was told. 'But keep the jokes for another time.'

'Yes, sir.'

Chapter 3

'But you need to make plans, Daddy!'

His daughter's voice echoed in his ear. It was really extraordinary, Ian Carter thought, how much like her mother Millie sounded. There was that same imperative note, with a hint of impatience, and the unspoken charge that he was a ditherer.

A fragment of long-ago conversation, held while he and Sophie were still man and wife, echoed in his brain.

'I am not a ditherer!' he had told her. 'I am a senior police officer, CID, and I do not dither!'

'Then make up your mind! I have to give Belinda and George an answer.'

'Belinda and George can go skiing perfectly well without us.'

'But they've invited us! It's a chalet party. It will be lovely! Don't be such a misery, Ian!'

'It's only September!'

'They have to confirm the booking now or they'll lose it!'

'They'll find someone else to join their party.'

'But they want *us*!' His then wife's voice had risen to a wail.

Remembering it now, Carter thought that, just possibly, he had been selfish to refuse to allow her to confirm a place in the chalet party. At the time it had been because, he told himself, he genuinely feared an outbreak of lawlessness might force him to drop out of the party at the last minute. Also, it was not true that the others wanted them both. They wanted Sophie. They were less keen on his company. The awareness that he was a police officer of any sort put a brake on their drinking and merry-making. Nor had George ever forgiven Carter for not helping out 'an old pal' when he, George, had accumulated an indecent amount of points on his driving licence.

Moreover, Carter reflected now, still sitting at his desk with his phone pressed to his ear, it was perfectly true that Christmas tended to see a crime spree: all kinds of mayhem, from drink-driving to outright murder. Families gathered at Christmas. Relatives, hardly thought of during the greater part of the year, got together, and remembered old times and absent friends and other family members. At first, they remembered them fondly. As the drink flowed, they started to remember the grudges, the embarrassment of having given the wrong present, of having forgotten that someone was on a special diet.

'*Daddy!*'

'I'm still here, darling.'

'You'd gone quiet. I thought perhaps we'd been cut off. Or you'd fallen asleep!' she added – unnecessarily, it seemed to him.

'I'm at work. You must realise that. I've got other things to think about than spending Christmas in France with you and your mother and, well, with Rodney. Oh, and your baby brother, how is he coming along?'

'Mum's sent photos. I'll email them to you. He looks just like Rodney.' Millie smothered a giggle.

Carter could have replied that most babies looked like her stepfather. The fellow looked like an oversized baby himself.

Whatever had Sophie seen in him? Well, whatever it was that had drawn her to Rodney, it was clearly because of something, or many things, Carter had failed to offer.

The present equivalent of that long-ago argument about Christmas in a Swiss chalet was a present-day lively discussion of a suggested extended family gathering in France. (It wasn't an argument. He didn't argue with his child; mostly because she was impervious to his refusal to fall in with any of her plans. Now, where did she get *that* from?)

'Look here, Millie,' he said firmly. 'Tell me honestly. Is it *your* idea that I should join you all in France at Christmas? I can't somehow believe it's your mum's idea. I don't suppose Rodney wants me there, either, hovering like Banquo's ghost at the banquet!'

'Rodney likes you,' said Millie, evasively.

Does he? Well, I don't like Rodney. 'I don't think, Millie, I'm sorry, I just don't think I'd be comfortable with you all.'

'Mummy says, if you don't want to stay with us, there's a dear little *pension* just round the corner. You could sleep there and join us during the day!'

Yes, that's the sort of excruciating idea Sophie would come up with. What did that make him, Carter? An elderly relative released from a retirement home for the day?

'I don't think the *pension*'s a good idea, Millie.' He did his best to sound firm without snapping.

'Oh, you wouldn't be on your own there, Daddy. Belinda and George will be sleeping there and joining us during the day, as well. Mummy wants a house party, only the house isn't big enough.'

Well, isn't that just the icing on the cake? Belinda and George, probably both of them as tiresome now as they ever were – and George still moaning, after all this time, about his suspended licence.

'Really, Millie, it's not on, sweetheart.'

'Well, think about it, Daddy, promise me!'

'Shouldn't you be in some class at this time of the morning?' Carter decided to take the initiative.

'Oh, I am, we are. It's Art Class. We're in the local park. Miss Huxtable drove us here in the minibus. We're sketching autumnal subjects.'

'So, what are you sketching and how come you're on the phone instead?'

'Because I've finished. I sketched the gardener's wheelbarrow. He'd been lifting dead plants, but he went off somewhere and left the barrow, and the dead plants, and his garden tools. So I re-arranged them and made them my subject. It's a very boring park.'

'And where is Miss Huxtable?'

'Sitting on a bench checking her smartphone . . .' A pause. 'Oh, she's finished and she's got up. She's looking this way. Got to go, Daddy! Bye!'

The call ended abruptly, leaving Carter sitting at his desk and staring at the instrument resentfully.

'Rodney likes me, does he?' he muttered under his breath. 'Considering he took my wife off me, he's got a damn cheek!'

But he ought not to be feeling uncharitable towards Rodney. All this had to do with his ex-wife. Sophie's way of arranging things had always been to Sophie's convenience. That Millie, although nominally resident with her mother and stepfather, should go to boarding school in England, wasn't so that Carter could see more of his daughter, and she of him. It was so that Sophie, with Rodney and their baby – what was the kid's name? Ah yes, Tristan – so they could play nuclear family without the embarrassment of a thirteen year old (almost fourteen) from Sophie's earlier marriage. He wondered whether Millie realised that. Was that why she was so keen for him to join them? He was desperately anxious that Millie be happy. She always acted happy. Not the same thing.

Jess Campbell was coming down the corridor towards his office. He knew her footstep. On impulse, he called out, 'Inspector Campbell!'

The door opened. Her trim form and mop of auburn hair appeared, and she half entered, hand still on the door handle.

'Some problem?' she asked warily.

'No, well, not anything officially a problem . . .'

She came into the room, closing the door behind her, and took the chair he indicated. He leaned back in the seat behind the desk and they stared at each other.

'My daughter's been on the phone,' he blurted. 'She wants me to go and join her mother, stepfather and little brother in France at Christmas.'

'Oh, I see,' said Jess. 'Will you go?' Her eyebrows twitched.

'No, it would be – embarrassing. I shall have a job to persuade Millie; but it's just not on. Somehow she's got to understand that it's more complicated than she chooses to believe.'

'Millie's smart,' said Jess. 'I think you'll find she understands . . .' She paused. 'She worries about you. It's natural.'

They both knew well that Millie's answer to her father's single status lay with the two of them. Millie had met Jess, summed

42

her up and decided that she was the one her father needed. But Jess didn't see it that way, Carter was sadly aware. He wished she did. Their working relationship had developed into a sort of friendship, including the occasional pub meal. There had been moments when . . .

When what? Well, nothing, because he, Carter, threw up a mental barrier in his own mind, affecting his actions. There were even moments when he felt as he'd done years ago, when attending the school prom. He could still recall the shock when girls he'd known only in school uniform suddenly filled the room like a flock of multicoloured parrots, rendering him speechless and gawky. Millie was growing up at an alarming rate. In a few short years she would be joining that band of parakeets. So few years – and he would miss most of them. Yet he was about to turn down the opportunity to spend Christmas with his child.

Here I am, he had told himself, a divorced man in early middle age, and it is high time I stopped being a singleton. Other men in his situation formed new close relationships. Mostly, they did so successfully, in his experience. He had thought once that any barrier to making a closer relationship with Jess would come in the form of her friendship with the pathologist Tom Palmer. Jess had always insisted that Tom was 'just a friend', but friendships can grow into something more complicated and so, as long as Tom was around, Carter felt anything could happen.

But Palmer was settled now and getting married in a few weeks' time. There had been a window of opportunity there, but he, Ian Carter, had muffed it, and now?

Now into the gap had walked that doctor pal of her brother, and not just any rival, but one who had appeared very much in the shape of the wounded hero of romantic literature. Mike Foley had worked tirelessly for a medical charity in a war-torn area of Central Africa. He'd been invalided home, partly because he had fallen victim to one of the very diseases he sought to cure in others, but also from overwork, exhaustion leading to a sudden collapse. 'And you can't beat that!' Carter had told himself with a snarl of frustration. To make matters worse, Jess's twin brother, also a doctor working in the refugee camps, had asked Jess to keep an eye on his pal. Jess had taken the invalid to meet her mother, because, as she explained it, her mother longed for news of Simon. So all the cards were in Foley's hand. All he had to do was play them. But there was, as Carter understood it, a snag.

Foley himself was an unappreciative blighter (this was Carter's private view of it all), who did not return Jess's interest, or not in any way Carter could understand it. He just kept on saying he was now fit and wanted to return to his work in Africa, even though the charity was uneasy about sending him back there. It made Carter want to grab a handful of the guy's shirtfront, stricken hero or not, and demand to know what he was playing at.

But, hey, whatever arrangement Jess and Mike had worked out between them, it was none of Carter's business. Jess was a tough and capable officer. She was also sparky and attractive. She was definitely neither a fool nor a pushover. Her private life was her own. If he tried to interfere, she'd tell him to keep out of it. Quite rightly.

He saw a flicker of concern in Jess's expression. He'd been silent too long. Oh, good grief! If he didn't get a grip, he might just as well put in for early retirement.

'Was there something else?' she asked now suddenly. She leaned forward slightly, her lively features beneath the cap of auburn hair expressing a polite, very official interest. But there was a personal curiosity behind it. He heard it in her voice.

He floundered. 'What?'

'When you called me in here, was there some other problem? Or was it just to tell me about Millie's phone call? Only you seemed to be drifting for a moment there.'

'Sorry,' he apologised. 'No, no, of course not! I was just—' What had he been doing? Not for the first time, he turned to work for a plausible excuse. 'As a matter of fact, I have been wondering how Paget is getting along with the rest of the team. I know Phil Morton will be missed.'

'I'll miss Phil,' admitted Jess. 'But I'm glad he got his promotion. I think Ben Paget will be fine. I'm not quite sure why he applied to join a force in another part of the country. Perhaps he thought it would secure his promotion. Or he didn't get along with his colleagues where he was. He's not exactly chatty; but that's probably because he's new. He's sizing us all up, I think. But he seems a pleasant sort, and yes, he should do excellently.'

'Only,' Carter said slowly, 'his old colleagues seem to be missing him. I've had a rather odd phone call from Trevor Barker.'

This was true. The call from Bamford had come in a few minutes before Millie phoned and delayed Carter's response to Barker's request.

'He's wondering if we might be able to spare Paget and send him back there for a week. He's got a murder on his hands, and feels the need of another experienced officer. What do you think?'

She looked startled and then disapproving. 'What happens if we find we need him here during that week? Frankly,' Jess added,

'I think it's out of order. If Inspector Barker can't manage, he ought to request extra help in the usual way.'

Carter shrugged. 'I'm inclined to agree. It's hardly fair on Paget to send him back, even for a week. Besides,' Carter smiled suddenly, 'it might give him the idea that he's indispensable in Bamford; and I'm sure Trevor Barker didn't mean to do that!'

He gave a decisive nod. 'I've already told him that I don't think I can spare Paget. But I'll call him again and confirm it. After all, we might find ourselves with murder on our hands here!'

'I hope not!' exclaimed Jess.

She retreated to her own office and found a cooling mug of coffee on her desk. Jess settled down to sip it and reflect on the conversation she'd just had. There hadn't exactly been a downturn in violent crime recently. There was always an element of the population that felt a good night out wasn't complete without a punch-up. As elsewhere in town and country, there'd been an increase in knives being used, where once it would have been bottles. This had led to serious injuries and, yes, in one recent case death, a young life taken. Victim aged seventeen, the knife-wielder only sixteen, a tragedy for all concerned.

There had been several domestic 'incidents'. Usually, the women had come off worst in these; but lately a quite elderly and here-tofore respectable lady, pillar of her local church flower club and famous organiser of charitable events, had turned on her husband of fifty years and battered him senseless with a brass candlestick. Expressed opinion in her community was that the offender had 'gone off her head'.

The candlestick had been brought from the church by the attacker. Asked why she'd taken it home, she had replied that she always did. 'From time to time, you know, to give it a good polish. Those big old ornamental candlesticks take ages to do properly. I like to sit at my kitchen table and make a decent job of it!'

She had certainly made a good job of beating up her life's partner. Jess suspected years of secret domestic abuse. Nearly always, the woman in the partnership was the victim. But not every time. Men who suffered seldom came forward to admit and complain. The humiliation would be too great. In addition, that generation and social group 'didn't talk' about such things.

Asked if she could give an explanation for her actions, the wife had simply replied that she had 'not been sleeping very well lately'.

But a murder? No, they hadn't had what you'd call an intentional murder, planned by a determined and remorseless killer, for a little while. Not since that flurry of homicide centred in and around Weston St Ambrose. They were probably due one. Hopefully, it wouldn't happen anywhere near Weston St Ambrose next time.

The coffee was too cold to be enjoyable. Jess relinquished it unfinished. Her mind had begun to move down a different, though not unconnected track. Relationships were tricky things. When Mike Foley had first arrived on the scene, Jess had realised that her brother, Simon, Mike's co-worker in a camp for refugees in what remained, despite official denial, a warzone, had fully intended that his sister keep an eye on his old friend. On Jess's part, she'd become more involved than was wise. Mike had never made a secret of his determination to go back to the camp and take up where he'd left off. The relationship might be good while it lasted, but last it wouldn't. Sometimes, like the coffee she'd abandoned, a relationship wasn't hot enough to start with, and eventually it had to be discarded.

There was always an 'if'. In the case of the coffee, *if* Ian Carter had not detained her, keen to discuss his troubles with his daughter and ex-wife, she would have arrived early enough to find the mug still hot. Ian didn't approve of her semi-detached relationship with Mike. Blame Ian for her missing her elevenses. But was Ian Carter also the problem in the relationship with Mike? Jess didn't want to pursue her ruminations any further.

'Stop daydreaming!' she ordered herself aloud. 'Do some work!'

Chapter 4

'Did you sleep well, dear?' asked Prue that morning, when Miff limped down to breakfast.

'Um, yes, thank you, Auntie. Really well.'

No, really badly. He could hear – or imagined he could – the rustling, outstretched arms of that damn spooky oak tree all night long. It invaded his dreams, turning them into nightmares in which BMW man, unseen but ever-present, pursued him across an alien landscape, always on his heels.

He felt better after he'd demolished a really splendid breakfast, a feast of bacon, eggs, sausages, tomatoes, toast with a choice of marmalade or jam, both home-made, and pots of tea. He wondered if the Blackwoods ate like this every morning. He suspected they didn't. It was in his honour.

'I thought, Auntie, that last night someone mentioned a shop in the village.'

'It calls itself a supermarket,' rumbled Uncle Henry. 'We had no shop at all before that. Even so, when it was first proposed, some people got up a petition against it.'

'Why?' asked Miff, intrigued.

'Eyesore,' said Henry briefly.

'Well, it is, a bit,' agreed Prue. 'But it's really useful. Turn right,

49

as you leave here, and just keep walking. You'll come to it just before you reach the Rosetta Gardens estate.'

'Watch out and avoid that,' advised Henry. 'The Rosetta Gardens has a bit of a reputation.'

'What for?' asked Miff with interest.

'There's always trouble there, police called out, that sort of thing. Fights, rowdy parties, drugs, at least one of the tenants has been in prison, to our knowledge,' confided Prue. 'His daughter was murdered locally, and it hasn't been the only murder. Oh, you wouldn't believe what goes on here sometimes!'

Miff dropped his knife. It fell to the floor and he took his time scrabbling to retrieve it. When he sat up again, he said in as controlled a voice as he could manage, 'Murder?'

'Oh, yes,' said Prue. 'Really very sad. We were all very distressed. It had a big effect on the writers' group and rather, well . . .'

She looked at Henry in appeal.

'Rather knocked us all for six,' said Henry gruffly. 'Although there is some talk of getting the group up and going again – the writers' group, I mean. It's been proposed we change the name to "Writers' Circle", to make a fresh start. If we do, I suppose you might like to come along, Matthew? Since you are planning a book. Of course, we all write fiction of one kind or another. Your book sounds much more serious.'

'It's only at a very early stage,' Miff said quickly. He didn't want to be drawn into a literary discussion right now, so asked, 'Got any good pubs hereabouts?'

Both Blackwoods shook their heads.

'Very ordinary,' said Henry.

'Nowhere really nice to sit and enjoy a quiet drink,' added

Prue. 'The best is the lounge at the Royal Oak, which is a small hotel and has a restaurant. Otherwise, there's only the Black Horse. That's very – basic.'

The lounge at a small country hotel didn't sound Miff's sort of place at all. Probably the sort of establishment that gave itself airs. On the other hand, it might take on casual labour, clearing up, that sort of thing. Or they might even need a barman. He could try there for work. For a pint, the Black Horse might prove a possibility. Miff liked the sound of 'basic'.

After breakfast, he set out to find the supermarket. When he did, he thought it was probably contravening the Trade Descriptions Act. It really wasn't much more than a convenience store. Nevertheless, he went in. For one thing, he needed to buy a razor to preserve his clean-shaven appearance, and for another, such places were often good for local information.

On entering, he passed a stout, bearded old boy who was coming out, carrying a newspaper and a plastic container of milk. He was wearing what looked to Miff like a Christmas sweater, only well before the event. It had prancing reindeer on it.

'Good morning!' boomed the wearer.

Miff returned the greeting. That was the country for you. People wished complete strangers a 'good morning'. In towns and cities, they ignored you. Old ladies ran their shopping trollies over your foot. Surly kids deliberately bumped into you. Their buggy-pushing mothers glared. Nobody cared.

Here, either they cared, which was a warming, kindly thought. Or, equally possible, they were prey to a curiosity that could become a nuisance. He had been marked down as a stranger. The bearded old gent would pass the word. Lock your doors!

The store's floor area was square, with stacks of shelves set in rows, narrow ends towards the tills. That way, the staff could see straight down between them, in case any customer was thinking of pinching a packet of biscuits. There were some freezer cabinets against the far wall. Miff managed to find a packet of disposable razors, and approached the tills. Only one of them was currently in use, in the charge of a short girl wearing an overall on which was pinned a brooch telling the customer her name was 'Debbie'. She had been watching Miff since he'd entered, with an interest that was so intense it was avid. Face to face with her now, he saw she had a round face with bright eyes, a snub nose, and a shock of hair dyed bright orange. The hair stood straight up, as if she'd been plugged into an electric socket. She reminded him of a squirrel.

'Hello,' she said cheerfully. 'You're new!'

He would have to get used to this sort of thing before the novelty of his presence wore off. 'Yes,' he said. 'I arrived last night.'

She grinned at him. 'Then you must be the guy my Auntie Glenys saw sitting on the Blackwoods' doorstep.'

'Oh? A neighbour of theirs, is she, your auntie?'

'No, not really. She lives on the Rosetta Gardens estate.' (Aha, Weston's haunt of riotous living and unlawful activity!) 'She'd been to visit my grandma in the old cottages down by the river.'

'A real local, then, your grandma!' Miff wasn't sure why he'd said that. But a reply of some sort seemed expected of him.

'We all are,' retorted Debbie, a touch snappishly. 'All the Garleys.'

'How many of them – I mean, how many members of your family does that make living here?'

Debbie screwed up her snub nose as she made a mental count. 'Twenty-three,' she said at last.

'Twenty-three? What – all in one family?' Miff asked tactlessly. 'I mean, all living in one village?'

'Well, cousins and that, you know,' explained Debbie. 'Some of them are Fallons. Most of those live at Long Weston, just down the road. But Garleys and Fallons are all related, so we're one family, really. We sort of marry each other.' After a tiny pause, she added, 'And that.' She didn't specify what 'and that' meant, but Miff thought he could guess.

'And do all the ones here, apart from your grandmother, live on the Rosetta Gardens estate?'

'Of course not! Some live in the other cottages by Grandma's. There's a row of four cottages down there and all but one of them have Garleys and Fallons living in them. Only Uncle Bert and Auntie Glenys live out at Rosetta. I'm in their spare room at the moment,' she added.

He fought the urge to ask why. He didn't know or care why. It didn't matter to him. He was in the Blackwoods' spare room. That did matter. All the same, Miff found himself asking, 'Who lives in the one cottage your lot haven't taken over?'

'Morgan does. He pots.'

'Potty?' queried Miff cautiously, seeking clarification.

Debbie considered her answer. 'Not really, just squiffy all the time, you know . . .' She mimed upending a glass or bottle. 'He makes pots.'

Debbie stopped chattering and waited, squirrel eyes fixed on

Miff. He realised he was expected to lay his cards on the table, in return for her information. 'The Blackwoods are my uncle and aunt. I'm visiting for a bit.'

He had family locally. It gave him credibility, as he had reckoned it would. Debbie was impressed. So she should be. Her mouth hung open and he could imagine her logging the information in her memory banks, to be passed on to every customer who came in the store today.

Miff wondered briefly about the other locals. Henry and Prue were normal – compared with the ones he'd met or heard about so far. They didn't wear Christmas sweaters out of season, they weren't permanently 'squiffy', and they didn't make pots. They wrote novels never to be published.

'It's like this,' continued Miff in a confidential tone, resting his elbow on the counter and leaning towards her. Debbie's eyes took on that squirrel sheen again. 'I'm looking for work. Odd-job man, fixing things.'

She shook her head. 'Garleys and Fallons do all that sort of work.'

Miff realised that he hadn't considered that Weston St Ambrose, and probably Lower Weston as well, were run by a Mafia-type extended family operating a closed shop. He straightened up. He'd have to ask at the Royal Oak if they wanted a barman.

Debbie was studying him shrewdly, top to toe. 'You can't have come here just to look for work and visit your uncle and aunt.'

'Why not?' demanded Miff, nettled.

Debbie gave him a knowing grin. 'Obvious.'

Why it was obvious to her, Miff had no idea. But he was uneasy. He'd come here for anonymity and cover: increasingly, it seemed neither were possible. 'I've come to write a book!' he said on the spur of the moment.

'What sort of book?' demanded Debbie.

'Non-fiction.' Debbie was frowning, so Miff added, 'A comment on social conditions in the deprived inner cities.'

'Who's going to read that?' she retorted.

Miff had no answer to that. Probably it wouldn't leap off the bookstore shelves. But then, he hadn't written the wretched thing yet.

Debbie pursued the point. 'If that's what you're doing, no wonder you're looking for work!' Suddenly she pointed at a notice-board by the door. It had various odd scraps of paper pinned to it. 'There's something on there, I think. Have a look, why don't you? Only you gotta pay for that razor first.'

Miff paid for the razor, noticing that Debbie's fingernails were each painted a different colour. Then he went to study the noticeboard. Bingo! On one square of paper was printed: *Assistant needed, part time only. Minglebury Garden Centre. Contact proprietor Sam French.*

He glanced towards Debbie but another customer had come in and an argument had arisen concerning some tomatoes purchased the day before.

'They was reduced!' Debbie was defending the supermarket's reputation.

'They were furry!' declared the customer. She was a large-boned elderly woman with grey hair chopped in an uneven bob. She wore a baggy skirt and a hand-knitted cardigan that was longer in the front than at the back. She continued, 'They *were* reduced, Debbie, *were*. I struggled for five years to impart some knowledge of basic grammar to you, but obviously, I was wasting my time. But that's immaterial. Just because you reduce the price, Debbie, it doesn't mean you can sell rotting tomatoes.'

'If they was furry, you'd have seen it when you bought them, so would I!' argued Debbie, clearly spoiling for a really good fight, and not intimidated by the challenge. Nor was she to be bullied into improving her grasp of English grammar.

'Don't argue with me, Debbie Garley! The ones on the top of the box looked all right. But the ones underneath them were furry!'

'I don't know anything about that, Mrs Porter. They looked all right to me. You should have used them straight away. If you buy reduced fruit and veg,' Debbie was warming up nicely, 'then you shouldn't leave 'em lying about. It only makes sense!'

'I'll thank you not to give me backchat, Debbie Garley!'

'I'm only pointing out the obvious, Mrs Porter, and I'm not in your English class any longer, so it's no good shouting at me!'

Miff was tempted to stay and see how it played out, but he had something to do. He unpinned the card about the job and put it in his pocket. Then he left the combatants to it and went back to the Blackwoods' home to ask them where he could find Minglebury Garden Centre.

It was located, the Blackwoods informed him, on the opposite side of Weston St Ambrose to the supermarket (and Rosetta Gardens estate).

'And it's only very small. We've called in there a couple of times, haven't we, Prue? We bought some tomato plants from them back in the spring. And some geraniums, didn't we?' Henry appealed to his wife.

'Oh, yes, we did,' she agreed. 'A very nice young couple were running it. They have a coffee shop of sorts. It is only tea or coffee and a limited range of sandwiches and scones. Glenys Garley was in charge of that when we were there.'

Miff felt quite pleased with himself because he knew who Glenys Garley was.

'That's the aunt of the girl on the till at the supermarket – Debbie?'

'My goodness, Matthew, you have been finding things out!'

'Well, I called in there . . . There was another customer there. Debbie called her Mrs Porter.'

'Oh, lord . . .' mumbled Henry. 'Yes, you'll soon find out who we all are, Matthew. But be warned, Garleys are *everywhere*. It's like a bush telegraph system.'

'Auntie Glenys,' said Miff, 'I mean, Debbie's Aunt Glenys, saw me sitting on your doorstep yesterday evening.'

'She was cycling home from the garden centre, I dare say,' Henry snorted. 'Nosy old bat.'

'Now, Henry, that's not quite fair. It's a good thing that people keep an eye open. Like Neighbourhood Watch.'

'Glenys Garley saw a stranger on our doorstep but she didn't do anything about it, did she? Other than spread the word around the Garley gang.'

Discord was in the air.

Miff said quickly, 'I'll just walk down to this garden centre. I understand they need a helper.'

'I'll drive you down there, Matthew. It's a fair walk.'

'Jenny Porter, that's the customer you saw in the supermarket, she knows all about the history of Minglebury,' Prue informed him. 'She's read it all up and she gave a talk to the writers' group once, didn't she, Henry? There's nothing there now except farmland and the garden centre, but in the early Middle Ages, it was a hamlet. It was one of those places where everyone died in the Black Death. That was the end of Minglebury. People were superstitious then. No one would live where the plague had been, in case it was in the soil.'

Just the spot for a garden centre! Miff thought. He realised how naïve he had been in thinking he could come to Weston St Ambrose to escape being pursued by a murderer. Did no one here die peacefully? He was beginning to feel like the guy who went to Damascus to escape a rendezvous with Death; and got there to find the Grim Reaper grinning at him.

'Right,' he said. 'Thanks, Uncle Henry.' He thought about asking them if they knew an old bearded guy who wore Christmas sweaters out of season. They probably did, but it could wait. He'd find out soon enough.

Chapter 5

Far away, in Bamford, Alan Markby had nothing more on his mind than lifting the onions in his garden for winter storage. Onions always did well in this soil. So did parsnips. He would be digging those up soon. The early September sun shone on his back, the birds fluttered in the trees. His wife, Meredith, was in the house working away on the latest of the detective yarns she'd taken to writing since retiring from her government work. Put simply, all was right with his world.

'Alan?' He looked up and saw his wife had approached unheard and was standing by him. Today's sunlight picked out the blond hairs mingling with the grey and sparkled her untidy mop with gold. She had her hands in the pockets of her jeans and a quizzical expression on her face. 'You've got a visitor,' she said.

'Who?' he asked suspiciously, because when Meredith had that look on her face, he was about to be considerably inconvenienced in some way.

'Her name is Harmony Button.' Meredith's mouth twitched. 'She said you'd remember her. I've never set eyes on her in my life.'

'I've never met anyone called Harmony!' Markby protested immediately. 'Are you sure about this?'

'I couldn't make a mistake about a name like that. She insists you knew her father – or, as she refers to him, her "old dad". Also her brothers, you knew them, too.' By now his wife was controlling her laughter with the greatest difficulty. 'Alan Markby! You've been leading a double life. Own up!'

'Button!' exclaimed Markby. 'There used to be a local family called that, petty crooks to a man and woman, with a spot of burglary thrown in. But it was years ago. How old is Harmony and what does she look like?'

'Well,' Meredith stared up at the sky, 'I'd say she's late thirties. She has a mass of jet-black hair, and is, um, generously built. She's also what my mother used to call "made up to the nines". I am assuming that's for your benefit. It can't be for mine!'

'Well, she might be one of the younger ones, grown older,' Alan muttered. 'There were a lot of kids. Her old dad himself would now be at least my age. What on earth does she want with me?'

'Aha!' Meredith retorted, grinning. 'That's what we both want to know!'

'Speak for yourself, my girl. I really don't want to know anything about this. I suppose I have to go and speak to her?'

'That's why she's here. She's sitting in the kitchen drinking tea and eating all the biscuits.'

'Give me a chance to wash my hands and rack my brains. Tell her I'll be there directly. I do wish you'd asked her what she wants.'

'I did, but she wouldn't tell me. She said she wants to speak to Superintendent Markby.' Meredith leaned forward and added in a low, theatrical whisper, 'She says it's personal!'

'But I'm not a superintendent any longer! I'm not any kind of police officer! I've retired!' howled Markby in despair. But his wife was already on her way back to the kitchen.

Harmony was waiting for him, still seated at the table with the emptied biscuit tin before her. She made a handsome sight, he had to admit, with the cloud of black hair and her blue eye shadow, heavy mascara and scarlet mouth. She rose ponderously to her feet as he entered, her jewellery glittering and the folds of a generously cut tent-shaped garment undulating. He was put in mind of a Spanish galleon getting under sail. She had gone to considerable trouble to prepare herself for this visit and he supposed he ought to feel flattered. Instead, Markby felt a growing alarm. What on earth did she want?

'You won't remember me, Mr Markby,' she greeted him. 'But you will remember my old dad.'

'Harry Button,' he replied. 'I take it your father is Harry. How is he, these days?'

'Can't get about much,' she told him, 'that's why he sent me. We discussed it in the family. Gary or Declan could have come, but Dad said, it had better be me.'

Ah, yes, Gary and Declan. As youngsters Declan had been as artful a rogue as you could meet, and Gary had been a tearaway and local thug. Amazingly, in latter years, both had morphed into owners of businesses. Markby seemed to remember Declan ran a scrapyard, a familiar eyesore on the outskirts of the town. Gary was into a different class of scrap. He sold 'antiques'. *Antiques*, for pity's sake! How had that happened?

Perhaps, thought Markby, both had decided it was better to stay out of gaol. After all, they must have seen little of old Harry, their father, when they were growing up. Harry Button had been in and out of the nick like a yo-yo. Nowadays, old Harry must be retired.

Curious, he asked, 'You have another brother, I think, Michael? Am I right? And a couple of sisters?'

'Michael's in prison,' she informed him.

Markby raised his eyebrows and looked at her enquiringly.

'He did the dress shop on the square one night, on his way home from the pub. He must have been tight, or he wouldn't have been so daft. He should have known they wouldn't leave anything in the till. So he helped himself to a load of jewellery they had on display. Nothing real, you understand, all fake. But some of it was pretty, glittery, you know. He was selling it at a car boot sale, when he got picked up.'

Oh, so at least one of the Button sons had kept up the family interest in burglary. Costume jewellery, eh? Harmony was wearing several pieces of that. When she moved and the light struck them, she flashed like a set of warning lights.

'Bad luck, really,' continued Harmony with a sigh. 'The cops were looking round the car boot sale for some stuff stolen somewhere else. They recognised Michael, saw all the stuff spread out for sale, asked him where he got it . . . and it all went wrong.'

'Oh, I see.' Markby could see that his wife, standing behind the visitor, was stifling a giggle. He gave her a severe look. Crime was no laughing matter.

'And one of my sisters has trouble with her feet, so she couldn't come.' Harmony was pursuing the update on her family. 'Anyway, it's the other one I've come about. Amber. She's the youngest. I mean, she's the youngest in our generation. There's grandkids, of course, and great-grandchildren too. But I'm just talking about us, Mum and Dad's kids.' She added, 'Mum died three years ago and Dad lives with me.'

There was a pause while Harmony resettled herself at the table and stared meaningfully at her empty mug.

'I'll make some more tea,' offered Meredith. 'I expect you could do with a cup, Alan.'

He felt he could do with something rather stronger, but he'd have to fortify himself with tea.

'You got a nice house here,' said Harmony suddenly. 'Used to be the vicarage, right?'

'Yes, that's right.'

'My brother Gary, he's got contacts in the antiques trade, if you're interested in that sort of stuff, this house being old and that.'

'Thanks, but we're okay for furniture, at the moment.' Antiques, my foot. Anything Gary was selling would have been made within the last year or two in the Far East and artfully 'distressed' with a hammer in Gary's lock-up. His unease increased. He suspected Harmony had just made the first move in a game of bargaining tactics. Gary can get me a Louis XV desk and, by the way, there's something I can do for the family . . .

'What is Amber's problem?' he asked. He had no intention of getting involved in anything to do with the Button clan, but he was curious. It was the ex-police detective in his make-up. He had to know. From the corner of his eye he saw Meredith give him a slight frown. He added, 'Although I don't think I can help you, um, Harmony.'

'If any of us knew what her problem was,' replied Harmony, 'I wouldn't be here, would I? She hasn't come near any of us for months. Dad, well, let's be honest . . .'

Markby wondered whether any of the Buttons truly appreciated the wider meaning of 'honest'. However, in family matters, they might apply different standards from those they used when dealing with the public at large.

'Amber was always Dad's favourite. That's why he's taken it so bad that she's cut herself off from the rest of us. And because he lives with me, I hear about it day and night.'

Harmony sighed and picked up her refilled mug. 'Thanks, love,' she said in Meredith's general direction. 'He won't give up. "Go and find her," he keeps saying. "She's in trouble, I know it." So, I've been looking and asking. So have Gary and Declan and Maria, when she can get out because of her feet. You should see her bunions.'

'Maria's bunions?'

Harmony nodded. 'It's all because of those shoes she wears. Over seven months gone and staggering about on them heels, but that's Maria for you. It's Amber I'm here about. None of us can find hide nor hair of her. It's like she's vanished, you know. It's like . . . like a spaceship came down and took her.'

Alarmed, Markby asked, 'Harry doesn't think a spaceship came down and took Amber, does he?'

Harmony set down her mug with a clunk on the tabletop. 'Of course he doesn't! He's wandering a bit but he's not seeing things or gone quite potty. It'll be a man, that's what it'll be. With Amber, any trouble is to do with a man. She's got no sense when it comes to men. Picks one loser after another.' For some reason, Harmony turned and addressed the next sentence to Meredith. 'You know what I mean, love, don't you?'

Startled, Meredith mumbled, 'Yes . . .'

Having made an appeal to the sisterhood and got backing for her theory, Harmony turned back to Markby. 'First off, I went to where she's been living. She's been lodging with old Mrs Clack in Station Road. She lets a couple of rooms, you know, to make ends meet. She's only got her old-age pension otherwise. I don't know how the old folk manage. I mean, Dad's with me, so with his pension and what my partner and I—'

'We were talking of Mrs Clack!' Markby interrupted, because with Harmony in full flow, it was difficult not to be borne away on a stream of narrative.

'That's what I said!' snapped Harmony. 'Old Myrtle Clack was no use. She said she'd been wondering where Amber was, too. Because the date for the next month's rent was coming up, and she'd not seen Amber nor heard from her. I explained who I was and she let me go up and look in Amber's room. She came with me, mind! Watched me like a hawk all the time and looking through everything as I was doing it. She was trying to find something that would tell us where Amber was, she said. But she was just being nosy.

'All Amber's clothes were still there in the wardrobe, and her make-up and hairbrush on the dressing table. Even her earrings were there in a little painted box she got in Spain, and her passport in a drawer with her undies. But no Amber, and nothing to suggest where she'd got to. So Mrs Clack said, if Amber didn't come back or send the rent, I should come and clear the room out. She'd need to relet.'

'Where does your sister work?' asked Meredith.

Harmony turned her head to study Meredith afresh. 'Work? She don't work. She's on the social. Well, she's had jobs, you know, now and then. But she never keeps them. I think her men friends give her money sometimes.'

Harmony cleared her throat and added with unexpected delicacy of tone, 'But she's never been professional, you understand.'

Alan and Meredith murmured politely that they understood, although Meredith looked sceptical. Markby managed to keep his expression bland.

Reluctantly, Harmony admitted, 'She does pick up blokes in clubs and bars. But that's just her way. She could never get herself organised, Amber. Anyhow, the next thing was, Dad was watching the local area news on the TV and there was a report of an unidentified body found in one of those old warehouses. Young woman. Naturally, he decided right off, it must be Amber. So that's why I've come to you.'

With this, Harmony had reached the end of her explanation, and sat back, watching him expectantly.

'Harmony,' Alan said carefully, aware of Meredith's eyes on him, 'I am very sorry, of course, to hear of your family troubles. I sympathise with your father. I understand how worried you all must be. But I have long been retired from the police force and, since I'm no longer a serving officer, there's really nothing I can do myself to help. I can't interfere.'

Harmony broke in. 'You helped Dilys Browning and her brother when there was all that fuss about a body in the spinney!'

'That was different. It was connected with an old unsolved case of mine from years back. Your problem is different . . .'

Harmony uttered a long, slow, menacing hiss. 'What's different?'

Alan ignored the throwing down of the gauntlet, to continue, 'If your sister Amber is missing, you should report it to the police station here. They will record it as a missing person and—'

'And do sod all!' snapped Harmony. 'I'm talking about my

family, Mr Markby. Since when does a Button go into any cop shop and make a report about anything?'

'Never been known, I dare say,' Markby continued calmly. 'But that's what you have to do. And if you have reason – as your father believes possible – to think that the unidentified body found locally in a disused warehouse could be that of your sister, then you *must* tell the police.'

Harmony simmered for a moment or two, glowering at him. Then she announced, 'I'm not going to the cops on my own! They won't listen to me. It's no use you saying they will, because I'm telling you they won't! You gotta come with me!'

The last thing Trevor Barker needed or wanted in his office was the former Superintendent Markby turning up to make a report and stir things up. They'd already been through all that once in the Browning case. 'I really can't go with you, Harmony. It would be – awkward.'

Meredith, who had been listening while propped against the Welsh dresser, straightened up. 'It's all right, Harmony. I understand. Alan can't go with you. It wouldn't be tactful. But I'll go.'

Harmony swivelled on her chair and looked Meredith up and down. 'You'll come with me to the cops?'

'Certainly. And they'll listen to me, won't they, Alan?'

'Why not?' he replied with a sigh. 'I do.'

'Listen, Harmony,' Meredith said, stopping her companion on the police station steps. 'Before we see anyone and make any kind of report, you do understand that it's not an offence for someone to go missing? People do it all the time. Ask Alan. And sometimes they come back without any explanation.'

'They don't leave all their clothes behind,' said Harmony.

'Yes, sometimes they do. They leave a husband and children behind, and good jobs and all kinds of responsibilities. I want to be frank, Harmony, you don't mind?'

'All the same if I do, I suppose?' retorted Harmony.

'There has to be some evidence or good reason for suspecting foul play, or the missing person has to be underage or very elderly, vulnerable somehow, before the police take any action. They're not there to patch up private problems. So, if perhaps you were thinking the police wouldn't treat the report of Amber's disappearance seriously, and not start any searches . . . Well, you wouldn't have had the idea of saying she might be the dead girl in the warehouse, just to get the police interested?'

'No,' said Harmony simply. 'It's Dad that's got it into his head she's the dead girl.'

'And you understand you may have to go and look at a corpse, at the morgue?'

'You're still going to come with me, right?' demanded Harmony.

Meredith sighed. 'Yes, if you want me to.' Not exactly how she'd planned to spend the rest of the day.

'Of course I want you to! That's why I came to see your husband, isn't it?'

Inspector Trevor Barker leaned back in his chair and surveyed his two visitors with poorly disguised trepidation. Meredith wondered which of the two of them, herself or Harmony Button, caused him the most concern. He looked from one to the other of them, undecided whom to tackle first. Meredith tried for a confident and encouraging smile. Harmony drew herself up and her eyes sparkled with challenge.

'Well, er, Meredith,' began Barker, making up his mind. 'I'm pleased to see you, of course, but this matter of Amber Button's whereabouts could have been reported at the desk.'

'No, it couldn't!' snapped Harmony before Meredith could reply. 'I'd have been told to go away!'

'Well, I don't think so, Ms Button,' protested the inspector. 'We take any report seriously—'

'Not from any of my family, you don't!' retorted Harmony.

Barker drew a deep breath. Meredith wondered whether he would say they generally received reports *about* the Buttons, rather than from one of them. But he had turned back to her. 'She could have gone away for a few days. There have been some cheap package holidays on offer in local travel agents'. It's getting towards the end of the season.'

'What? Decided to take off for Majorca without a clean pair of knickers or her passport?' Harmony demanded with heavy sarcasm.

Barker resolutely ignored her and continued to address himself to Meredith. 'It's true we have a so far unidentified corpse. Would Ms Button be willing to attempt an identification?'

Harmony, not to be excluded by being addressed in the third person, moved forward to loom over him. 'You can talk to me direct, you know! I'm not deaf, and I'm not daft. You're not a judge, neither. Meredith ain't my counsel. You got a question, ask me direct!'

'You brought Mrs Markby with you to act as your spokesperson!' retorted Barker, stung into defending himself.

'So as you'd listen to *me*, not just to *her*!'

Meredith took Harmony by the arm and gently persuaded her back into her chair.

Barker decided that brisk and businesslike was best. 'All right, then, Ms Button, are you willing to let us take you to the morgue, to see if you can make an identification of the corpse we have there?'

'Why? How many murdered bodies have you got there? If it's a dead woman, it'll be my sister!'

'Someone has to make – someone has to go and look!' Barker was losing control of his temper. Distressed and frightened relatives were one thing. He had a procedure worked out to deal with them. Harmony Button was another kettle of fish altogether.

'It's necessary, Harmony,' Meredith told her.

'All right, then, let's go!' Harmony got to her feet and strode to the door.

Meredith took the opportunity to whisper hastily to Barker. 'She wouldn't come without me. She's frightened, I think. She's been looking for her sister and her elderly father is distressed. Also, I think she's frightened of being in a police station, her family being known to you all.'

'She's pretty frightening herself!' returned Barker. 'I'm quite glad you're here, Meredith. We'll take a squad car and get down there.'

Markby sat in the gathering twilight gloom in the sitting room with a glass of whisky at his elbow and conducted a mental argument with his conscience.

'Listen!' he told it. 'You know what Trevor Barker was like when I went to see him about Josh and his sister and that bracelet? If I had gone to see him with Harmony Button and some story about a missing sister, Trevor would have given me very short shrift! At least, in that other affair, I had some evidence by way of the bracelet, and it was all on file as an unsolved case. This is Harmony Button with some yarn about a missing sibling. Goodness only knows, perhaps Amber Button just wants to put some distance between herself and the rest of the clan. She may have a dozen good reasons.'

'You should still have gone yourself,' his conscience retorted. 'Not left it to Meredith. It was you Harmony came to see!'

'Meredith is good at this sort of thing. She used be a consular officer.'

'You,' sneered his conscience, 'used to be a copper!'

'A police officer, yes. A social worker, no!'

'Then why didn't you send Harmony to see someone at Social Services?'

'And why don't you just keep quiet!' Markby told the voice in his head, and could imagine his conscience sitting there with a sneer on its face, knowing it had won the argument.

He had switched on a couple of lamps by the time Meredith came back.

She looked tired and threw herself into the opposite chair. 'Pour me one of those, please?' She indicated his whisky.

Markby did as he was bid and, handing her the glass, said, 'I'm really sorry. I should have gone. I was passing the buck and I had no right to do that.'

'It's okay. I volunteered.'

'You've been gone for over three hours. I'm guessing you had to go to see the body?'

She nodded. 'Harmony identified the deceased as her sister, Amber Button. She'd been strangled. It wasn't pretty.'

'Oh damn,' muttered Markby. 'I shouldn't have put you through that. Harmony was very distressed, I suppose? It's what she'd feared. But actually to see . . .'

'She was very upset, certainly. She didn't break down. That's not her way. Instead, she addressed the body, like at a Russian funeral, only less spiritual and more disrespectful. "You stupid cow, now look what's happened!" was how she began. But that wasn't the worst of it. She insisted I go with her afterwards, to break the sad news to their father.'

'How did Harry take it?'

Meredith was silent for a few moments. Then she said, 'He has limited mobility. They've bought one of those armchairs that help you stand up. You know the sort of thing? The sitter presses a button and the chair pushes him up into a standing position.'

'I know what you mean.'

'He's a very small man now; I suppose he was once bigger. Muscle wastage and so on. The chair is capacious and he looks lost in it. He just sat there and cried. Didn't say much, hardly anything. Just wept.'

'And the family have no idea, *really no idea* who . . .'

'I don't think they do. If they had any idea, they would have sorted it out for themselves before now. Going to the police means they are desperate. Harmony just keeps saying it will be one of Amber's men friends. Amber picked wrong 'uns. Anyway, then Gary and Declan turned up, the brothers. She'd texted them from the morgue. They brought their wives with them, both women dressed in their best clothes – formal occasion, you see. The men had found leather jackets, and a bottle of whisky for their father. They promised him they'd find out who killed her. I think they'll make real trouble for Trevor Barker. They want vengeance. Harmony got on the phone to Maria, the sister with the bad feet, and they were expecting her to join them all with her husband. It's only a small house and it will be bursting at the seams. I left them to it. They'd forgotten me by then, anyway.'

After a pause, Markby said, 'That's all you could do, Meredith, and it was more than enough. It's Barker's case now.' He added after a moment, 'I should have taken Harmony more seriously. None of the Buttons would approach anyone even remotely connected with authority unless they were genuinely worried and had done all they could to find their sister. Amber's obviously been a part-time prostitute for years. They must have been expecting something like this.'

Meredith said thoughtfully, 'In that case, what about the land-lady, Mrs Clack, who "lets out a couple of rooms". Has she actually been supplementing her pension by running a brothel?'

'Trevor Barker will have his work cut out if he wants to look into that. He'll check her out; but the old girl will never admit a thing, and it will be difficult to prove. He'll have his problems with Gary and Declan Button, too. You said they wanted vengeance. I suspect they want blood!'

Henry Blackwood dropped Miff off at the entrance to the garden centre. Miff said he would find his own way home. When Henry had driven away, he studied the scene carefully. This, he decided, had once been a small farm. There was a rambling cottage with a roof in need of attention. It sagged in the middle. There were other outbuildings: a large shed and a couple of barns, one of which bore a notice proclaiming it to be a coffee shop. That would be Auntie Glenys's lair. These buildings lined three sides of a large area laid out with raised platforms for plants and plant pots. The open area to the front had a gravelled space for car parking. There was a greenhouse. In a far corner, to the rear of the premises, stood what might once have been a stable. Parked alongside it, he could make out a muddy and ramshackle old Land Rover. It had the air of not having been moved in a long time; it may even have crawled there to die. At the roadside boundary of the property a large wooden board proudly proclaimed the legend 'MINGLEBURY GARDEN CENTRE prop. Sam French'.

There were a few people wandering around in desultory fashion. Miff presumed them to be customers and, nearby, a sturdy female in jeans and a mud-stained gilet was working at one of the raised platforms. Miff approached her.

'Excuse me,' he said, 'I'm looking for Sam French.'

The girl looked up and peered at him through an untidy fringe of fair hair. He supposed her to be his own age or there-abouts. She wore no make-up and her face was freckled and sunburnt. She straightened up, wiping her soil-encrusted hands on a handy piece of cloth hanging over the edge of a bucket.

'I'm Sam French,' she said.

'Oh,' said Miff, taken aback. 'Oh, right. Well, I've come about this.' He extracted the card advertising for help from his pocket. 'It was on the noticeboard at the supermarket. My name is M— Matthew Ferguson.'

'You got out of Henry Blackwood's car,' said Sam.

Could one draw breath in this place without someone taking note? 'Yes, he's my uncle. I've come to stay for a bit – and write a book.' He added, 'A social commentary on homelessness and its impact.'

This reason for being in Weston St Ambrose sounded even thinner now he told Sam than it had when he'd told the Blackwoods and Debbie Garley. Sam had a shrewd look in her blue-grey eyes and he suspected she didn't believe a word. But she had seen him with Henry, so she couldn't dismiss the whole thing. He decided it was best to come clean. 'Well, it's what I've told Henry and Prue, anyway. I might even do it.'

There was a spark of amusement in the blue-grey eyes. 'Would you like a cup of coffee?' she asked. 'And we can discuss it.'

They collected their coffee from an interested Glenys Garley in the barn but carried it over to the cottage, where Sam had her office, to drink.

'Because,' explained Sam, 'Glenys is really great in so many ways. But she's not discreet and she does, well, eavesdrop.'

'I've been told about the Garley messaging service,' Miff said.

The office had once been a sitting room. Although it now boasted a computer and a wall lined with shelves stuffed with catalogues and gardening books, it also had its original armchairs, and the sort of television set Lord Reith might have recognised. Sam banged the seat of an armchair vigorously, raising a small cloud of dust.

'It gets in,' she explained, 'from outside. And I don't have much time for housework.'

She sat down in the other armchair and Miff took the one she'd kindly prepared.

'Do you know much about gardening?' she asked.

'Not a thing,' admitted Miff. 'But I'm willing to learn, and I'm okay with moving heavy stuff about and so on.'

He felt rather sheepish saying this because, compared with this healthy and very fit female, he must look pretty weedy and useless. She looked as strong as a horse, as the saying went. She had nice eyes, though, he decided.

'What did you do before you came here to Weston?'

Now for it. He might as well confirm her suspicions. She'd hear about it anyway, because there were no secrets in Weston St Ambrose. The Blackwoods might have been discreet, for family's sake, but Mrs Porter would tell everyone and, once he gave the talk to the writers' circle that he'd so rashly agreed to, everyone would know. Besides, she'd been studying him as he'd been assessing her. She'd already have judged him a drop-out.

Miff drew a deep breath. 'I was living rough.'

'Researching your book?' That quizzical look was back in her eyes.

'Not doing anything much,' he confessed. 'The idea for the book came later.'

'Have you never had a job?'

'Oh, yes. I worked in a bank, in the City, in London.'

Sam blinked. 'Then how on earth did you end up sleeping rough?'

'Believe it or not, by choice. I knew I had a good job. Parents were as happy as could be. The job was quite interesting at times. The people I worked with were a decent crowd. It was just, you know . . . upward and onward, and so on. One day I thought, this is it. This is the rest of my life. I shall end up fat and prosperous, and my life will have slipped away. I knew I had to make a decision. Stay or walk. So I walked.'

'Never regretted it?' asked Sam after a pause.

'Never, I can honestly say . . .' Miff paused. 'Well, not until recently, but that was because of something unforeseen. I'd rather not tell you.'

'Fair enough. I suppose your parents were upset when you left your job.'

'Both absolutely furious. They moved to Portugal. I don't mean they moved only because of me. They already had a holiday home and were thinking of retiring there. But when I took to living on the streets, well, it sort of made up their minds. They packed their bags and went. They couldn't face the rest of the family and the neighbours, I suppose. I ought to feel guilty, but I can't say I do. Call me selfish if you want.'

'I won't call you selfish. You felt you had to make a decision.' Sam paused. 'My partner, Stuart, did the same thing. I don't mean he walked out of here to live rough. Or I don't think he's doing that. He walked out because he'd had enough of the garden centre, and of me, too. I have to accept that. He just went. Anyhow, it's difficult from the practical point of view, running the place on my own. I've got Danny Garley working here. He's pretty good – if you make sure he's not hiding away somewhere having a smoke. And Glenys runs the coffee shop as a concession. But I have to run everything else. I suppose,' Sam eyed Miff thoughtfully, 'if you worked in a top-notch merchant bank, sorting out this office would be a doddle for you?'

Miff glanced round the crammed, dusty room, and grinned. Hastily he wiped away the smile. 'Probably,' he said.

'And lend a hand out there from time to time?' Sam waved towards the window and the trays of plants.

'Anything you want.'

'I can't pay very much.'

'Basic wage more than sufficient,' he told her. 'Can I ask one thing? I am living with Henry and Prue at the moment. I think my welcome might wear a bit thin after a while. Could I camp out in one of the barns? I've got my sleeping bag and my tent.'

'You can have a room here.' Sam waved a hand towards the ceiling. 'Got a couple of spare beds.' She frowned. 'We inherited the furniture when we bought the place. The beds are old and the springs not very good.'

'No problem. I have been sleeping in a tent.'

She held out her hand. 'That's agreed, then?'

They shook on it.

'I'll bring my stuff over with me tomorrow and move in here then,' Miff said. 'I'd better stay tonight with Henry and Prue.'

Sam grinned. 'Now you can write to your parents and tell them you have another proper job.'

'I'll let Uncle Henry do that. They – my parents – have told everyone I'm doing voluntary work in Central Africa.'

'Honestly, Matthew . . .'

'I'm usually called "Miff". Only my family call me Matthew.'

'Why "Miff"?' she asked.

'From my initials,' he told her. 'M.F. Miff, you see. It wasn't my idea,' he added defensively. 'I got it at school, somehow. Someone thought it was witty. Don't ask me why. Kids think anything is funny.'

'Well, Miff, I was going to say, you've obviously inherited your very inventive mind from your parents. You really should write that book.' She indicated the computer. 'You could use that, if you want.'

'Oh, the damn book,' said Miff with a sigh. 'You know, Sam, that book is going to be a real problem.'

And in saying that, he spoke the truth. It became immediately apparent when he returned to the Blackwoods' home, to tell them the good news that he would be moving out the next day. What's more, he had found gainful employment.

But they already had another visitor; and his news would have to wait. Miff recognised the grey-haired female customer from the supermarket who'd been having a disagreement with Debbie about some tomatoes. She sat in the armchair that Miff had already realised his uncle favoured, with her feet planted firmly on the carpet, and surrounded by a scattering of cake crumbs.

'Ah, Matthew!' exclaimed Henry. 'This is Jenny Porter.' He sounded harassed.

Mrs Porter looked Miff up and down and fixed him with a gimlet stare. 'I saw you in the supermarket.'

'That's right,' agreed Miff, holding out his hand. 'Nice to meet you, Mrs Porter!' He gasped as his fingers were seized in a grip of iron. 'Get the matter of the tomatoes sorted out?' he asked, retrieving his crushed palm.

'Of course I did!' she snapped. 'Debbie Garley knows better than to try any nonsense with me. They were furry!' Mrs Porter turned to the Blackwoods. 'The ones on the top of the box were all right. But the ones underneath were absolutely furry and the shop had no right selling them. I told Debbie so.'

'Get your money back?' asked Henry.

Her complexion darkened. 'No, but I did get a replacement box of tomatoes.'

'I hope the new box is all right,' murmured Prue.

'It is! I took them all out and checked them over before I left the shop!' Jenny Porter turned to Miff. 'I am told, Matthew, that you are writing a book!'

'Well, I haven't actually written anything yet, you understand,' explained Miff. 'I've been doing research and making notes.'

'Very sensible,' said Mrs Porter with a nod of approval that took all three of the others by surprise. 'Now then, I have been discussing with Henry and Prue what kind of programme we can put together for our writers' circle, once we get up and running again.'

'Well, as a matter of fact, Jenny—' Henry began but was cut short.

'I absolutely agree with Peter, that we should start up again.' Mrs Porter rolled over his words. 'And the sooner the better. We have left it far too long. I've sounded out a couple of other people and got some new recruits. Peter says you and Prue are happy with Wednesday being the day, on a fortnightly basis, to begin on the first Wednesday of the coming month, right?'

'What, oh, yes . . .' muttered Henry.

'So I have suggested to your uncle' – Mrs Porter turned back to Miff – 'that for our inaugural meeting of the new term, as you might call it, you could tell us all about *your* writing!'

'But I haven't written anything yet!' yelped Miff.

'Then tell us about your research. How you've gone about it. Your experiences on the streets and the interesting characters you've met.'

Miff could only gaze at her in horror.

'So that's all right, then!' she said cheerfully. 'I'll let Peter know you're happy to come along and talk to us. We shall all look forward to it.'

He was trapped. He couldn't even do as he'd done when trapped in the warehouse with BMW man; or a couple of years earlier, when trapped in that merchant bank. He couldn't run, because he'd promised Sam he would move into her spare room tomorrow and get to work sorting out her accounts. She'd already seen the boyfriend scarper, the one she'd opened the centre with. A second desertion so soon would be cruel. There was nothing for it. He'd have to start writing that book – or at least start thinking seriously about it. What else could go wrong?

Miff did not spend a good night. Far from getting used to the soft bed, his body was rebelling even more. Eventually, he decided to unpack his sleeping bag from his pack over there on the chair, and unroll it on the floor. It was while he was doing this that he heard the distant sound of a siren. An emergency vehicle, certainly, but called for what purpose? He stood up and went to the window. It was difficult to see anything because of that wretched tree, but he heard voices below in the garden. Miff opened the window and leaned out. Someone was down there with a torch.

'Hello?' Miff called out.

Two figures moved further from the shelter of the house so that he could see them. The torch beam flashed briefly over him.

'Only us, Matthew!' called up his uncle.

'There's a fire somewhere!' Prue added.

Miff pulled on his jeans and a sweater and went down to join them where they stood in their dressing gowns.

'Oh, Matthew,' Prue greeted him. 'Did we wake you?'

'No, I was—' Better not to tell her about the sleeping bag on the floor. 'I heard the siren.'

'Fire engine!' said Henry. 'It's over there, the fire.' He pointed.

Sure enough, in the distance the night was lit by an angry red glow.

'Isn't that about where Reg Prescott has his farm, Henry?'

'It's in that direction, certainly, and the distance would be about right.'

'I do hope,' Prue said, 'it's not the farmhouse. Or even one of the barns.'

The wail of a second siren filled the night air.

'They've sent out backup,' said Henry. 'It must be serious. Reg has probably got hay stored in one of the barns and it's gone up. Oh, well, there's nothing we can do. We'll hear about it in the morning.'

They trooped back indoors and stood in the kitchen looking indecisively at one another.

'Anyone like some cocoa?' asked Prue.

Her suggestion was greeted with enthusiasm.

Once he was settled at the kitchen table with them, his hands clasped around a large mug of cocoa, Miff brought up the subject that had been on his mind.

'Oh, by the way, Uncle Henry,' he said, 'I meant to tell you earlier, but that woman was here and you were talking about your group—'

'Jenny Porter?' interrupted Prue. 'She does mean well, you know, but she's a bit – forceful in her way.'

'You told us you had taken a job at the garden centre,' Henry said. 'Right after she left, you told us all about that.'

'Yes, but the thing is, I don't think I mentioned there's a spare room there, in the cottage. It goes with the job, so, well, I'm very grateful to you both for taking me in as you have. After all, I just turned up . . .'

They chimed in to assure him that it was a delight to see him after so long.

'But,' said Miff firmly, as soon as he got a chance, 'I think I'll move my stuff over to the garden centre and stay there. Is that all right with you?'

'You're more than welcome to stay here, Matthew,' his uncle assured him.

'You're very kind, Uncle Henry, and it's a generous offer. But I really think it would be better if I moved out. I never meant to impose on you long term.'

Hardly the truth. He had meant to stay as long as possible. But that was before reality stuck an oar in.

Prue leaned over the table towards him, her face filled with concern. 'It's not because of Jenny, is it? You don't mind her asking you to speak to the writers' circle?'

'Oh, no,' lied Miff. 'I don't mind a bit.'

'It's not much,' apologised Sam.

It was a fair description of the bedroom she had shown Miff into. The bed was topped and tailed with brass rails. Miff thought it might have some antique value.

'The mattress isn't as old as the bed,' Sam assured him. 'We thought, Stuart and I – we thought we might get the occasional visitor, parents and so on, so we bought the mattress new. It was cheap, on offer. I think the shop was closing down. We burned the original one because it was past it. The bed frame itself and all the other stuff in here came with the house. It's like I told you. Someone died here.' In consternation she added quickly, 'I don't mean someone died in that bed. I meant, the previous owner died in the house, just of old age, I think. Whoever inherited the estate didn't want any furnishings and couldn't be bothered to clear it out. We bought the whole thing, lock, stock and barrel. Did I tell you that when you came yesterday? At the time, it seemed a good buy. It included the barns and space for the garden centre . . .' She paused. 'Oh, well, I'll leave you to settle in.'

Alone, Miff studied the room. He decided the walls had been papered about thirty years before. In parts the paper was peeling. There was more than a suggestion of damp. He opened the wardrobe door, more than half expecting to find it full of the deceased owner's clothes, but found it empty – except for a lingering smell of mothballs. He proceeded to a chest of drawers. An attempt to open the top drawer was thwarted when the knobs came away in his hand. He tried the second drawer down. Same result. He now had a collection of drawer knobs but no storage. With little hope he tried the lowest and last of the trio of drawers and, to his surprise, managed to drag it open without damage. It was empty and lined with newspaper. Curiously, he examined the newsprint and found sports coverage for July 1990.

Miff retreated to survey his new accommodation. He wasn't surprised someone had died here, probably of depression. But then, it seemed that there wasn't a spot in Weston St Ambrose where someone hadn't met his or her end in dramatic fashion.

Two framed but foxed prints hung on the walls. They were both entitled 'Coaching Days and Coaching Ways'. One showed passengers clambering into a stagecoach outside an inn. Their luggage had already been stacked atop. That one was subtitled 'Setting Off'. The other showed the same passengers, having exited the conveyance, trudging up a steep hill behind the struggling horses. Their heads were bowed against a stiff wind that tugged at their coats. That one was called 'Walking the Hill'.

'Merrie Olde England!' observed Miff aloud.

Chapter 6

Mixed with the fumes of petrol and oil was the stench of burnt flesh. It was an unmistakable odour that would cling to hair, skin and clothes. Jess pressed a handkerchief to her nose. An infernal barbecue had taken place here overnight as the van burned. That was how she couldn't help but think of it. The picture in her head was that of some mediaeval painted descent into hell. Fiends prodded along the sinners, naked and wailing, as they wound their way towards the inferno below. People had believed that was how it would be, back in the Middle Ages. The righteous would soar above to glory, but oh, for the others . . . Yet this belief didn't stop them sinning. Perhaps they'd clung to the notion they would have time to repent and be shriven. They must have known it couldn't always work out so neatly.

She would shower as soon as she got home that night, wash her hair and scrub her nails. Her clothes would all go into the washing machine. Her wellington boots would have a bath of their own. None of it would erase the stink. You couldn't put this smell in a washtub and rinse it away.

'Feeling queasy, ma'am?' asked Ben Paget beside her. There was concern in his voice and expression.

'Only temporary,' Jess told him firmly.

Paget nodded. He was a burly, fair-haired figure and looked

like a countryman. As far as she knew, he wasn't. But it prompted her to add, 'You would have been spared this if you'd stayed in Bamford!'

Paget shrugged. 'We had something like this after a three-car pile-up on the motorway last year. That was just down to someone driving too fast in heavy rain and poor visibility. But there's always some daft bugger who puts his foot down . . .' After a fractional pause, Paget added, 'Daft blighter, I should have said.'

Jess managed a faint grin. 'Don't worry about my sensibilities, sergeant! I'm pretty tough!'

'Yes, ma'am,' said Paget.

This wasn't the aftermath of a motorway smash of the sort Paget had referred to. Someone had driven the van through an opened gate and torched it, after removing the number plates. The police didn't yet know whether removing the plates had been in the forlorn hope of delaying identification of the body; or because number plates had a value of their own in the criminal world. Provided the vehicle's identifying number was still engraved on the engine block, they'd be able to trace its owner. Had the arsonist not realised that? There was something about the removal of the number plates that was unsettling. It was as if the setter of the blaze had been leaving a message saying, 'Look, I'm an amateur.' But they knew the opposite was true. This was the work of someone who had known full well what he was doing, and how to go about it. This was a murder scene.

The field sloped down from the gate so that where Jess and Paget stood, twenty feet away at a lower level, they looked up towards the burnt-out metal shell. The rear doors were still opened wide, the metal too hot to touch for more than a few seconds without protective gloves. Even at a distance, they could still feel a ripple of heat.

It had not been until the fire was well out, the wreck hosed down, that a search of the interior had been possible. That was when the fire crew had found the remains of a body.

They had not initially realised the van had had an occupant because the grim contents had been in the back, hidden under a twisted metal frame, once a sofa bed. It was when the fire scene investigators lifted out the bed that the gruesome secret had been discovered. Even then, it had taken several minutes for the reality of the find to become apparent.

'It's an old bed frame, isn't it? The sort that folds up and turns into a settee?'

'That's not!' said another man, pointing. 'That's a leg bone, a human one.'

Then they could see that what had been taken for the remains of a piece of furniture were, in reality, far more than that. Not only had the bed been in the van, but also a human body, now barely recognisable, the charred bones difficult to distinguish from the blackened metal frame and the coiled metal springs of the bed, between which they nestled.

In horrified silence, the men had stood around the discovery, speechless, as first their eyes, and then their brains, had worked out that here they had a huddled skeleton suggesting the figure had been tied hand and foot, the arms pulled back behind the spine.

The police had attended the original scene of the blaze as distant observers, and to prevent the intrusion of the curious. Fire fascinates the general public. Drawn by news of something unusual and dramatic, the ghouls would inevitably find their way to the spot. Those who turned up for this one had been fewer than might be expected, because this was out in the middle of the countryside, after all, and it had been after dark. They had been told they were causing an obstruction and ordered to clear off.

Once the police had been informed of the skeletal remains, and the two officers in the squad car had gone down and seen for themselves, a well-rehearsed process moved into action. The experts arrived. A doctor had been called to certify death, even if all he had to view was a blackened skeleton. In the circumstances his visit had lasted only a few minutes.

From then until now, in late afternoon, the field had been the scene of constant but disciplined activity. The scorched earth had been trampled by the feet of the team meticulously searching for the slightest clue. Now the scene of crime vehicles and fire service investigators had also left. Everything had been measured and photographed, the surrounding area searched. Lastly, the corpse – what remained of it – had been carefully removed. That had been a slow business and, even with the greatest care, the skeleton had snagged on the bedsprings and cracked apart. Tom Palmer, the pathologist, would have his work cut out trying to make sense of it all. Now they just had to wait for the recovery vehicle that would carry the wrecked van away to be examined under forensic conditions.

Deserted now, the scene was ringed by police tape that gave it the appearance of an arena. Something awful had happened here, something that was not the result of accident but of an act of evil. And the smell. That remained – and would do for many days.

'Poor sod was baked like in an oven!' observed one investigator to Jess. 'Let's hope he was already dead when the fire was started, not just trussed up and shoved in there alive.'

'Dead or alive when he went in there,' muttered Paget, 'it's a murder now.'

Jess Campbell and Ben Paget had been among the last to arrive at the scene. Their work began now that the others had finished. Both were glad to turn their backs to the scorched earth and hedges. They were almost the only people there now. The field was as good as deserted. One solitary police car, with a couple of officers in it, remained on the farm track beyond the gate. They were there to make sure the scene wasn't tampered with, or invaded by hunters in search of macabre souvenirs, or the dedicated takers of selfies, even though there was nothing of interest left now for either.

'What made you decide to move to Gloucestershire?' Jess asked Paget, for want of something to say, she thought, and probably prompted by Carter's enquiry about how the new man was settling in. It was, in the present setting, a mundane, unimportant question. But at least it could be answered – unlike all those other answers the investigation would demand – and it was a way of not thinking for a few minutes about that crackling blaze. Plus, it was a good time to ask. They'd all been curious about their new colleague. Dave Nugent, in particular, seemed to think Paget's arrival presented him with some kind of challenge.

Unexpectedly, the hitherto taciturn Paget became loquacious. He, too, was probably keen to talk about something other than the grim scene around them.

'I've always wanted to work in Gloucestershire. The family originally came from here. In the school holidays, my parents used to drive me down to stay with an uncle who farmed not that far from here, like him!'

Paget nodded to where, on the far side of the field, a figure waited by a quad bike: Reg Prescott, who farmed this land.

'Both my parents were in business and they couldn't take much time off. So, they left me with my uncle and aunt and I had a whale of a time. I always hankered after coming back to this part of the world and when I heard there was need of a replacement sergeant, I applied to transfer to the Gloucestershire force. Bit of luck, really . . .' Paget paused and added wryly, 'Well, I thought it was!'

They set off to walk towards the observer as Paget spoke, and now reached the disgruntled figure of Prescott. He greeted them with, 'How long is that wreck going to stay there? You're not expecting me to pay for it to be removed, I hope? People do – fly-tippers and that. They leave their mess and think the farmer will clear it up for them!'

'Removing the wreck is all part of our investigation, Mr Prescott,' Jess told him. 'You won't be getting the bill.'

No, he wouldn't get the bill; but he had got the Bill. Such a stupid tasteless joke, but it had popped into her head. Don't lose it, Jess! she ordered herself.

Prescott appeared marginally appeased but had another cause for grief. 'I shan't be able to turn the cattle out here for who knows how long. And look at the state of the ground up there, all churned up! People trampling about all over the place, vehicles in and out. Good pasture now a sea of mud.'

Jess ignored his grumbles to say, 'I don't think we have a formal statement from you yet, Mr Prescott.'

The farmer stared at her in amazement. 'What statement? What about? I called the fire brigade, that's all. Rather, my wife did. I don't know anything else.'

'All the same, we'll need a statement. What time you noticed the fire and so forth. Did you hear anything?'

'I didn't hear a thing, not at first. The wife woke me up. I didn't know it was a vehicle on fire, just that there was a fire. Just after midnight, it must have been. I told her to call out the fire engine, threw my clothes on, and drove up here on this thing!' Prescott indicated the quad bike on which he sat. 'I saw when I got near it was a van. It was well alight. I couldn't have got anyone out. I didn't know anyone was in it! I thought it would be joyriders. Bloody maniacs, they are. They pinch a car in town, drive it out here and then torch it. Then they phone one of their mates to come out and pick them up.

'Them mobile phones,' added Prescott, 'handy gadgets, I grant you, but they make everything worse. They wouldn't torch the van if they had to get home in it, would they? They'd drive it back to town and dump it in a back street. But not now, oh no! Now they can have even more fun! Set it alight, then just run off a little way, call up on a mobile, and hide until their friends come out and collect them like a ruddy taxi service.'

'Yes, Mr Prescott. Perhaps Sergeant Paget here could accompany you to your farmhouse and take a proper statement?'

Prescott leaned back and studied the sergeant for the first time. 'Paget, eh? You're not a local man, are you?'

'I wasn't born in the county. But I used to have family hereabouts.'

Reg squinted at him. 'It's the name, see? You wouldn't have

anything to do with old Jim Paget, used to farm over Abbots Weston way?'

'He was my uncle,' Paget told him.

'Well, I'm blessed,' said Prescott, cheering up. 'Yes, I'll give you a statement. Come on up to the house. My wife will put the kettle on. I remember Jim. They've built houses all over his land now, you know.'

Without further ado, the farmer set off on the quad bike.

'There you go, Ben,' said Jess to him. 'Just like old times!'

As Superintendent Carter and his officers in Gloucestershire began the investigation into the body in the van, many miles away in Bamford another murder victim's last days were subject to scrutiny by another force.

At least Inspector Trevor Barker and his team had a name for the body discovered in the warehouse, and they could begin to track the late Amber Button's last movements. For Barker this meant he would have the Button family, as represented by Harmony Button, buzzing round him like a demented and determined wasp, until they got what they considered to be results.

'We all want to know who did it!' declared Harmony.

'Yes, Ms Button, so do we . . .' Barker had told her several times.

'Then get on with it!' stormed Harmony.

'Keep her away from me!' he had ordered everyone else in the building, in a vain attempt to escape. Some chance. No one else wanted to confront Harmony, either, nor was that lady easily deflected. Barker had become her target. His underlings, after token resistance, still sent for him.

For Emma Johnson the morning's programme had begun with a visit to the victim's landlady, Myrtle Clack, in Station Road.

Station Road proved to be a street of 1930s brick villas, semi-detached, with a narrow passage between each pair leading to the rear and probably the dustbins. As Emma stood outside the one belonging to Mrs Clack, she reflected that she had walked down this street many times on her way to the railway station, but never taken note of its name. Arriving at the house, her eye was taken by a new-looking notice taped to the front door. It was hand-printed in large letters, using green wax crayon: Do Not Ring Or Knock. No Callers.

Did this mean no one was home, or just that the occupants were unfriendly? From the corner of her eye, Emma saw a curtain twitch at the bay window. She pressed the bell firmly, then stooped to push open the letter box and shout through it, 'Police!'

She waited. Nothing happened for a couple of minutes and she was about to ring again when she heard shuffling steps approaching the door on the other side. It opened about two inches and an angry eye could be seen pressed to the gap.

'How do I know you're police?' demanded a voice.

Emma produced her warrant card and held it to the gap. Some muttered words followed from the occupant. The door opened fully to reveal a very small, very thin, elderly woman in blue-and-white patterned trousers, a hand-knitted sweater and slippers. Her hair was dyed a purplish shade and tightly curled. Her face was heavily powdered and her withered lips daubed with bright pink lipstick.

'Mrs Clack?' asked Emma, trying not to look taken aback.

'I put the notice on the door,' returned the woman aggressively, 'because they keep coming. I've had them all. There's people who know I've got a room vacant now and say they want to take it. They're not serious, most of them. They just want to snoop. There's young whippersnappers who say they're from newspapers. And there's Buttons.'

For a moment, Emma didn't connect the last word with the surname of the murder victim and wondered briefly where buttons came into it. 'Buttons?' she ventured.

Mrs Clack glared at her. 'Yes, Buttons! That's what her name was, my lodger. Amber Button. The one who got herself murdered. Not that I'm surprised. She was a tarty bit of goods. Anyhow, her family keep coming here. First I had someone who said she was her sister. That was when she'd gone missing but we didn't yet know she'd been murdered. "How do I know you're her sister?" I asked her. I mean, I didn't *know* she was her sister. Amber never mentioned any sister to me. So the woman showed me her driver's licence. And she did look a bit like her, too, a big girl with a lot of black hair. She insisted on going upstairs and searching the room for clues. That was her word, "clues". I went with her, mind! I wasn't about to allow her to roam about all over the house, poking her nose into everything. Anyway, she didn't find anything. I told her the rent was due. I told both the men who came the same thing. Pay the rent, I told them, or clear out her things. I need to let the room again.'

'Who were these two men?' asked Emma.

'I told you, Buttons! Her brothers. They went away and then, yesterday evening, they came back with the sister – Harmony, the one who came before. They went upstairs and cleared the room, took everything away in a couple of bin bags.'

95

'Damn!' muttered Emma. 'I'm sorry to hear that, Mrs Clack.'

'Why? Here! You sure you're a policewoman? You look a bit young to me!'

'Would you like to see my warrant card again?'

'No!' Mrs Clack dismissed the offer. 'I was expecting a man.'

'Were you? Well, I'm sorry to hear that the occupant's belongings have been removed, because I was hoping to look around the room myself, even send a fingerprint expert over.'

'You won't find any fingerprints,' said Mrs Clack, drawing herself up to her full height. She reached the middle of Emma's chest. 'I cleaned it all with bleach. I made a very good job of it, if I say so myself!'

Emma didn't say anything immediately but thought of several words she would like to have said.

'Nothing should have been touched . . .' she protested weakly, at last.

'I didn't know that, did I?' challenged Mrs Clack. 'No one told me. If you wanted it left, you should have told me. And you should have paid the rent, and all. It's due.' She leaned forward and peered up into Emma's face, her eyes fixing the visitor with a malevolent stare. 'I've only got my pension,' she said. 'I need the rent.'

'Mrs Clack!' Emma decided it was time to get a grip on the situation. 'I would like to go up and see the room, anyway.'

'Help yourself,' returned Mrs Clack sourly. 'Being the police, you'll do that anyway, I dare say!'

She led the way up the stairs. They encountered the smell of bleach well before they reached a small back bedroom. Most of the floor space was taken up by the furniture: bed, narrow wardrobe and dressing table. Emma had to sidle between these to get to the back window and look out. Unsurprisingly, it gave on to a neglected scrap of garden, patrolled by a feral-looking tabby, and the railway embankment. As she watched, a train swept past at eye level.

'Not much space, not much privacy!' she muttered. 'Do you mind if I ask how much rent you're asking for this room?'

'You interested in taking it?'

'No,' admitted Emma. 'I'm just curious.'

'Curiosity killed the cat!' snapped Mrs Clack. 'Policewoman or not, if you're not interested in taking the room, the rent's no business of yours.'

Emma decided to overlook this. Mrs Clack was clearly spoiling for a fight. 'How about visitors?' she asked. 'Did Amber have many visitors?'

For the first time, Mrs Clack appeared slightly defensive. 'Some,' she admitted. 'I don't keep track. None of my business!' Her combative manner returned. 'The world would be a better place, if folk minded their own business!'

'Do you let out any other rooms?'

'I do – young girl from Romania. She's at work now, so you won't be able to bother her!' Mrs Clack gave a triumphant nod.

'I'll come back tonight,' Emma told her. Before Mrs Clack could explode with a new outpouring of outrage, Emma added, 'Forensics will come over and take a look around the room, anyway. Expect them sometime today. So I'd be glad if you don't clean any more – and do not, of course, relet it. Not until we tell you that you can.'

Mrs Clack's angry protestations ringing in her ears, she beat a retreat.

'Too late, sir,' she told Trevor Barker on her return to base. 'It's been cleared out. The family came and removed all the victim's belongings. Oh, and the landlady has cleaned everywhere with bleach.'

'Bleach?' Barker leaned back in his chair and stared at the sergeant. 'Bit extreme, don't you think?' He folded his hands on his desk. 'Now, just what do you think Mrs Clack was so keen to scrub away?' He paused, before asking, 'What about the other lodger, in Mrs Clack's other rented-out room?'

'She's Romanian and she's at work until after six. I'll go back this evening, sir.'

'No, I'll go,' said Barker. 'Mrs Clack will be expecting you, so it will throw her off if I turn up.'

But Mrs Clack was not easily 'thrown off'. Since Emma's morning visit, her fury seemed to have grown in strength and virulence, and her determination to defend her home against official intrusion remained unyielding.

'Who are you, then?' she first demanded, seeing not her earlier female visitor but a strange male in plain clothes who had turned up just as she was sitting down to watch her favourite soap. 'Are you selling anything? Because I don't want anything. And I'm not filling in no surveys, or joining any religions, or signing up to make regular donations to any charity. I haven't got any spare money. I'm a pensioner.'

'I'm a police officer,' said Barker.

'Ho! Are you? I've already had one of those here. Young girl. How do I know you're real?'

Having, with great difficulty, stemmed the flow and persuaded her to inspect his warrant card, on which his senior rank was revealed, the luckless Trevor Barker was subjected to a further barrage. Mrs Clack went to town. He had first to put up with listening to a harangue about the inadequacy of Mrs Clack's pension, and the need to relet the free room as soon as possible. It was followed by a diatribe about how much the police got from her council tax payments – and what did they do with it all? It was with great reluctance that she agreed Barker could come in.

'It's not respectable,' she snapped, when told he would like to interview her other lodger, Eva Florescu, upstairs in her room. 'Inspector or not, you shouldn't be calling on single women in their own homes.'

'But Miss Florescu is here?'

'Yes, I told you she was here. I told her the police had been this morning and would be coming back. I told her it would be a young woman, because this morning it was a woman. Where is she? Why are you here? It's not respectable.'

Barker shrewdly judged that her unwillingness had nothing to do with any possible impropriety. It was rather because it would be more difficult for Mrs Clack to eavesdrop on the conversation if Eva didn't come down to Mrs Clack's claustrophobic sitting room, where a hatch in the wall communicated with the kitchen and the loitering house owner.

In the event, the interview produced very little. Eva Florescu was a small, slim girl with dark curly hair and elfin features. Definitely, thought Barker, she'd catch the eye. She was also frightened, defensive and monosyllabic. Barker was offered, and took, the single upright chair by the window. Enterprisingly, Eva had seated herself on the bedside cabinet, having first removed a cheap lamp and deposited that on the bed. From this perch she eyed him as though Count Dracula himself had entered the room. Barker didn't doubt she was concealing something, but what it was, well, who knew? During the whole conversation, her eyes flickered around the room as if some hiding place might be found, some nook or cranny into which she might creep and escape him.

She'd be hard put to find a refuge in this room. It was smaller than the room next door, previously rented by Amber Button. Barker wondered if this meant Eva paid less rent, but guessed it probably didn't. It just meant that it was more cramped. The view was the same as Emma Johnson had described from Amber's room. The old-fashioned fireplace framed a coin-operated gas fire. Along the mantelshelf, above it, were arranged numerous photographs. Most were of a family group, some featuring Eva herself and, presumably, her parents and siblings. There was also an icon depicting an austere bearded saint in priestly robes. Barker had no idea who he was. But he felt the religious guy fixed a disapproving painted gaze on him.

'My English is not so good!' was Eva's opening statement; it proved to be her stock reply to any question.

'We can bring an interpreter,' offered Barker.

'No need, I do not know anything,' was the sullen response.

It was possible she was just afraid of the police for no other reason than the power she considered them to have.

Barker tried another tack. 'Look, Miss Florescu, I'm not from the Home Office. I'm not here to find out if you're here legally.'

That got a spark of response.

'I am legal!' said Eva indignantly. 'I came here with EU passport.

I pay British tax. I work for proper company, cleaning houses. I have applied for settled status. It is not my fault Britain want to leave EU. I want to stay. You can check all this.'

'I don't need to check all that. I only want to know about the young woman who rented the other room from Mrs Clack. You knew Amber Button, surely?'

Eva tilted her head and surveyed him. 'I only see her on the stairs. We say "Good Morning!" or "Goodnight!"'

'You never went out with Amber to, say, a bar or a pub?'

'I work very hard,' retorted Eva. 'I am cleaner, like I tell you. I work for proper company. It has office in Church Street. You can ask them there – Mr Billings. I work all day. I do not go out in the evening.' She indicated the bearded saint. 'I do not go to pubs. I am respectable girl.'

'Did you ever see a visitor come here for Amber?'

Eva shrugged. 'I mind my own business.'

'All right then, did you ever hear a man's voice, through the wall? Don't tell me the walls aren't pretty thin between this room and the one next door!'

Eva hunched her shoulders. 'Oh, voices, they mean nothing. I don't hear words. My English is not good enough.'

'But you did hear a man's voice from time to time?'

'I come home late from work. Amber went out every evening.'

'What about weekends?' Barker insisted.

'Then Amber go out all the time.'

Barker gave up. Perhaps he should have sent Emma, after all. With the painted holy man giving him a distinctly sardonic farewell glare from the mantelshelf, or so it seemed to Barker, he left.

*   *   *

Later that evening, at home, he complained wearily to his wife. 'Hear no evil, see no evil, speak no evil! That's what the old woman Clack and her really rather attractive Romanian lodger have decided to do.'

His wife took a charitable view. 'Well, if the poor girl works all day as a cleaner, she must be very tired by the evening.'

'She's also scared out of her wits. Listen, don't tell me a young girl like that doesn't ever go out in the evening!' He paused. 'On the other hand, perhaps she doesn't need to!'

'Meaning?' asked his wife.

'Oh, come on, Sally! I mean perhaps both Amber was, and young Eva still is, working from home of an evening! It'd take more than a picture of a saint to put paid to that. She'd probably turn it to the wall.'

'But what about the landlady, Mrs Clack?'

'Mrs Clack,' Barker retorted, 'is very keen to supplement her pension!'

'Can you prove it?' asked Sally. She was a police officer's wife.

'At the moment? Not a chance. Ever? Well, perhaps. But not likely.' Barker uttered a muffled growl. 'It wouldn't be so bad, but if Harmony Button doesn't get the result she wants from me, she'll go straight off to find Markby and his wife and harangue them into action. Wouldn't you think a man like Alan Markby would know better than to let himself be used by the Button family? As for his wife, well, perhaps she thinks all this is good research material for those books she writes about a piano tuner, for crying out loud! Whoever heard about a piano tuner as a detective?'

'They're very popular, those books of hers,' said Sally Barker. 'They told me at the library that readers love them.'

'Books like that,' said Barker sternly, 'encourage people, who should know better, to think detection is for talented amateurs! For goodness' sake, why doesn't Alan Markby tell his wife so! She ought to know more about police procedure, being married to a retired senior officer! If you have a murder on your hands, you don't send for a piano tuner. Would people ask a police constable to fix their pianos?'

'They're entertainment . . .' protested Sally, who had read and enjoyed Meredith's books.

Barker scowled. 'But what I really can't understand is why Markby seems prepared to put up with the Buttons!'

Sally found an ingenious reply. 'You know, Trevor, perhaps that might turn out to your advantage.'

'How?' he asked shortly.

'If Harmony is pestering Alan and Meredith, she's not pestering you!'

'Ah . . .' murmured her husband, struck by this notion. 'You might be right, Sal.'

Later, passing through the hall on his way upstairs to bed, Barker paused to peer into the mirror there, tilting his head to check on his hair. He was sure that, in the twenty-four hours since Harmony had come into his life, it had started looking even thinner.

Chapter 7

Sadly, for Barker, the following day began equally badly and, as the hands on the clock crept round with irritating slowness, it got worse. It wasn't yet ten o'clock before he found himself under siege. He stared with barely concealed dismay at his visitor, Mrs Myrtle Clack.

'Oh, no!' he'd said on being given the news that she was in reception, wanting to speak to him. 'I had enough of her last night. What on earth does she want to see me now for?'

'Perhaps,' suggested Emma Johnson, 'she's thought of something useful?'

'Sergeant Johnson, if old Mrs Clack thought of anything at all helpful to the police, she'd go to any lengths to hide it. We are not popular in her book. You can decide for yourself why.'

'Will you see her?' asked Emma. 'She won't go away and she won't speak to anyone else. Oh, and she said it was all your doing.'

'What was all my doing?' demanded Barker.

'She won't say. She'll only speak to you.'

'Oh, show the old bat in, then.'

Mrs Clack was dressed for the occasion in a red coat and black patent leather boots, her make-up freely, if inaccurately, applied to her wrinkled visage. Purple curls quivering with rage, she stood before him and voiced her grievance – at length and, apparently, without pausing to draw fresh breath.

Emma Johnson, who remained to lend support to her beleaguered boss, attempted twice to interrupt the flow of the visitor's harangue, and then gave up.

'You've got no right!' raged Mrs Clack, shaking a small clenched fist at the inspector. 'You come to my house unasked . . .' Here she paused to swing round and point a trembling finger at Emma. 'First her, then you – Mr Inspector or whatever Barker! Then a whole lot of people, up and down my stairs, wearing out my carpet and turning that back bedroom inside out, taking photos and doing I don't know what up there. It's not surprising, is it, that now she's gone?'

'Who has gone?' asked Barker as Mrs Clack paused for breath.

'My other lodger, young Eva! It's not surprising, seeing as you frightened the poor kid off! She was a very good tenant, was Eva! Always paid the rent regular on the first of the month. Money exact, down to the last penny. Never asked for more time or any such nonsense! And she's packed her bags, cleared out and gone! So now I've got both my rooms empty and have to find a couple of new girls, I mean, lodgers for them both! And it's all down to you!'

'Why new girls?' asked Emma Johnson sharply. 'Why not let to men? Or let the two rooms together, as a unit, to a family?'

Mrs Clack looked Emma up and down before replying. Then she said briefly, 'Girls are less trouble and keep the place clean and tidy. Men make a mess and bring drink in. Families I can do without. Families mean kids, wearing out the stair carpet, racing up and down, yelling and making a racket.'

'What about men visitors?' asked Emma casually. 'Do you allow your women tenants to have them?'

'Their private lives,' returned Mrs Clack austerely, 'are their own concern. They can have whatever visitor they like, provided they don't move anyone in permanent. If they did that, I'd have to increase the rent! Of course, they mustn't make any noise!'

'Have you asked Eva's employers if she turned up for work this morning?' asked Barker.

'No. I don't need to. She's gone, cleared her stuff out of the room! It makes no difference to me where she's *working*. It's where she's *living* – and it isn't with me any longer, so there!'

She took a step nearer the desk and pushed her face closer to Barker, who leaned so far back in his chair he was in danger of toppling over. 'I've only got my pension!' she snarled. 'I'm a poor old lady and got no one to support me! I've got to let my two rooms. And now they're *both* empty! What are you going to do? That's what I want to know. What are you going to do about it, eh?'

Barker ignored this to ask, 'Have you a forwarding address for Eva?'

'Course not!' snapped Mrs Clack. 'She's trying to get away from all the fuss and to-do. She doesn't want you lot chasing after her with your never-ending questions! No more do I! I don't know what happened to Amber Button! Well, I know now she got herself murdered. But I didn't know it when she first went missing. Nor did Eva know what had happened to Amber. I asked her that myself. She said she didn't, and she was a very honest girl! You lot want to be out there!' Myrtle directed a pointing finger at the window. 'Out there, looking for clues!'

'That's what the forensic team have been doing at your house, Mrs Clack.'

Barker realised as he spoke these words that he might perhaps have phrased them differently. He braced himself for another onslaught. But when Mrs Clack spoke, it was quietly and – he had to admit – far more alarming than when she raged.

'Are you saying that Amber Button died in my house?'

'We don't know where she died, Mrs Clack, and until we do—'

'She died where you found her!' snapped Myrtle. 'In that warehouse, where else? Go and search that with your forensic team!'

'We have and, actually, we don't think Amber died there. We think . . .'

There was another silence.

'Think what?' asked Mrs Clack ominously.

'We are pursuing our enquiries, Mrs Clack. Now then!' said Trevor Barker, standing up and taking back control of the situation. 'We appreciate that all this has caused considerable disruption to your household. But this is a murder enquiry, and it can't be helped!'

'I'll see you out,' said Emma and guided the visitor to the door.

Here Mrs Clack paused to look back and announce, 'I am a respectable widow and I've got my rights, too, you know! I'll thank you to remember that!'

With that, at last – and to Trevor's great relief – she was gone.

'Blasted nuisance, that girl Eva doing a runner,' he said to Emma when she returned alone. 'I'm sure she could have told us something. Forensics not come up with anything from that house?'

'Still carrying out tests, sir. But the landlady did clean it all out with bleach, you remember.'

'Oh, I remember, sergeant! I shall remember Myrtle Clack to my dying day!'

Hesitantly, Emma said, 'I suppose Eva Florescu *has* just moved away. I mean, she's not another missing person, is she?'

'First try the cleaning company she worked for. I've got a note of it here. It's a place in Church Street, run by a fellow name of Billings. Thank goodness I remembered to jot it down before I left. If she's done a flit from Station Road, she's probably given in her notice there, and moved on somewhere else. But she might have gone into work today and, with luck, we can catch her wherever she's doing her cleaning. Or someone among her co-workers might know where she's gone, even if her employers don't. She was definitely scared, and perhaps we shouldn't be surprised she's bolted. If we can't trace her,' added Barker moodily, 'then put her down as missing. Put out a request to the public. Police anxious to talk to her, the usual sort of thing.' Barker ran a hand nervously over his head when he had finished speaking. No wonder he was losing his hair.

Edward Billings's day had started earlier than Barker's, but just as badly. He'd arrived at the office of the cleaning company he ran with his partner, Sergio, bright and early, at a quarter past eight. If you're in business, you have to be up with the lark. He'd tried to get this message across to Sergio, but with only mixed success. Sergio got up all right, but then disappeared to the shops, to buy food, or on other mysterious errands. Fair enough, Sergio made the coffee before he left, but still, Edward breakfasted alone most days. He usually made scrambled eggs, because that was about the limit of his cooking. Sergio was a first-class cook, had even worked as a chef, but he didn't cook breakfast. He went to find a coffee shop where he could sit, drinking espresso, and reading the news bulletins on his smartphone, or texting his friends back in Italy. To balance this, Sergio cooked for them both in the evening and, whatever he presented as the meal for that day, it was unfailingly delicious. But to achieve that, said Sergio, you have to shop early in the day, when the stuff has been freshly put out, and hasn't been picked over by other customers. So that was another reason for his absence in the office when an emergency arose.

Reputation was everything in business, and if you were in the business of supplying cleaners, you had to hire people who knew what they were doing and were absolutely reliable. So it was extremely annoying to have this young woman standing there in front of his desk, announcing that she wished to leave.

'Is there a particular reason?' asked Edward, hoping it wasn't workplace harassment. Well, neither he nor Sergio would have harassed her. But they employed male as well as female cleaners. One of the men might have got a bit fresh. The girl, Eva, was pretty, if you like that sort of thing. 'I think you'll find we pay very well compared with—'

'It is personal!' declared Eva. 'I do not wish to talk about it. It is emergency!'

'I'm sorry to hear that,' said Edward cautiously. 'Well, if you must, you must. Were you thinking of leaving at the end of the week? Could you carry on until the end of the month? We'll have to find someone else.'

'I go now,' said Eva calmly. 'You give me P45 please!' She held out her hand.

'Now!' gasped Edward. 'What, right this minute?'

'Yes, yes, now!' snapped Eva.

'This is very unreasonable, Eva . . .'

She leaned over his desk, glaring at him. 'I have told you, I go now!'

Blast Sergio! Probably sitting in some café, drinking coffee and watching the world go by! Why couldn't he be here and lend Edward some support?

'Very well,' he said, capitulating. Frankly, if she was going to act like this over anything, he couldn't wait to see the back of her. And now he looked at her again, she wasn't that pretty. Shrewish, that was it, if not downright aggressive.

Thus it was that, when Emma Johnson arrived to enquire at the cleaning company later, it was to discover that the bird had already flown from there, as well.

'I don't know where she's gone!' protested Edward, staring at her in dismay. 'Believe me, Sergeant Johnson, if I could help you, I would. She came early this morning, and announced she was giving up the job and wanted her paperwork. I asked why she was going, and she just said, it was personal, an emergency, and she had to leave town. All I know is, she isn't here and we have to find a replacement.'

'Perhaps I could speak to your other employees? They might know where she's gone.'

It wasn't surprising that the girl had moved quickly. But it was a signal that she might be difficult to track down. Emma's boss, Inspector Barker, wouldn't like this. There wasn't much he did like these days. If he'd had more hair, he'd be tearing it out. It was making life difficult for all of them.

'I'd rather you didn't,' said Edward apprehensively. 'They won't like it. They're all foreign. They might not understand. And if they do know, they won't tell you.'

He was probably right. 'Look,' said Emma, 'if you hear anything, get in touch with us, right? We really want to find Miss Florescu.'

'Why?' asked Edward, suspicion, mixed with dread, in every line of his face and his body language. 'What's she done?'

'As far as we know, nothing. But we need to talk to her, that's all.'

Nothing? Huh! The response went through Edward's mind like the headlines along the bottom of the screen during the television news. As if this CID officer would be here if the girl hadn't got into some sort of trouble! The sergeant could have telephoned ahead, but no, she'd marched into the office, announced her purpose and demanded to be taken to Edward. It had all the hallmarks of a raid. The news that the police had been in the office would spread like wildfire. Half his employees would probably fail to come in tomorrow. He'd have to tell Sergio, of course, that the police had been. Sergio had found another reason to be out of the office. Visiting a prospective client, he'd claimed. He was never there when wanted.

'Something's wrong, must be!' Edward said, that evening, when he'd finally got his partner cornered.

Sergio, who was scowling into a saucepan of boiling pasta, shrugged. 'It doesn't matter, does it? If she's gone, it's out of our hands. We don't have to worry about it. It's not our problem. All we need to do is concentrate on finding a replacement. What we should not do, is make it our problem. The cops will find her. They have their methods. They don't need us to help them.'

'I hope you're right.'

'I am right,' said Sergio with easy confidence. 'Ah, yes, this is al dente. It's ready!'

It was left at that.

It was destined to be a difficult day for everyone. For the Markbys it had started well. Harmony and the Button family in general had now become a problem for the local police. Alan finished taking up the onions, and turned to other garden tasks. Meredith had spent the day hard at work on her latest book. It was now nearly suppertime and, at the back of her mind, the need to leave the computer and make for the fridge was looming large. Secretly, she hoped Alan would realise how busy she was, and would take over, because he, frankly, was good at making scratch meals, or interesting sandwiches, or whatever the moment called for. She was at a tricky point in the plot, and she didn't really want to break off.

But something was happening at the rear of the house. She could hear voices. One was Alan's and the other . . . surely not?

'Sorry,' said Alan, appearing in her study. 'But Harmony is back – and this time she insists on seeing *you.*'

Meredith sighed and made her way to the kitchen, where she found Harmony Button enthroned on what threatened to become her regular chair. As before, she was heavily made-up, and bedecked with jewellery, although dressed head to toe in mourning black. She cut an impressive figure, but this didn't disguise her real distress.

'You've got to come back with me again!' she greeted Meredith.

'Back to see your father?' asked Meredith apprehensively. 'How is he?'

'How do you think? He don't speak, don't eat, don't do anything but sit there and cry. It'll finish him, that's what all this will do. Especially now.'

'Why now?' asked Meredith with a sinking heart. She recognised the signs of panic.

Harmony twisted her fingers together and twiddled with the gold rings adorning them. She was flushed and perspiring, although it wasn't a particularly warm day. Her mascara was smudged. Meredith wondered whether she'd been weeping.

'Because now my brother Gary has gone missing, as well! That's why you've got to come with me again, to the police station, and report it.' She leaned forward. 'I don't know what's going on, but something awful *is* going on! It's like, one by one, we're all being picked off! Why?'

Meredith made calming gestures. 'Are you sure he's missing, Harmony? Surely not? I saw him myself, the other day, at your house.'

'He didn't come home last night or the night before!' Harmony snapped. 'He might come home late from the pub sometimes, but he's never not come home at all! He's got family. He didn't come home again last night, and no one knows where he is today. We've waited until now to see if he turned up. But he hasn't – or phoned – and now it's late. His van has gone. He's driven some-where. But he wouldn't go far and not let my sister-in-law know about it! I mean, if he'd gone on business, to see about a bit of antique furniture, he'd have left a message, or phoned, or something! I tell you, he's gone missing, just like Amber did. I daren't tell my dad.'

Harmony drew breath. 'So you've got to come with me to see that inspector again. If I go on my own, they always try to fob me off. Tell me their enquiries are "in hand", whatever that means! And that Barker hides in his office and won't come out.'

Meredith turned to her husband. 'Alan, this time you must come with me. I couldn't face Trevor Barker again so soon with . . . with the news.'

'It's late,' Alan reminded her. 'Barker won't be at work. He'll have gone home.'

'I want to report it!' shouted Harmony.

They both stared at her.

She flushed and muttered, 'Sorry! But I am very worried – and there's Dad, you see. If we don't find out where Gary is soon, I'll have to go home and face Dad – and my sister-in-law, Katie. That's Gary's wife. She's in an awful state. I mean, after what happened to Amber, you can understand it. Gary might not be the perfect husband, you know, but he's a family man and he wouldn't just go missing and not send word!'

So they all three went to the station and reported the mystery of Gary Button's whereabouts to the duty sergeant.

'He's believed to be driving a Ford Transit van,' Markby told them.

'It's white,' added Harmony. 'He hasn't had it long.'

'Gary's business doing well, then, is it?' asked the sergeant. 'He still doing the house clearances?'

'He's an antiques dealer!' snapped Harmony.

'Then that's it!' said the sergeant. 'He's heard of some place throwing stuff out and he's gone there to see what he can find.'

'Even if he did,' retorted Harmony, now simmering like a pot coming to the boil, 'he'd have told his wife where he was off to. And he'd have come back! He's missing, I tell you!'

'But he's been gone barely forty-eight hours,' protested the duty sergeant unwisely. 'Had a row with the missus, had he?'

Harmony's roar of fury brought other officers running to the front desk in support of their colleague.

'It's all right!' Markby assured them. 'Ms Button is upset. Please tell Inspector Barker first thing in the morning that Gary Button's whereabouts are unknown and it's a cause for concern. He's brother to the murder victim, Amber Button.'

One of the younger officers who had arrived in support was unfortunately overheard muttering to a colleague, 'Done a runner, has he?'

After that, it took three of them to manhandle the outraged Harmony out of the station and back into Alan's car.

'I think,' he muttered to Meredith, 'we'll risk disturbing Barker's quiet evening and tell him the news now, before he gets into work tomorrow morning. He might arrive to find Buttons camped on the doorstep. We'll take Harmony home first.'

Harmony sat in the back of the car, carrying on a non-stop litany of complaint, until they reached her house. As she clambered out of the car, the Markbys caught a glimpse of a small, thin, furtive figure who darted into the back garden as soon as he saw them.

'My partner, Chas,' said Harmony briefly. 'He don't take any interest in my family's problems.'

Ann Granger

'Chas more likely doesn't want the police taking any interest in his activities,' observed Alan to Meredith as they drove to Trevor Barker's house.

They were received by Sally Barker with, 'He's just got in. He's had a difficult day. They've lost the other girl who lodges with Myrtle Clack.'

Barker was slumped in front of the television, staring resentfully at the third screening of the same very old film in a short space of time.

'You'd think you'd get something else for your licence fee,' he greeted them morosely. Then, apparently becoming aware of the visitors' identity, he scrambled to his feet. 'Sorry, I just thought it was Sal coming back.' He looked from one to the other of them. 'What's happened now?' he asked resignedly.

'Gary Button has gone missing,' said Markby.

He hadn't been sure how Barker would react. Surprise? Shock? Fury? As it was, the inspector fixed him with a morose stare, then picked up the remote and turned down the sound.

'Really missing?' asked Barker suspiciously.

'According to his wife and his sister,' Meredith told him. 'We've just reported it at the station. He's believed to be driving a white Ford Transit van and he's been absent since yesterday morning.'

Barker studied the screen on which the actors carried on silently. 'Makes no difference,' he commented, gesturing with the remote. 'We don't need the speech. We've all seen this film at least twice, and that doesn't count when it was new and some of us saw it in the cinema!'

He gestured at the visitors to sit down, as his wife put her head round the door and asked if they'd like tea or coffee? They opted for tea, and Sally disappeared.

Trevor Barker flopped back in his chair and stared up at the ceiling. 'This business with the Button family is threatening to turn into one of these old films. We've all seen it before and know the basic plot by heart. But this, well, it does at least have some element of surprise! Who's going next, do you reckon? Declan? Old Harry Button himself? Is someone going to spirit Michael over the wall, out of prison? I suppose it's too much to hope that, next time, whoever is masterminding this will take Harmony?'

'It'd take a bold man,' said Markby, 'and he'd probably send her back. I think Harmony is safe.'

Barker nodded and sighed. 'You must remember the Button clan, Alan. They were very active in your day. A long line of burglars, petty thieves and used car dealers, they always operated just on the wrong side of the law, until recent years when a couple of them have turned legit.'

'I remember,' said Markby. 'But they weren't big-time crooks. It was a bit of dodgy dealing, petty theft, breaking and entering, and football hooliganism.'

Barker thumped his fist on the arm of his chair. 'Exactly! That's my point. They never showed any ambition to go big time. They messed with nothing that would get them into trouble with the serious criminal underworld. No straying on to the turf of some mysterious Mr Big. Right, Alan?'

'Right,' agreed Markby.

'What's more, Michael apart – he was always more of a dedicated professional, as you might say – they have been showing signs of going straight, well, straight enough. Michael might be doing time, but there's Gary with his antiques business. So far that's been clean. Declan has also kept out of trouble for the last few years. So, what the hell could they have got themselves into that means, one by one, they're vanishing into thin air? Okay, Amber has turned up, but she's turned up dead. I went to talk to Mrs Clack's other lodger, the Romanian girl, Eva. She was frightened and she's hiding some information. We'll hope to get it out of her eventually, but it might take a while, because just at the moment, we don't know where she is! And when we do find out what she's hiding, it might not help us much. It might not even have anything to do with Amber's death. But I'd still like to know what it is.'

Barker turned his head towards his visitors. 'By the way, Myrtle Clack – who is half cracked, in my view, and who is not otherwise noticeably keen on high standards of house cleaning – scrubbed out Amber's room with bleach before we got there.'

'Did she?' Markby was startled. 'You've still sent in forensics?'

'You bet!' retorted Barker. 'I told them to take that room apart!'

Chapter 8

'I don't see,' Miff said at last, 'how you and what's-his-name, Stuart, ran this business together for as long as you did, or how you've managed to keep going on your own! Look, I'm not trying to insult you or anything. I don't mean to be unkind. But honestly, I've come across all kinds of office systems, back when I was part of the rat race, before I escaped. Some have been better than others. But you don't have *any* kind of system. How do you manage?'

'Not very well,' admitted Sam. 'I'm okay with plants!' she added.

Miff picked up a catalogue. 'What's this about Christmas trees? We're not at Christmas yet.'

Sam, now on a subject she was sure of, cheered up. 'Oh, we have to order now from the growers, or we won't get what we want – or else we'll get what no one else wants, which is worse. We don't grow our own, you see. We haven't got the space. Actually, I should have ordered last month, but things have rather got on top of me. That's why I decided I had to advertise for more help . . .' She paused and added, a little shyly, 'So I was really pleased when you turned up.'

'I don't know anything about gardening or garden centres! I told you.'

'But you know about office work. And you're Henry Blackwood's nephew.'

'What difference does that make?' asked Miff, puzzled.

'It means you're okay. Henry and Prue are okay. So, you are!'

Miff quenched the guilty spasm that assailed him by grabbing the catalogue again and riffling through it until he found the relevant page. 'Norway Spruce,' he said, 'Nordmann Fir, Fraser Fir . . . what's the difference? I mean, apart from price?'

'The needles, mostly. Norway Spruce is what we sell most of, because it's the cheapest. But it's the first to lose its needles. The other two cost more, but look nicer, and don't lose their needles so easily. To be honest, most people want Norway Spruce so that is what we stock in the run-up to Christmas. But we have to put in our order with the growers now.'

Miff sat back with a sigh and gazed at the box full of assorted receipts, handwritten reminders and sundry information.

'I know it's boring,' said Sam. 'That's why I avoid it. I expect you'd like to be writing your book.'

'No,' replied Miff honestly. 'If I ever do write it – and if it ever gets published . . .' He met her anxious gaze. 'Neither of those things are likely, by the way. Anyhow, Debbie at the supermarket is probably right and no one would want to read it.'

'You've got to have confidence!' Sam told him brightly. 'It's like when Stuart and I started up the garden centre. We had confidence.' The brightness faded. 'Our parents subbed us. We didn't think it would be such hard work. Well, of course we knew we would have to struggle for a while. But when we found ourselves working all hours, Stuart got depressed.'

So far, everything he'd learned about Stuart had led Miff to form the opinion that anything Stuart touched would be doomed to failure. He'd seen the guy's photo, propped behind the old clock on the mantelshelf in this office. The pic had shown a spindly, studious-looking type with spectacles and a drooping fringe of hair. This photo had since disappeared. Perhaps he ought not to think harsh thoughts about the poor sod. Stuart's garden centre was a bit like Miff's book. It must have seemed like a good idea at the time.

Sam was looking a bit down at the moment.

'It's okay!' Miff told her encouragingly. 'I'll sort it all out.'

'You'll sort out your book, too. And for goodness' sake, don't let Debbie Garley put you off.'

A long, hard day was over. Outside, the garden centre was dimly lit by a couple of lights, but beyond that, the world was shrouded in the kind of darkness Miff was learning to associate with country living. You couldn't see a damn thing out there beyond the gates. He and Sam sat in the two sagging armchairs in the office with a mug of tea apiece and the remains of their supper on plates on the floor.

'There's no time to cook,' Sam had explained. 'And I can't cook, anyway. I eat whatever Glenys has left over in the coffee shop.'

Tonight that had meant chewing his way through dried-out sandwiches, soggy sausage rolls and dark-coloured squares of mixed ingredients called, apparently, 'rocky road' cakes. You couldn't fault the name. Miff had tried one and nearly cracked a tooth.

'Can't she make anything else?' he asked now. 'I mean, other cakes.'

'She does make other cakes, but they've all sold. The rocky road ones were all that was left.'

'Perhaps Glenys ought to take a hint!' muttered Miff.

Sam leaned forward and said earnestly, 'I mustn't upset Glenys, and honestly, Miff, please don't you do it, either. If she goes, no one else will take on the coffee shop. Anyway, the Garleys all stick together. If we offend Glenys, Danny will walk out, too.'

Miff had met Danny Garley when that youth roared into the garden centre, early on the first morning, on a motorcycle that must have cost far more than he should have been able to afford on what Sam paid him for working here. Danny was a stocky, bullet-headed, unsmiling figure who, when he dismounted the bike and took off his helmet, proved to have a way of lowering his head and looking up at the person in front of him from beneath ginger eyebrows. His gaze was neither hostile nor curious; but it certainly wasn't friendly. Inscrutable wasn't the half of it. It was like being studied by a robot. It added to his simian stance and walk.

''Ello,' he'd greeted Miff. 'I heard about you from Auntie Glenys and from our Debbie. Moved in here, have you?'

'Yes,' said Miff, because it seemed the easiest answer and also because, with the Danny Garleys of this world, it didn't do to try and explain.

If the explanation didn't go right over their heads, it got jumbled up in their brains and this, in turn, could lead to their deciding they'd been disrespected. He well knew, from his time living rough, that the type could turn aggressive for very little reason. As it turned out, he didn't need to explain because Danny already had enough information to be going on with.

'You were chatting up our Debbie in the supermarket.'

Miff almost argued with that, but decided not to bother. If that was what Debbie had told her family, then so be it.

'Going to write a book, ain'tcha?'

'Might do,' replied Miff cautiously.

'I don't read,' said Danny. (Miff wondered if that should be 'can't read'.) 'I was never any good at it at school. You know anything about bikes?'

'No,' said Miff.

'Thought not!' said Danny cryptically. He remounted his steed and rode off to the ramshackle former stable. He probably kept his bike in it.

'What about the droid out there?' Miff asked Sam now. 'The demon motorcyclist, is he reliable?'

'His Auntie Glenys keeps him in order.'

'I see . . .' Miff hesitated. 'Do you like this place, Weston St Ambrose?'

Sam thought about this. 'It's okay. It isn't dull. You might think it is when you first come here. But, really, quite a lot goes on.'

'Henry and Prue told me there was a murder. The daughter of some guy on the Rosetta Gardens estate.'

'Oh, yes, the murder. Yes, I remember that! That was drama for you, if you like that. Actually, there has been more than one murder around here.' Sam didn't seem fazed by the thought.

'The place seems to attract gruesome goings-on,' said Miff moodily. 'Mrs Porter says that there was once a village here in Minglebury, in the Middle Ages. But they all died in the Black Death.'

'It was somewhere around here,' Sam admitted. 'But it might not have been right on this spot. I like to think it wasn't. Although Jenny

Porter told me that, about twenty years ago, some archaeologists came and dug trenches on that big field beyond our boundary line. They found a few old bones but nothing very interesting. They thought it was the site of a burial pit for the victims. But they weren't sure. It had all been ploughed over so often.'

There was a silence.

Then Sam said hesitantly, 'Glenys told me they found a body in that burnt-out vehicle, the one on Reg Prescott's land. They didn't know anyone was in it when the fire alarm was raised. That's awful, isn't it? I hope the poor soul was already dead when the van was torched.' She shivered. 'It doesn't bear thinking about. I wonder who it could have been?'

In that regard, progress was being made. Well, in one way, at least – not so much in another. Superintendent Carter also had his troubles. Office politics were boiling up like Sergio's spaghetti back in Bamford.

'I'll tell you something about that place, Weston St Ambrose,' said Dave Nugent to Ben Paget. 'You'd think it was a sleepy old spot. But it's like one of those villages in a horror film. One half of the locals is forever plotting against the other half. Strangers are reputed to turn up and never be seen again, sucked in like into a black hole.'

'Really?' asked Paget, sounding intrigued.

'You'd better believe it, mate. There's always something going on there. Talk about weird. Aha!'

Nugent was sitting in front of a computer, his favourite workplace, and now sat back with a satisfied smirk. 'You want my opinion?'

Paget, knowing he was to be told it, anyway, waited silently.

'Removing the number plates wasn't done to prevent us finding out who the owner is. It was meant to confuse us, lead us up the garden path.'

'How so?'

'We're meant to think that whoever torched the vehicle is just another car-nicking low-life. But, if you want my opinion, he's not. This isn't your average teenage joyrider. Not with a body in the back.'

Paget was not unaware that Nugent had been less welcoming than the others since his arrival. Not unfriendly, just wary. Perhaps he should put down a marker. So he said now, 'Whoever torched the van could still be a run-of-the-mill joyrider. He might have nicked the vehicle, not realising there was a body in it. It seems to have been covered by some sort of furniture, a sofa bed. Off drove chummy, thinking himself very clever, and unaware he had a passenger.'

'Unlucky sod, then, isn't he?' snapped Nugent, and leaned forward to peer at the screen.

Paget decided to cool the situation. Newcomers always got the blame if an established team started squabbling among themselves.

'I don't mind working at a computer for a limited time,' he observed. 'I haven't got the enthusiasm for it you clearly have. I mean,' he added generously, 'I haven't got your gift. I'm better out in the open air.'

Nugent swivelled on his chair and grinned up at him. 'Yes, quite the country boy, we hear! Practically a local man!'

So much for bonhomie. 'If you mean I spent some summer holidays with an uncle on his farm, when I was a kid, that hardly

Ann Granger

makes me a local!' said Paget brusquely. 'I stopped going there once I got well into my teens and lost my liking for muck and smelly animals. It's Reg Prescott, the owner of the land on which the car was torched, who's decided I'm practically a long-lost relative.'

'What, related to Reg Prescott?' asked Nugent incredulously.

'As near as dammit. He knew my uncle. That means he also knows of a horde of cousins, some of whom I remember dimly, but most of whom I've never heard of. Plus some more remote family members, and, because they intermarry round there, it means I'm practically related to everyone else to some degree. Reg hasn't yet traced a direct link between him and me, but he's working on it! His wife has already remembered that her grandmother had a sister married to a Paget.'

Nugent said thoughtfully, 'Well, if he does find one, you might get taken off the case. Conflict of interest and all that.' He sounded as though the idea appealed to him.

'Suits me,' said Paget moodily.

Nugent indicated the computer. 'You can trace your family tree on one of these, you know.'

'I told you,' said Paget, 'Reg Prescott's already doing that! And he doesn't need a computer.' He wandered off.

Later, Dave Nugent tapped on Carter's door. He obeyed the summons to enter and found himself in the company of the superintendent, Inspector Campbell and, to his surprise and displeasure, Sergeant Paget.

Now then! thought Nugent. How did Paget wangle his way in here? He's the newcomer. If they need a sergeant's input, they have me and they have Stubbs. We've both been here long enough to know the territory. Ben Paget should be keeping his head down and taking notes. But he's a bit too keen and too ambitious.

The three people in the room had clearly been discussing the case of the body in the back of the van, and all three now looked at Nugent expectantly.

'Give us some good news, Dave,' Jess encouraged him.

'Can do!' said Nugent with forced cheerfulness, managing to position himself so that he faced his boss and the inspector, but had his back to the new boy, excluding him. He may have been cut out of the discussion that had been going on, but he was here now and wouldn't be sidelined again! 'I don't know who the body in the back of the van is – or was. But the registered owner of the vehicle is one Gary Button, who lives at a place called Pitchett's Green, near—'

'It's near Bamford!' interrupted Paget excitedly, from behind Nugent's shoulder. 'I know it! It's not really a place, just a collection of former farm buildings now used for small businesses. I know of Gary Button, too! One of the businesses is an antiques dealer's, set up in one of the barns. Gary Button runs it. He lives with his family over the shop, or rather, next door to it.'

Dave Nugent, fuel thrown on to the flames of his earlier displeasure, now found his moment of triumph stolen by someone who was clearly setting himself up as a rival. He turned and glared at the interloper.

'Antiques? Legit?' asked Jess.

'More or less. I'm no antiques expert,' Paget told her. 'I don't think Gary Button is, either. Let's say, his stock looks like a collection of antiques. Old junk, I'd call most of it. House clearances, that sort of thing.'

'So you have actually visited this antiques place yourself, talked to Button?' Carter demanded. 'What took you there?'

'We'd had a tip-off, at Bamford, about some stolen items taken from large houses in the county. We were told they might have found their way into Button's store. But when we went out there, we drew a blank. There was nothing there on our list, or we didn't find it. He had receipts for the other stock. Some of it had arrived from China not long before. Quite a bit of it was French. Seems Gary likes to go over to France and hunt around the flea markets there.'

'What about Button himself?'

'He's a member of a well-known local family, some with convictions, and others without records, but operating in a grey area, if you know what I mean. Wheeler-dealers. Anything you want, a Button will find it for you. Where he finds it, that's another matter.'

'Bamford, eh?' mused Carter. 'That will be Trevor Barker's manor. Okay, Paget, well done. You and Nugent follow it up. Has the van been reported stolen?'

When the two men had left the room, Carter tapped his fingers on his desk and asked Jess, 'What are the odds? We no sooner clear up one case involving working with Barker and his officers, before here we are again. Poor old Trevor wasn't pleased to see us last time. He's not going to be delighted to hear from us again.'

'And then there's Alan Markby,' Jess reminded him.

'Oh, he can't be involved in this, surely?' said Carter – as it turned out, inaccurately. He glanced at the door and asked in a lowered voice, 'Am I imagining it, or has our newcomer started treading on toes? Dave was gradually turning puce in the face while Paget was telling us about Gary Button. I thought he was about to have some sort of an attack.'

Jess agreed. 'I did notice. Paget's new. I suppose he wants to make a good impression on you. To be fair, he did have the information we needed about Gary Button. I think Dave's feathers may have been ruffled.'

'We need a team, working together!' returned Carter shortly.

'I did think Paget was settling in well,' Jess told him a little ruefully. 'I said as much to you, didn't I?'

'Yes, you did, and I thought the same. To make it worse, I gather Paget has distant relatives around the place.'

'He's connected – very distantly, he insists – to the wife of Prescott, the farmer, on whose land Button's burnt-out van was found. Paget didn't know about any family link, until Prescott asked him about his name. It shouldn't be a problem.'

'We'll have to watch the situation.' Carter sighed. 'If Paget has family interests, we may have to take him off the team for this one. He won't like it, but Nugent will! I hate office rivalries. They have no place in police work. This is a murder investigation and it requires a team working with, not against, one another! Everyone needs to concentrate. Squabbling sergeants, one of them newly promoted to the rank, each trying to mark their turf like a couple of rutting deer, is not what we need right now. What's more, Dave Nugent has not only been here longer, he's the computer expert around the office.'

A tap at the door heralded the return of Nugent, who marched in again, his earlier air of triumph restored. 'Not only has the vehicle been reported missing, sir, but the owner's disappeared, too. Gary Button was reported missing by his sister on behalf of his wife.'

If Nugent had been equipped with a flag, he'd be waving it now. He couldn't resist a quick glance over his shoulder towards the newcomer, Paget, who'd followed him and was standing in the doorway, shaking his head incredulously.

Okay, new boy! thought Nugent. This is how it's done! You think, with a brand-new promotion under your belt, you're going to waltz in here and start giving us the benefit of your extensive professional experience. Just because you know where this place Pitchett's Whatsit is. Well, listen and learn!

Paget wasn't telepathic but he'd recognised that look on Nugent's face as Dave made for the superintendent's office. That was why he'd made sure to follow on his heels. This was the moment when he, Ben Paget, had to seize the initiative or he'd be playing second fiddle to Nugent throughout this investigation. And that wasn't going to happen. He now had a chance to make his mark, and he wasn't going to pass it up. Besides, he wanted to know what was going on.

'It might be Gary's van,' he conceded generously. (Nugent scowled.) 'That type of vehicle gets nicked all the time,' continued Paget. 'But the body being Gary's? No way. He sells dodgy antiques, like I said. He can't have got himself murdered because someone found out a Ming vase he bought was a modern fake. Unless he went back to Gary's place, and smashed the vase over his head.'

Nugent opened his mouth to argue but caught a look from the superintendent that told him to shut up.

'Good work!' Carter said briefly and dismissed the pair of them with a nod.

When they'd gone, he turned to Jess. 'Well, then! It looks as though, once again, we'll be investigating in partnership with Trevor Barker and his officers. You don't suppose . . .'

He and Jess stared at each other.

'At the moment,' said Jess, shaking her head decisively, 'I don't see how Alan Markby could be involved in this. I mean, it's not a cold case of his, it's a brand-new one . . .'

'It's just . . .' Carter hesitated. 'Well, if Markby is to be involved, we'll hear about it soon enough.' A thought struck him. 'When you were based at Bamford, back in Alan Markby's time, did you ever encounter this Button family?'

She shook her head. 'Personally? No, I didn't. I do remember the name. Superintendent Markby, as he was then, certainly had a couple of run-ins with them. I dare say that Trevor Barker has had his dealings with them since that time.'

Carter sighed. 'Well, no use putting it off! I'll get on to Barker and tell him we have a burnt-out van registered to Gary Button of Pitchett's Green, near Bamford.' He glanced at her. 'Do you want to wait and hear how he takes it?'

Jess grinned.

The reception of this news fairly made the phone tingle in Carter's hand. Even Jess could hear the outraged response.

'What do you mean? You've got Gary's Button's Transit van, burnt out!' yelled the luckless Barker. 'What's it doing down in your neck of the woods?'

'Yes, Trevor, I am afraid that's right.' Carter drew a breath. 'Also, I have to inform you that there was a charred body in the van, in the back, under the frame of a sofa bed. Of course, it's not yet been identified.'

There was a sound at the other end of the line as if someone had hit the top of a desk with his fist. It was followed by muttered imprecations. Then Barker was back.

'That Button family,' he howled down the phone, 'are a blasted nuisance! One of them was recently found murdered, one of the girls. Her sister reported her missing and later identified the body. Then the sister was back, to report her brother Gary missing. Don't ask me what's going on, I don't know! All I know is that both reports were made by the same sister, Harmony Button, and on both occasions she was accompanied by Meredith Markby, Alan's wife. You might know her better as Meredith Mitchell. She writes detective stories, if you please! Before that, she was some sort of civil servant.'

'Why was she with . . . what name did you say – *Harmony*?'

'Harmony!' confirmed Trevor Barker. 'And if ever a baby was given the wrong name, that's the one! Harmonious, the lady isn't!'

'But why was Meredith with her?'

'Oh, well,' snapped the goaded Barker. 'That's simple. When the family had trouble, they went to Markby first! Never mind official channels, the regular police force! No, Harmony Button went to Markby because, years ago, he nicked her old dad a couple of times.'

Barker was silent for a moment and Carter heard him draw an audible, deep breath. Then he asked more calmly, 'Will you be coming up here to check it all out? If you've got Gary's burnt-out van and, possibly, the remains of Gary himself?'

'First, we have to establish that the remains taken from the van are those of Gary Button. We'll try for DNA, of course, from the bones. But the high temperature of the fire and general incineration of the material means that any DNA obtained from them is likely to be severely degraded. The lab will do its best, of course, but it might take some time and not turn out to be definitive. On the other hand, we do have a complete set of teeth. Our pathologist has reported extensive dental work to the front teeth, upper and lower, and a healed fractured jaw. At one time in his life, several years ago, our subject was in a violent confrontation of some sort. The family can probably tell you when that happened.'

'Okay, I can check that out for you,' Barker said. 'But if it's recent dental work you're after, I doubt Gary went regularly for check-ups at the same dental surgery. Not something he'd bother with. We'll have to ask around every dentist in the area.'

'To go back to the DNA,' Carter went on, 'if any usable material is recovered, that is. The lab will need a sample from a close relative for comparison. How about that sister, Harmony? Would she be prepared to give a DNA sample? Or is the old chap, Gary's father, still alive?'

'He is, and there are two other brothers, one of them in the nick as we speak, and another sister. Getting a DNA sample for comparison shouldn't be a problem. But I'll have to tell the family why we need it, and why we want to know if and when he was ever in a punch-up resulting in a need for extensive dental work.'

'Do you mind doing that? Obviously, the wife will have to be told that there is a possibility her husband is the victim. But until that's established, tell them as little as possible—'

'You haven't met Harmony Button. She won't be fobbed off,' Barker's voice in his ear told him, echoing with deepest gloom.

'Then tell her we've found the torched van and a body inside it. She'll understand you can't be sure of the identity. That would lead neatly into a request for a DNA sample. You know as well as I do that recovering usable DNA from a badly charred body is difficult – especially if the underlying tissue and muscle have gone, as they have in this case. But suppose we're lucky and the scientists can get something for us, and if the DNA comparison shows that the body is that of Gary Button, we'll let you know at once. In the meantime, the teeth might be a better bet. As for whether I'll need to come up to see you, no, I'll—'

Carter glanced at Jess. 'If it's okay with you, I'll send Inspector Campbell to liaise with you, if and when the need arises. She knows both Markby and his wife. The Button family might be more free with information if Alan Markby vouches for Inspector Campbell.'

He put down the phone and smiled at her. 'Okay, Jess?'

Chapter 9

'A Christmas Fayre!' said Sam. 'We spell it F-A-Y-R-E.'

Miff stared at her, appalled. 'Where? How? Doing what? Run by whom?'

As he spoke, he knew the answer to the last question.

'Us!' said Sam happily.

It was coffee break time in the office. Sam was perched up high, wedged in the window recess in the thick stone walls, where there was a seat. She sat with her back to one wall, knees bent at forty-five degrees, and feet pressed against the facing wall. She was sipping from a mug with a horse's head painted on it, and had kicked off her boots at the door. She wore mismatched socks in rainbow colours. The sun picked up highlights in her spiky hair and made her resemble some woodland sprite.

'You know all about that sort of thing, do you?' asked Miff suspiciously. 'Because I can tell you now, I know zilch! I know less about running a Christmas Fayre, however you spell it, than I do about writing a book, and that's saying something!'

'But you can run an office!' countered Sam, gesturing with the mug at the general surroundings.

'I've never even been to a Christmas Fayre,' argued Miff.

'Well, we can use the spare space in the coffee shop barn. We'll put up decorations inside, and fairy lights and so on, outside.

Glenys can make Christmassy biscuits and cakes. We'll get in some Christmas stuff to sell, garden-related gifts . . .'

'What's a garden-related gift? A fork wrapped up in fancy paper? A set of gnomes, painted to look like Father Christmas and his elves—'

'That's a good idea!' broke in Sam enthusiastically. 'And if we get the gnomes unpainted, just the figures, we can paint them ourselves. That would make it cheaper for us. Great!'

'No, it's not!' howled Miff. 'Sam, I can tell you now, if you ask me to paint gnomes, I'll leave! You won't see me for dust!'

'Oh, *you* won't have to do it!' she assured him. 'Some of the Garley kids can do it. Debbie's artistic. She'll organise it. We wouldn't have to pay them much.'

'Debbie? What, the one who works in the supermarket?'

'That's right.'

'Sam,' Miff tried for a calm, reasonable tone. 'Have you any idea what gnomes painted by Debbie would look like? Every colour of the rainbow.'

'They'd be a novelty!'

'Granted. But not Christmassy.'

'But people do like that sort of thing,' argued Sam.

'They probably do in Weston St Ambrose,' admitted Miff.

But Sam was planning busily. 'Danny Garley is a biker. He could get some of his mates to paint gnomes in biker gear.'

'Sam,' said Miff, appealing to her reason. 'About the same number of people would like a set of biker gnomes in the garden as would be likely to read my book – if I ever write the damn thing.'

'You mustn't give up on your book!' she told him earnestly. 'You've just got to buckle down and do it.'

'I've got to do something before the first Wednesday of next month, when I give a talk to the writers' circle here.' Miff decided to make a stand. But Custer had tried that – and look what happened to him.

'Look here, Sam, writing a book takes time. So does putting together a talk in front of this local lot. Now you hand me the job of organising the Christmas Fayre, on top of everyday stuff.' He made a dramatic gesture encompassing the office as a whole.

'You organise your talk,' Sam told him, undeterred. 'I'll go and talk to Glenys and Danny about the Christmas Fayre.'

Miff threw in a last objection. 'Where do we get these unpainted gnome figures from?'

'Oh, that's not a problem,' she assured him. 'Morgan Jay makes them.'

'Who on earth is Morgan Jay?' asked Miff, before he realised the first name was familiar. The inebriated neighbour of Debbie Garley's grandma, that's who Morgan was, must be.

Sam confirmed it. 'He's a potter. He has his studio in a cottage by the river. Mostly he makes flower bowls and vases, and cats, because cats sell well, he says. So do owls. Every so often, when he feels like it, he makes a few gnomes. Generally, it's when he's had a go at the whisky that he turns to gnomes.'

'He sells these things?' asked Miff incredulously. 'Where?'

'Oh, on market stalls sometimes, country fairs, and places like our Christmas Fayre will be.'

'How old is this potter guy?'

'Hard to say,' Sam frowned. 'He's sort of ageless. He's always looked the same. He's what people call "a character".'

'Couldn't Morgan paint them? I mean, if he's made them in the first place, it seems sensible to let him finish the job.'

'It's better if we supervise the painting of them!' said Sam firmly. 'Morgan's fine painting the vases or the cats. I wouldn't like to let him loose painting the gnomes.'

Miff didn't ask why. He didn't really want to know. He wondered if he could possibly return to Henry and Prue and ask to move back into their spare room. All they wanted him to do was write a book.

'DNA?' asked Harmony suspiciously. 'All right, I know what it is. I'm not stupid, you know. I watch the detective series on the telly. Dad likes them. What I want to know is, what do you want it for?'

Trevor Barker drew a deep breath. This was going to unleash a storm. Mentally he battened down the hatches. 'I have to tell you, Harmony, that your brother's van has been discovered.'

'Where?' demanded Harmony. 'Whatcha mean, his van? What about Gary himself?'

'Now, I want you to try and keep calm.' Trevor raised his hands, palms turned out towards her. 'Because it's possible I have some bad news—'

'He's been in a smash!' she interrupted. 'Where? I listen to local radio. It didn't say nothing!'

'No, not a smash . . . The fact is, the van has been discovered in Gloucestershire.'

Harmony opened her mouth but Barker forestalled her, holding up his hand. 'I'm sorry, Ms Button, but it isn't good news. The van was burnt out . . .'

Harmony was calm enough, but it was a very dangerous sort of calm. Barker thought that if you were wandering through the jungle, and you found yourself facing a tigress, then the sort of assessing look he was getting from Harmony was probably akin to the scrutiny you'd get from the tigress. It was working out how to tear you limb from limb. He wished he'd brought Meredith Markby with him. She seemed able to handle Harmony. He'd only brought Emma Johnson, and she was looking far from happy.

Moreover, because of the fear of upsetting Harry Button – paterfamilias of this motley crew – the police officers were not allowed in the house. They had to sit in a partly collapsed greenhouse in the Buttons' overgrown garden. Barker had been granted the only chair, a rickety canvas-seated one. Emma was propped against the bench laden with cobwebbed stacks of empty plant pots. Harmony stood, arms folded across her ample bosom. An unfriendly-looking cat had squeezed in too, and studied them with baleful yellow eyes. Emma liked cats, but even she hadn't tried to pet this one.

'You said it wasn't a smash,' said Harmony in a low voice, like a tiger's growl.

'We understand – or rather, the police in Gloucestershire have informed us – that it was torched. It happened out in the countryside, on farmland. The fire was spotted from the farmhouse and the fire brigade alerted. Later . . . later, they found a body inside . . .'

'And you're saying it's my brother Gary's body?' Harmony's tone sharpened.

'We don't know that yet. I'm asking you to provide a specimen of DNA so that the lab can make a comparison to that taken from . . . from the remains. Then we'll, um, know for certain.'

Harmony wetted her lips. 'What sort of remains? If it's a body they've found down there, wherever it is, why not say so? Remains? What are they supposed to be?'

Barker didn't want to say bluntly that they had a jumble of bones from a broken, blackened skeleton that, according to information received from Ian Carter, had needed to be disentangled from a cat's cradle of twisted metal. On the other hand, there was no way he could disguise the reality of the situation.

'I mean, DNA from the charred body the police have in Gloucestershire. Harmony, you need to bear in mind the fire was fierce and, well, all they have down there are the bones and teeth – so we have to establish for certain this is your brother.'

A glitter showed in Harmony's eyes.

Barker hurried on. 'Firstly, could I ask if you know whether Gary used a particular local dentist? Or whether Mrs Katie Button would know?'

'Sitting in the driver's seat, was it, this body?' asked Harmony astutely, ignoring his request.

'No, it was in the back of the van.'

The tigress uttered a warning snarl. 'Well, Gary wouldn't be in the back of the van, would he?'

'Ms Button, we need to find out. Can you help? Do you know the name of a dentist, or are you – or would one of your brothers or your other sister – be prepared—'

'No need to involve the whole family, is there, until it's certain? You can ask Katie about a dentist, but ten to one, she won't know, or remember. How long will it take to make this DNA comparison of yours? How long until we'll know for sure?'

'These things can take a little while. The labs have a lot of samples coming in from all over the country . . .'

'And in the meantime, what do we do?' The growl was louder. Harmony pushed her upper body and face towards the police officers. Barker wondered if she really was about to spring on him. The cat, too, was shaping up for attack, its tail twitching and its body low to the ground.

Emma Johnson spoke. 'We were hoping, Ms Button, that you would come with us to see your sister-in-law. She will have to be alerted to the possibility that—'

'That what?' snapped Harmony. 'That she's a widow? That her kids are orphans? How am I supposed to tell Dad?' She turned and flung out an arm to point at the upper storey of the house where, presumably, the old man's bedroom was located. 'It'll kill him. He's not got over Amber. None of us has!'

'We realise the strain this puts you under—' Barker was not able to finish the sentence.

'*Oh, you do, do you?*' roared Harmony, full throttle. 'That's a fat lot of help, that is. Strain? There's Amber murdered, Michael in prison, Gary missing, and now you say he's probably been burnt to a crisp in his van? How? He wouldn't just sit there and let someone torch it! Or are you saying he was carrying something that might have made it blow up? Gas bottles or something. He doesn't deal in that sort of thing. He deals in antiques!'

Barker wondered how to phrase the next piece of information. 'It is possible the victim – if it's Gary – was, well, he was already dead when the van was torched. We don't yet know. The police in Gloucestershire will be investigating but they will keep us informed . . .'

Harmony straightened up, suddenly under control. 'He was murdered, you're saying? Like poor Amber?'

'Possibly, Harmony—'

He was interrupted. 'Before we go to see Katie, Gary's wife, we need to go and get Meredith!' Harmony told him briskly. 'I need Meredith with me. Okay?'

'Well, if Mrs Markby is willing . . .'

'She'll come with me, I know it. We'll go and get her now, all right?'

There was no denying it. Harmony had put herself in charge. Trevor Barker was prey to a reluctant admiration for her. She was one of those indomitable women who, through the ages, had coped with war and disaster and managed to keep the family's head above water, somehow. Like the wives who waited at the pithead in the old days when there had been a mining disaster, he thought. Or a wronged woman like Boadicea, who got in her chariot and charged the Roman army.

One thing was certain. She was not going to be easy to control.

'Okay, this is it,' said Miff.

Sam, seated cross-legged on the floor, nodded encouragingly. 'Go on, then.'

'Good evening, everyone,' began Miff, and stopped. 'I feel a complete idiot.'

'If you say that to them, they'll think you are an idiot. Keep going!' Sam ordered.

'It is very kind of you to invite me to talk to you tonight about my book, or, as I should say, my planned book. I haven't yet written it.' Miff stopped again and looked up. 'I plan to pause there and, with any luck, they'll make encouraging noises.'

'Or they might just tell you to get on with it!'

'Oh, all right. As you may already know, before coming here to Weston St Ambrose, I had been living on the streets for the past two years, getting to know the rough sleepers and their stories. It has been a real eye-opener and I feel I would like to share their histories with a wider world. Thereby – is "thereby" okay? Not too pompous or archaic?'

'No, carry on, the sort of people who go to the writers' circle here – Peter Posset and his chums – use words like "thereby".'

'Thereby bringing their world to the attention of the rest of us. Of course, I have changed the names to protect individual identities. My hope is that, by telling their stories, I can help find a solution to a very real problem, one that any of us can see for himself, or herself, any day of the week in our towns and cities. We should not ignore it. We *can't* ignore it. We should be asking why it has arisen, and what can be done.'

'That's very good,' said Sam. 'You are sure you are just writing a book, are you? You're not thinking of standing for parliament?'

'There are already enough people wanting to be MPs and mess up the country, just let me write this bloody book. And can you stop interrupting? Save the comments for when I've finished. At this rate, I never will!'

'Okay, carry on.'

'Right, well, yes, where was I? There are many dangers in sleeping rough. Some of the people I had encountered had suffered violent attack, verbal abuse, severe medical problems, both physical and mental . . .'

'Why did you stick it for so long?' asked Sam. 'It must have been dangerous! And so – uncertain, uncomfortable . . .'

Miff frowned. 'I felt free,' he said. 'It was marvellous. I was beholden to no one, only myself. I could go where I liked, do what I liked. Nobody ever asked me why or how or where . . . I got chased by drunks several times, caught by some occasionally, and got done over. That wasn't nice. But I went to Casualty with my cuts and bruises; and they cleaned me up, and gave me sandwiches and cups of tea, so that was all right. Generally, nobody bothered me or bothered about me. I just did whatever I felt like.'

'Oh,' said Sam dolefully. 'I suppose that's what Stuart wanted, to be free.'

Stuart again. The man who probably grew seeds in yoghurt tubs when he was in pre-school; and later thought running a garden centre involved no more than that. 'Can we leave Stuart out of this? I know you were hurt by his desertion, leaving you in the lurch here at Minglebury and all the rest of it. But the guy's gone, and for goodness' sake, don't waste your time brooding over it. It's his loss, not yours!'

Sam brightened. 'You really think so?'

'Yes, I do!' This was going in a direction Miff didn't want to take. 'Let me get on with rehearsing my talk, okay?'

'Yes, sure, sorry to interrupt. Sorry to bother you with my hang-ups about Stuart.'

'And stop apologising! "Never apologise. Never explain." Benjamin Jowett said that.'

'Who's he?'

'He was a guy at Oxford in the nineteenth century. Loads of other people have said it since.'

144

'How do you know Benjamin Whatsit said it?'

'I've spent a lot of time in libraries reading books of quotations and that sort of thing. They have good central heating in libraries – because of the books, not because of the people. You need to know that kind of thing if you are sleeping rough.'

'Are you putting that in your talk?'

'I could, I suppose . . .' Miff frowned. 'Tell me,' he said, 'this chap Posset, who seems to run the writers' group . . .'

'What about him?'

'He's not a bearded type who wears woolly sweaters with Christmas motifs sprinkled across them?'

'Yes, that's Peter Posset. He knits the sweaters himself. His granny taught him how to do it when he was a kid. He was a bank manager before he retired.' Sam frowned. 'What a pity I didn't think about Peter.'

'Why?'

'I could have asked him to knit some Christmas sweaters to sell at our Fayre. But he wouldn't have time now. I could ask, I suppose. Or perhaps one of the Blackwoods could ask him? He knows them well. Could you, Miff, ask Henry or Prue if they would ask Peter if he'd have time to knit a couple of sweaters?'

'No,' said Miff. 'We'll have enough on our plates trying to sell Morgan Jay's gnomes, if he condescends to make us any.'

About an hour later, Miff was wandering around the deserted garden centre, can of lager in hand, before turning in. 'Just going out to check everything is all right,' he'd told Sam. But actually, he liked this moment in the deserted centre. It wasn't lonely, that was it. The thing about plants, he was beginning to realise, was that they were company. They were, after all, a life form. They breathed, in their own way. They grew. They reproduced. They died. An entire existence spent in a pot or a flower bed, or a vegetable patch. A lot of humans had lives that weren't dissimilar. He hadn't yet reached the point where he'd started talking to the plants. But he could understand how some people did.

The countryside all around was wrapped in the velvet darkness; but the area of the garden centre itself was dimly lit by what Sam liked to call security lights. They'd been triggered by Miff's perambulations. Miff thought that it was the lack of anything of any obvious great value that would deter any thieves, rather than the half-hearted glow from the lights. But at least it meant he could walk around without bumping into the raised wooden tables, laden with plants.

There were odd rustlings and scrabbling but he couldn't identify the origin. Glenys had complained several times of having to chase mice from the pantry. Then, yesterday morning, Miff had been summoned by a screech from Sam. He'd found her in the store shed, pointing with dismay at the floor.

Several large bags of peanuts were stacked against the wall. They were not fit for human consumption, for garden birds only, and they stocked them because many visitors to the centre were bird watchers. They liked to sprinkle the peanuts on their bird tables and lawns. One bag had sprung a leak. Something had chewed off the corner of the plastic sack and the nuts had spilled out across the floor.

'Something's been eating them!'

Danny Garley, wandering in to see what the fuss was about, said laconically, 'Might be mice, or you might have a rat.' He wandered out again.

'*Rat!*' wailed Sam.

'We're out in the country, Sam. Danny could be right,' said Miff. 'Mind you, you see plenty of them around in towns, particularly if you're living rough. Some street sleepers who are really hard up catch rats to cook.'

That didn't help. 'Cook?' wailed Sam. 'What, and eat?'

'Yes, if you're hungry enough, you'll eat anything.'

She stared him aghast. 'Have *you*?'

'Me? No, of course not! I'm not daft. You don't know what the rat's eaten before you eat it! Anyway,' confessed Miff, 'I haven't got to that stage yet, or didn't get to it, before I came here. There are people out on the streets who don't qualify for any benefit. Life's tough for them.'

Sam stared at him thoughtfully and asked, 'I know it's not really my business, but were you drawing benefits?'

'No,' said Miff, 'and I haven't ever applied. I don't want some clerk breathing down my neck and asking me if I'm available for work. Mind you, I paid enough taxes in the days when I worked in London. I reckon they owe me money.'

'So, what have you been living on?'

'When I retired from, well, I was going to say the "rat race"! But as we've been talking about rats, I shouldn't. So, when I decided to become an independent entity, I realised my assets, sold up everything – car, flat, contents, the lot. It left me with a rucksack, a sleeping bag, a mini tent and a change of underwear, but a stash of money in my bank account. I've been happily watching it dwindle ever since. I don't need much. Although, as I'm here working for you, I have the gloomy feeling that my days of freedom are nearing their end.'

'Thanks a lot!' snapped Sam.

'Sorry, didn't mean to offend. I like being here with you and messing around with the plants and so on; even sorting out that madhouse of an office you had when I arrived. I even quite like the idea of being an author, but I'm beginning to think that, if I am going to write anything, it should be something with more earning potential than this wretched book the writers' circle thinks I'm writing.'

'Do you want to know what I think?' Sam said suddenly, after a moment or two in thought. 'I don't suppose you do, why on earth should you?'

'Go on, tell me.' Miff resigned himself to the inevitable.

'It seems to me that you get bored. When that happens, you just walk away. When you got tired of life in the world of finance, you dropped out of that. Now, you've become tired of living on the streets, so you've started dropping out of that. Taking a job here, for example. Excuse my frankness.'

'Oh, my coming to Weston St Ambrose had nothing to do with getting fed up with street life!' admitted Miff gloomily. 'It . . . it was something else. I'd rather not say.'

At that, by common consent, they let the matter drop. In the end, Danny had been dispatched to get some humane traps from Uncle Bert who, it seemed, made them to his own design. There were small traps for mice and larger ones for rats. 'I'll bring a couple of both sorts,' promised Danny.

'If I see a rat, I'll be *sick*!' declared Sam. 'You and Danny will have to take care of the traps.'

The traps were strategically placed and baited with the last of Glenys's rocky road cakes. So far, they hadn't caught anything. There was no way of knowing whether this was because the traps were too humane, and the mice (or rats) just strolled in and out, or whether the rodents didn't fancy the rocky road cakes.

'Don't let Danny or Glenys hear you say that!' Sam warned Miff.

'Well, the traps are useless, anyway,' argued Miff. 'I know they've only been down one day, but we'd be better off with a dog about the place.'

'Perhaps we could get a cat!' suggested Sam.

All this had been earlier. A cat? thought Miff now. Cats hunted, fair enough. But tackle a rat? It would have to be a pretty big cat. He chuckled into the empty night. The surrounding dark didn't worry him so much now. Perhaps he was getting used to it. Or perhaps the panic, which had caused him to flee and take refuge in Weston St Ambrose, was less on his mind. He'd had a narrow escape, but he had given his enemy the slip. That was all that mattered. Miff leaned on the closed five-barred gate at the entry to the centre and gazed out at the narrow road and the irregular darker shapes of the hedges beyond. He was in danger of turning into a sort of yokel, that's what he was doing. Well, there were worse things . . .

A car was coming. The engine sound came from Weston St Ambrose. That was very odd, because few people drove out of the village at night. Beyond the garden centre lay only fields and, buried under them, perhaps, the bones of Minglebury peasants, victims of the plague. Disturbed air swirled around him. Headlights swept over him and, automatically, Miff ducked.

But as he did so, he glimpsed the car, before it disappeared round a bend. It was a BMW. Difficult to be certain in the gloom, but he was fairly sure it had been black.

149

Chapter 10

'We've had a bit of luck, Jess,' Ian Carter told her. 'I think we can now say we've identified our skeleton. He is, or was, Gary Button all right!'

'Got the DNA results already?' asked Jess. 'That was quick! They usually take a lot longer to come back to us!'

Carter was shaking his head. 'Oh, no sign of those yet. It'll be ages before we get a report back from the lab. Besides, they've already warned us, they might not be able to recover anything from the bones. DNA, if any is retrievable, will probably be too badly damaged.

'What we have got is a nice, old-fashioned dental record, courtesy of HM Prisons, for Gary Button. Once Trevor Barker managed to calm the family down enough to get some answers from them, they told him they believed Gary had his teeth "seen to", as they put it, while doing a spot of time at Her Majesty's pleasure, in a Young Offender Institution. Apparently, as a teenage dropout, Gary ran with a bunch of thugs. They liked to waylay the buses carrying supporters of visiting football teams, and set about them. Eventually, he earned himself a spell in detention and, when he went inside, they fixed his teeth for him. The work done was extensive and distinctive. Our man is Gary, all right.'

'When did he stop brawling for a hobby?' asked Jess.

'After his spell inside. Perhaps being injured himself concentrated his mind. Also, he got married and set up his antiques business, becoming almost a model citizen, or as near to it as he was likely to get. As to why he developed a sudden interest in antiques, it seems they taught him carpentry and basic furniture making in the institution. Someone must have told him there was money in the old stuff.'

'So I suppose the YOI would count Gary as one of their success stories,' observed Jess. 'But if he was absolutely keeping to the straight and narrow, how did he finish up as a charred corpse, tied up in the back of his own van?'

Carter rustled the papers on his desk. 'I've also got here somewhere, oh, yes, here it is!' He held up a sheet of paper. 'This is a printout of Tom Palmer's autopsy report. There are, in Tom's judgement, two blows to the skull in approximately the same spot. The first might not have been fatal, but a second one, on top of it, was.'

'Does Tom suggest what kind of a weapon was used? Or is it our old faithful, the blunt instrument?'

'Something irregular in shape without a marked sharp edge. Tom doesn't think it was a metal tool – a hammer, say, or a wrench. He suggests a large stone.'

Jess said thoughtfully, 'So someone actually wanted to kill him and the attack took place, probably, outdoors. The assailant picked up a handy large stone, or rock, and struck Gary twice with considerable force.'

Carter nodded. 'So it would appear. Tom's not swearing to it, mind you. As he states here in his report, it's often easier to describe what the weapon wasn't, rather than what it was. But a rock of some sort would fit the evidence of the dents in Gary's skull.'

'A fight?' Jess suggested. 'Between Gary and an unknown person. This person picked up a handy large stone and – *bam!*'

'Twice,' Carter reminded her. 'He meant to finish Gary off!'

'The question is, why?' Jess mused.

'Give us time. We'll find out!' replied Carter with a confidence he didn't, right now, altogether feel. 'But let's assume that's what happened. What happened next, we should be asking!'

'Okay,' said Jess briskly. 'If it's right, the assailant now has a dead body at his feet. He needs to hide it or, even better, dispose of it altogether. So he trusses it up, and places it in the van with a view to torching the vehicle. So at least Gary wasn't alive when he burned . . .' Jess frowned. 'Why truss up a dead body? Why not just throw it into the van?'

Carter leaned back, folded his hands and fixed his gaze on her. 'I've been giving this some thought. It's what they pay me for, after all!'

Jess suppressed a grin. 'Okay, what do you reckon?'

'Suppose we assume Gary and his killer meet somewhere, either by design or by accident, and there is a falling out of some kind. We now know that Gary wasn't a stranger to a scrap in the past. But this time, Gary, the new family man, turns away; and that's his mistake. Perhaps he should just have swung a fist, or been the first to pick up a handy stone, as he would have done when he was seventeen. Perhaps he doesn't turn away. Perhaps he stumbles and falls on his face. Before he can get to his feet, his opponent strikes him a violent blow on the back of the head. Gary is stunned and helpless. The assailant decides to get rid of him, once and for all. He strikes him again. How am I doing so far?'

'I'll buy it,' said Jess.

'Right, so now the killer needs to move the body and hide it. He decides to do the job properly and get rid of the van as well. But Gary's van isn't close by. The killer does know where it's parked, though. So he trusses up the body in order to pack it into the boot of his own car, drives to where the van is parked, and transfers the packaged body into the Ford Transit. As luck would have it, there is already a sofa bed in there. Gary had picked it up somewhere earlier on one of his hunts for saleable items. Incidentally, if we can find out where Gary got the sofa bed, it would be a big help in tracing his movements. I'll arrange for something to go out on local radio.'

'All right,' agreed Jess, 'I'm still going along with all that. But why take the trouble to push the sofa bed over on top of the body?'

'Because before he can set the van alight, our killer needs to drive it to a remote location, out in the country. He doesn't want the Fire Brigade on the spot immediately! It's very unlikely that anyone would stop him, and ask to look in the back, but our man is playing extra safe. In case the van is stopped, or has cause to stop, and someone opens the rear doors, they'll see the sofa bed and not the body.

'So, you'd better get up to Bamford, Jess, and see what more you can find out about Gary Button. We need to trace his every move from Pitchett's Green, near Bamford, to Reg Prescott's field near Weston St Ambrose!'

'I've got a few ideas of my own,' said Jess when Carter fell silent. 'What if Gary was in the area on business, driving around, calling at country houses and farms? Some families have farmed the same land since Queen Victoria was a girl. A lot of country houses pass from generation to generation. They're likely to contain any number of antiques. They've been in the family for so long, no one thinks of them as being valuable any longer. It's just an old picture, or Grandma's clock. Besides, you know what farmers are. Keep everything. Don't throw it out or update it, if it still works! Gary sounds the sort of dealer who goes about, knocking on doors, and buying up odds and ends from people who don't know if what they're selling is valuable or not. I've already asked Ben Paget if he thought that might be the case.'

'And what did Sergeant Paget say?'

'Actually, he said, "Yes, that's Gary, all right."'

Carter nodded. 'A distinct possibility, I suppose. It's something to ask his wife, at any rate, when you interview her. Give my very best wishes to Alan and Meredith. You're bound to run into them.'

So, here she was, a couple of days later, in Bamford, being welcomed by the Markbys with an invitation to dinner.

'I do hope you'll be all right at The Crown,' Meredith said. 'Honestly, Jess, we'd be more than happy to have you stay here with us. At least you wouldn't be kept awake by the drunks falling out of the bar late at night.'

'You might hear the odd one stumbling through the graveyard on his way home. They've been known to fall asleep among the headstones,' Markby put in. 'It comes with living next door to the church. But I agree with Meredith, it would be quieter here than in the town centre.'

'Inspector Barker arranged for me to stay at The Crown. I wouldn't like him to think I'm critical of his decision. I get the impression he's a bit touchy. I am on his turf, after all.' Jess smiled apologetically. 'But thanks for the offer.'

'It used to be my turf,' said Markby nostalgically, gazing into his wine glass.

His wife cast him a look, then turned to Jess. 'Trevor Barker is a very nice man. But I think he worries.'

'You want a stressful occupation? Join the police force!' said her husband.

'Whatever you do, should you meet my mother again, don't say that!' Jess begged him.

'Oh, yes, how is your mother?' Alan and Meredith enquired politely in that synchronised way that couples have, thought Jess.

'Wants me to settle down – with a man, she means.'

'I thought you and Mike Foley . . .' Meredith raised an eyebrow.

'He wants to go back to his medical work in Africa.' Jess did her best to sound casual but knew it didn't come out sounding that way.

'Is that altogether a good idea?' asked Markby. 'He came home pretty sick, didn't he? Touch and go?'

'Not quite "touch and go", but yes, very sick. Now he's better – so he reckons – and he can go back and pick up where he left off. The charity that runs the medical centre isn't keen. They've offered him a job in London, organising things at this end. He won't even think about it.'

'I suppose,' said Meredith, 'one can understand that. He feels he didn't complete the task he went out to Africa to do. He would like to see it through.'

'Oh, I understand it, well enough!' Jess managed a smile. 'I don't like it. But I've got to accept it.'

'Hang on in there,' advised Alan. He nodded towards his wife. 'I did, and she gave in eventually . . .'

'Watch out I don't poison your cocoa!' retorted his wife.

The Crown Hotel wasn't so bad. It could do with a lick of paint here and there, but the staff were obliging and the bed appeared comfortable. Besides which, and this was something Jess wanted to keep to herself, if she took up the kind invitation from the Markbys to stay with them, they would expect regular updates on anything she found out. That could create a delicate situation. Alan kept saying that he was 'retired', but at the hint of an investigation, a gleam entered his eyes.

'He's bored, but won't admit it,' Meredith had already informed Jess in the kitchen, before they sat down to eat in the Markbys' comfortable, rambling former vicarage. Jess hadn't been sure if it was intended as a comment or a warning.

'Trevor and I will be visiting Katie Button, Gary's widow, tomorrow,' Jess said now. 'And we'll call on Harmony as well.'

'Don't be surprised if, when you call on Katie Button, Harmony isn't already there, waiting for you,' warned Meredith. 'I should tell you that I was with Trevor Barker, when he went with Harmony Button to tell her sister-in-law the bad news. Harmony had insisted I go with them. It's a matriarchal situation. The oldest family member, Harry Button—'

'Old rogue,' interjected her husband. 'Nicked him several times myself, years ago.'

His wife drew a deep breath and glanced at him. 'Well, his wife died and he moved in with his eldest daughter, Harmony.

She not only assumed responsibility for him, she took over the mother's role and responsibilities for all the siblings, as well.'

'Of which there are now two fewer,' added Markby, 'since Amber was murdered, and now Gary. I agree with Meredith. If you call on Katie, you'll almost certainly find Harmony there. Or, if not, she'll arrive pretty quickly, as soon as the drums beat out the message.'

'How did Mrs Gary Button take the death of her husband?'

'She's . . . she found it hard to accept. When we went to break the bad news, she kept saying we had "got it wrong". I don't think even Harmony has been able to persuade her.'

'Two murders in one family, so close together, is enough to make anyone have trouble believing it. You think there is a definite connection?' Jess asked Markby.

'Ah, now, that would be a rash assumption without further proof. Coincidences happen!' he reminded her, reaching for the wine.

'Are the family unpopular in the town?'

'You know how it is,' he told her, 'the town has grown over the years and people have come and gone. But there is always a core of old families in communities like ours. Those who know about the Buttons might lock up their valuables when one of them is about. But they accept them as part of the landscape. If they all left, there'd be a gap. When Amber was murdered, there was a real sense of outrage. She was a bit of a tart but she was a local girl, one of the town's own. I dare say, it'll be the same for Gary.'

'He couldn't just have been a prisoner in the van, unconscious, say? Whoever fired it might not have known he was there, and didn't mean to kill him?' Meredith mused.

157

'We are pretty certain he was dead, or as good as, when the van was torched,' Jess told her. 'Tom Palmer, who takes care of most of our autopsies, had only bones and teeth to work with. But there is clear evidence of a double head wound; the back of the skull is fractured. Tom suggests a rock or large stone as a weapon. Something you might find lying around at the edge of a dirt road. Plus he was tied hand and foot.'

'Someone slugged him and then put him in the van?' Alan asked.

'We – well, Ian Carter – thinks so. Ian has a theory that Gary died some distance away from where the van was parked. The killer tied up the body to be able to manoeuvre it. We all want to believe Gary was dead when the fire was started. He probably was. If he'd only been unconscious, he might have woken up and become difficult to handle.'

They all sat silent for a few minutes, concentrating on the lasagne.

'What about that farmer, the one on whose land the van was torched?' asked Meredith.

'Reg Prescott? Well, he's a very well-liked local man, nothing known against him. I've got Sergeant Paget working on that. Paget had local connections in the area when he was a boy.'

'Did he?' asked Markby, startled.

'The relatives he stayed with are all gone now; and the farm they ran when he was a kid is now a housing estate. But Paget's uncle was a respected member of the farming community, and is remembered. What's more, there may be a family connection, a bit distant, but you know how they are in the country. So, as a result, the Prescotts have welcomed Ben like the prodigal returned!

It's not a question of his fishing for information. It's more that he's being deluged with it.'

Walking through the peeling pillars of the late-Georgian entrance into The Crown, on her return from the Markbys, Jess found the place humming with activity. They seemed to have quite a few overnight guests and the dining room had obviously been busy. There was a faint background smell of hot food about the whole place. Jess felt reluctant to go straight up to her room, although an early night probably would be best. But she turned aside from the staircase (the hotel lift was slow and unpredictable), and entered the lounge bar.

This was about a third full and she was the only woman. The other drinkers had the appearance of businessmen, or visiting site engineers and representatives of various companies involved in the development projects underway around the town. Most appeared to be in their forties, a little overweight, winding down after a stressful day. They sat in small groups, and many seemed to be old acquaintances. A couple of them looked up as Jess came in, and then looked down again.

Jess suppressed a smile. No, she obviously wasn't a local good-time girl on the hunt for customers. Not an Amber Button. But this was the sort of place where Amber might well have wandered in, looking to suss out the possibility of a lonely man with cash in his pocket and wanting some female company. Food for thought. It might be worth making a few very discreet enquiries. Always supposing Barker's officers had not already done so. Also, she wasn't on home turf, here. She'd have to make sure Barker didn't find out she was asking people about Amber Button. Amber was his case. Jess was here about Gary Button. But Barker's enquiries, it seemed to Jess, had become blocked at the first hurdle, at Mrs Clack's house. The landlady remained defiantly uncooperative and the only other witness there, the Romanian lodger, had disappeared into the wide blue yonder. So Barker ought not to be surprised that Jess was asking around. Not being surprised did not mean he wouldn't be very cross. He was a touchy fellow.

There were two women serving in here, one young and the other older. The older woman recognised Jess as a resident and came across to her.

'Are you all right there, inspector?'

Jess had taken the only empty armchair, tucked away in a corner behind a standard lamp. The waitress had spoken quietly, but every other guest in this room had ears trained to pick up any sign of a problem, from discontented brickies to investors losing confidence. Enough of those enjoying a quiet drink had caught the mode of address. They looked up quickly, assessed Jess again, and then fell to speaking even more quietly to their companions. The most innocent of civilians, thought Jess with amusement, can get a little twitchy when the police walk in. They start muttering and look furtive, like this lot around her.

'Can I get you something to drink?' the waitress was asking.

'Just a single gin and tonic, Gordon's gin, if you have it, and not much ice, please.' The fashion now seemed to be to cram the glass with ice, which melted quickly and rendered the drink tasteless.

The waitress departed on her errand. The other patrons had accepted Jess's presence now and, if they were curious as to why she was here, and they almost certainly were, they made a good show of hiding it. One of them was on his mobile phone. Jess caught a few words: 'So, what are you watching? Oh, *New Tricks*?'

The viewers loved police dramas. The style of these programmes varied, but the basic theme was always the same: a crime, a puzzle to solve, some action scenes in most cases, though not in all . . . Who did it? That was what it all turned on. That and the main detective's private life, which always appeared to be more fraught than the mystery he or she was trying to solve.

Sometimes, thought Jess, private life was more complicated than public drama, or real-life murder mysteries. At other times, the reverse was true. Often it was painfully obvious who the killer was. Most murders remained close-to-home affairs. But not always. Getting the evidence to put before a judge, that was another matter. And murderers were seldom interesting people. They were inadequate, insecure, frightened men, masquerading as bully-boys. Or respectable citizens outwardly and monsters within. They were human beings with terrible secrets to hide, prepared to go to any length to keep things hidden, even if it took a murder to hide the original secret. A sin to hide a sin. Then there were the jealous lovers, the desperate women trapped in loveless unions, the betrayed wives and cast-off girlfriends. Don't forget the greedy, the frightened, the trapped – and, occasionally, the evil – of both sexes.

But that man over there on his phone was anxious to reassure his wife that he was thinking of her, missing his evening in front of the telly, behaving himself, wherever he was phoning from.

She wouldn't be phoning Mike, to ask what he was watching, because the relationship with Mike wasn't in that category. He probably wasn't watching television at all. Nor had he phoned her to ask if she was okay. Each of them worked on the assumption that the other would manage without that kind of long-distance support. But it was another factor to support her instinct that she and Mike were not heading towards a shared future.

But even good husbands, thought Jess, watching the other guest wind up his call, get lonely. A conversation with whoever was at home was no substitute, might even increase the awareness of distance. They would have been Amber's natural prey.

The waitress had returned with the G&T. She also brought a small dish of peanuts as a bonus.

'You've been busy here tonight,' said Jess, signing the bill. 'A lot of people staying over?'

'Oh, yes, it's mostly to do with the new business park they're building on the edge of town. It brings in all kinds of people during the week – planners, developers, and engineers of all sorts. Sometimes they tell me why they're here. It's usually one of those.'

The man who had been phoning his wife was looking this way. He had a pink, shiny face, thinning fair hair and blue eyes with a sharp look in them. He could do with losing a few pounds but looked generally pretty fit. He was doing his best to hear what Jess was saying to the waitress. He might be bored and curious, now he'd wound up his call home, or it might be a little more than a passing interest.

'I see,' Jess said to the waitress, 'that I'm the only woman here. Do you get many women in the bar of an evening?'

'Oh, yes, if they're staying here. But tonight you're the only single lady guest.' The waitress wasn't a fool. She had understood what lay behind Jess's query. 'We sometimes get a single woman come in for a drink. We don't mind. It depends on how she behaves.' The waitress lowered her voice. 'Have you come to Bamford on account of Amber?'

Now the pink-faced man was blatantly listening, leaning sideways in his chair as he strained to catch the words.

'You knew Amber?' Jess wasn't in town because of Amber Button, not strictly speaking, but because of Gary. However, the two enquiries had to be linked. She didn't hesitate to ask the waitress.

The waitress allowed herself a grin. 'All the pubs and bars around here knew Amber! Our manager didn't like her coming here, though. If he caught sight of her, he'd let her know she should drink up and go. We're not a knocking shop . . .' She paused. 'Still, dreadful what happened to her. Hope you find who did it.'

The waitress departed to see to other customers. The pink-faced man was still staring at Jess. She turned and met his stare. He nearly fell off his chair in his haste to turn away and look unconcerned. But he got to his feet moments later and walked briskly out of the lounge.

Oh yes, thought Jess. And you knew Amber, too! Very well! Bet my next month's pay on it.

Miff sighed. It was late and he was doing the accounts. What that meant, in practice, was that he was calculating how fast the garden centre was going down the tubes. On the other hand, it was a challenge. If he could make the place a going concern, with Sam doing all the gardening stuff, and Miff keeping an eye on the expenditure, it would be a real achievement. But, after such a long time with no responsibilities, it now seemed that the whole world rested on his shoulders.

Besides the book, there was the talk to the writers' group, and now the Christmas Fayre. And, stupid though it no doubt was, he couldn't forget that car, the one that had driven past the garden centre as he was leaning on the gate with his can of beer. It was ridiculous, he told himself, to be stressing out over a glimpse of an unknown car, and in the twilight. But the truth was, so many things seemed to be going on here in Weston St Ambrose that he had very nearly forgotten about BMW man and what had led him to flee from Bamford in the first place. It could not, of course, be the BMW he'd seen parked by the warehouse in which a murderer had decided to dispose of his victim's body. Sure, the man would still be looking for him. But not here in this back-of-beyond spot. There was no way he could have tracked Miff here.

'I can't forget him, that's the trouble,' Miff muttered aloud to the computer screen. 'Any more than the murderous blighter will have forgotten me. I'm going to spend the rest of my life looking over my shoulder, twitching every time I see a black car, and generally turning into a nervous wreck!'

Behind him, Sam asked quietly, 'Why? What happened in Bamford, Miff? What made you leave and come here?'

Miff spun round on his chair. He had thought Sam was outside in the plant area, tidying up after a visit by a group of walkers in identical anoraks. But she was standing in the doorway of the office, frowning slightly, and looking worried.

'I know you don't want to talk to me about it,' she said, 'whatever it is. And it's not for me to quiz you. You wouldn't have to tell me the truth, anyway. Except that I think you probably don't tell lies. Well, yes, you *do*, of course you do. Take all that rubbish you told people about writing a book and working abroad when you were really living rough in the UK—'

'My parents invented the working abroad bit!' Miff interrupted, defending himself.

'Bet you never denied it, though. But that's not exactly telling lies. It's more – creative. And you are now going to write the book, aren't you? But you tell people whatever comes into your head. Anything to stop them asking questions.'

'Thanks for that interpretation of it,' Miff said with a wan smile. 'I like to think of it as creative, as well. The trouble with outright lies is that you have to remember what you've said. With fantasy, if what you've said doesn't fit with what you said earlier, you dream up a bit more, so it does. I admit, I do invent. I invent what I think people want to hear, what will make them happy, if you like. No point in worrying them. Nobody wants to hear bad news.'

Miff frowned. 'In early times, they used to kill the messenger who brought bad news. It meant a threat to their very survival was on the horizon. No wonder they were cheesed off with the poor guy. Not that much has changed, you know. Where I was working, before I walked off the career scene, everyone was so relentlessly upbeat all the time. Everything must seem to be going well, everyone doing fine, even when it wasn't the case. There were all these people being relentlessly positive, and all eyeing one another to see who had bought a new car or traded up to a bigger flat. Doing well, you see. Slap him on the back and buy him a drink. Hope he remembers you. Then there was the poor blighter who was still driving the same old set of wheels or, heaven help him, had moved to a less expensive part of town. They avoided him like the plague. Failure is catching. Kill the messenger.'

'Did they buy you drinks?' asked Sam.

'All the time. Loads of false bonhomie. I thought, sod this for a game of soldiers, and I buzzed off. Dropped right out. The word was put out that I'd had a nervous breakdown from overwork. No, I hadn't. But it was the only way they could understand it. "Ferguson, poor blighter, went right round the twist! He was heading for the top, you know. Then he cracked up." That was something they could understand. Nervous breakdowns happen. No one mentioned them – no more than any other unmentionable disease. Pretend it's not there . . .'

He paused. 'I must have worried my parents, I suppose. But they've cut me loose, and shoved off to Portugal, so they've coped with it in their own way. Or they're simply avoiding association with my failure. Perhaps they're just furious with me. They spent a lot on my education.'

Sam came into the room slowly and took her usual seat in the window embrasure. This time she sat with her legs dangling, hands pressed on the ledge, either side of her.

'I can't help, I suppose?'

'Believe me,' Miff told her fervently. 'You have helped already, more than you can imagine. You've given me refuge, a job, a hidey-hole, if you like.'

'So, you are hiding from something, then?'

'I'm hiding from someone,' Miff admitted.

'What will this person do, if he or she finds you?'

'He,' said Miff. 'It's a man.' He couldn't answer her question, because the reply would have to be, 'He'll kill me.' For the first time, it occurred to him that his presence here, or anywhere, might endanger someone else: Sam, Henry and Prue, Auntie

Glenys, even Danny, everyone and anyone he came into contact with.

'Perhaps,' he said, 'I should move on.'

Panic filled her face. 'Oh, no! Oh, damn! I shouldn't have asked you about it! Don't leave! I won't ask again, promise!'

'Okay, and in return, I promise I'll stay and arrange the Christmas Fayre with you, at least.'

'Thanks.'

Besides, he thought, he couldn't run for ever. He'd run out of places to hide. He'd have to pitch camp somewhere eventually, build a stockade, hope the enemy, in the shape of BMW man, didn't come charging over the hill towards him. Everyone ends up somewhere. He'd just never thought he would end up in a place like the Minglebury Garden Centre. But hey! he thought to himself. I might just end up on the streets for real. Not just in the amateurish way he'd been living there before, turning his back on his responsibilities. No, he might just end up unwashed, alcoholic and hungry, beaten up regularly by drunken yobs. It made the garden centre look like Shangri-La.

Chapter 11

'Meredith thinks that when we get to Gary Button's home, we'll find his sister Harmony there with Gary's wife,' said Jess the following morning, to Trevor Barker.

Her night at The Crown had not been as comfortable as hoped. It hadn't been the departing customers who had been the problem. It was the staff moving the furniture in the empty bar, beneath her room, to enable the cleaners to do their job in the morning. They did this by the simple means of pushing it along the stone-flagged floor, or picking up the chairs and slamming them down on the tabletops. Thus the latter part of the night had been punctuated by unearthly screeches, crashes and thumps. The bed had proved hard, the pillows thin and the pipes had whistled and clanked all night long. Air in the radiators, probably. A firm mattress was supposed to be good for you, or so she'd been told once. It had not been good for her spine. She ached all over.

In the breakfast room this morning, she'd walked in to see the pink-faced man of the evening before, finishing his bacon and eggs. When he saw her, he rose and made a rapid exit, leaving his cup of tea untouched. Perhaps he was just running late for his first appointment. Jess put him out of her mind for now. She had other fish to fry, as the saying went. She hoped she didn't starting yawning in mid-interview with the widow.

'Harmony? Put your money on it!' replied Barker now, briefly. 'She's bound to be there, or she'll turn up within minutes. Brace yourself. Harmony Button is a force of nature. She takes over; and she won't be impressed by us being police officers. Her opinion of the police isn't high, and, anyway, her family have always seen us as the enemy. Her brother, Michael, is currently in prison, by the way. Burglary.' Barker gave a snort of derision. 'He's not a very good burglar. Gets caught regularly, usually when he tries to get rid of his loot.'

'Tell me about Gary. He lives out in the country, it seems – or he did?'

They had left Bamford and were driving along a narrow B road. There were few places a car could pull over. Jess wondered what would happen if they met a tractor, head on. The annoying thing was she had once been based locally; she ought to remember this road, and many others. But the layout seemed mysteriously to have changed. Trees had been chopped down, and fields churned up ahead of works beginning. There was already a new estate of 'affordable' homes just outside the town. Once landmarks went, so did familiarity. It just wasn't the same place. Well, it was, but it was playing tricks with her memory, disguising itself. She was reminded of the businessmen in the lounge of The Crown. They were behind this transformation, she thought. This, they would insist, was progress. She was recalled from her musings by her companion's voice.

'I wouldn't call Pitchett's Green out in the country,' Barker was saying. 'It's where four roads intersect and there are several buildings, mostly old barns and a couple of cottages. Didn't you ever drive through it when you were based in Bamford?'

'If I did, I don't remember it,' she admitted cautiously. 'I might do, when I see it. You know how it is. If there hasn't been a crime committed there, it doesn't get logged in the memory banks!'

Barker laughed. 'True enough. Well, how to describe Pitchett's Green? There's a former pub, but long abandoned. It's boarded up and falling into disrepair. I gather applications for permission to demolish it have been unsuccessful. It's not beautiful, but it is old, and the local parish council objects to any further residential development. The access roads aren't up to it, anyway, as you see.'

Jess looked again across the hedgerows towards the destroyed fields. There might not be any access roads at the moment. But undoubtedly they were in some planner's computer. Barker nodded to indicate something ahead of them. 'Ah, we're here!'

They rounded a bend and Jess saw the place for herself. There were the four roads, forming a cross at this point, and central to them a patch of grass and an oak tree. The tree looked very old. Jess wondered whether Pitchett's Green had a sinister history. Gibbets had sometimes been set up at crossroads in ancient times. A large wood pigeon was patrolling the grass patch, occasionally pecking at something on the ground. It had noted the arrival of the car and was keeping a wary eye on it.

The pub was as Barker had described it, a sorry sight, its windows boarded up, its slate roof in a perilous state. For all that, an old man sat outside it on a dilapidated bench. He'd probably sat on that bench of a summer evening all his life, starting back when the pub had been a thriving drinking den. He still sat there, with an aged dog asleep at his feet, and watched, sentry-like, for the approach of strangers. He must live in one of the ramshackle cottages beyond the pub.

Some traces of knowing this place were being dredged up from

Jess's memory; but they were confused when Barker indicated, with a nod, a large barn conversion, located across the road from the pub. That certainly hadn't been here in Jess's time in Bamford – or, if it had, it hadn't looked like this. Its excellent state of repair and general appearance were in stark contrast to the former pub and the cottages.

There was a fenced area beside it; not a garden, more a holding area for an assortment of bits of masonry, old fireplaces, with their iron grates and tiled surrounds. A board announced 'Reclamations'.

'Gary's place!' said Barker. He pointed at the barn.

Jess's first thought was that a lot of money had been spent on converting what had been a farm building into a residence. Where there had been a wide entry, allowing carts or a tractor to enter, there was now a plate-glass window. The roof had been re-shingled and the outside treated with some wood preservative. Jess knew that such properties were highly desirable, for all their many inconveniences, and fetched high prices. Gary's business had been doing well.

Barker switched off the engine and they got out of the car. The pigeon flew up in a clatter of wings and took refuge in the branches of the oak. Between it and the old fellow over there, watching, unsmiling and unmoving, Pitchett's Green had an excellent warning system. Even the dog had woken and sat up, ears pricked, staring at them.

'As I feared, Harmony is here before us!' Barker pointed at a much scraped and dented Ford Focus pulled up before the house.

As he spoke, a door opened at one end of the building and a large woman, with a mass of hair, emerged. She sported outsized hoop earrings. Her plump legs were sheathed in black leggings, teamed with a voluminous purple top. She made a striking figure

171

as she stood by the grass verge, awaiting them. Good grief! Was that the widow? No, thought Jess, it was more likely to be . . .

'Harmony . . .' said Inspector Barker with resignation.

He and Jess proceeded towards the house in a manner, thought Jess, which would make it obvious to anyone watching that they were police officers. The old guy over there knew it, probably his dog knew it, and any well-concealed watchers in the cottages knew it. She had that prickling feeling in her spine that meant eyes were following their every move.

'Who's she?' asked Harmony brusquely by way of welcome, pointing a plump beringed finger in Jess's direction. Her hoop earrings swung and bounced. She had watched their approach, unsmiling and unwelcoming. Barker she knew. Jess was a newcomer, an intruder on the scene. That could be good or bad. Until she knew, Harmony was maintaining her defences.

Barker made the introductions in a formal manner. 'This is Inspector Campbell. She is heading up the team investigating your brother's death, in Gloucestershire.'

To Jess, he said, although she already knew it, 'This is Harmony Button, the victim's sister.'

Harmony peered at Jess from beneath heavily mascara'd lashes and mauve-shadowed eyelids. 'I've seen you before somewhere.'

'A few years ago, I was part of CID here in Bamford.'

'Knew I'd seen you,' said Harmony gloomily. 'Come on in, then.'

'How is Mrs Button today?' asked Trevor as they followed her into the house.

'How do you think? She still can't get her head around it. You'll see.'

Harmony led them into a large, raftered room, unexpectedly well furnished, and spotlessly clean. An electric fire, disguised to have the appearance of a wood-burning stove, had been switched on. It was efficient. Its fake logs glowed cheerily and the room was very warm. Jess wondered if the heating was because Katie was cold with shock. There were signs of children by way of a high chair against one wall and a brimming toy box. But there were no signs or sounds of the children themselves.

'Maria, my sister, has got the kids,' explained Harmony, pre-empting any enquiry. 'Sleeping over. They're okay. It's her – she's not.'

She indicated a sofa and the figure of a small pale woman huddled on it. 'She don't say much. You can try asking her questions but you won't get much out of her.'

'Harmony,' said Jess cheerfully, 'Inspector Barker and I would love a cup of tea.'

Harmony eyed her up and down. 'Oh, yes? I'll take myself off and make it, then, if that's what you mean. Take my time about it, too. I got the message.' She stomped out.

Jess went to take a seat on the sofa, next to Katie Button. Katie wore jeans and a sweater and her feet were clad in sand-coloured Ugg boots. The sleeves of the sweater were too long and the whole garment too roomy, so that the wearer appeared to be sitting inside it, rather than wearing it. Jess wondered whether, in fact, the sweater had belonged to Gary.

Gently, she began, 'My name is Jessica Campbell, Katie, and I'm a detective inspector. I'm really very, very sorry for your loss. I've come over from Gloucestershire as part of the investigation into your husband's death.'

She wondered whether the woman had even heard her. But

173

Katie turned her head and fixed Jess with large, pale blue eyes. They were strangely blank. Jess wondered whether Katie might be, as the country expression had it, 'a bit slow'. Her long, fair straight hair framed her face and she appeared very young. She was probably older than she looked – had to be, thought Jess. Meredith had told her there were four children.

'No,' said Katie in a very quiet but steady voice. 'You've got it wrong. You can't be investigating his death, because he's not dead.'

Oh, dear. 'I'm afraid, Mrs Button, that he is. I know what a terrible shock it is . . .'

Katie shook her head. 'He always comes home at night. He goes off early sometimes, and comes home late, but he always comes home.'

'Not this time, Katie, I am so sorry. The dental records—'

Katie interrupted her, still speaking very quietly but with a hint of determination. Her mind was made up. 'Then you were looking at the wrong ones. You looked at someone else's.'

'I'm afraid they can't be wrong, Katie . . .'

'Why not?' It wasn't really a question: it was a rebuttal.

Jess gave it another go. 'These are the prison dental records, Katie, from when Gary was a youngster. They're part of Gary's Young Offenders' Institution record; and they can't be the wrong ones.'

'Mistakes get made,' returned Katie. 'They give people the wrong babies in hospitals sometimes.' She frowned slightly. 'I got the right ones,' she said. 'I took a good look at them when they were born.'

Jess abandoned the questioned reliability of official records, and tried another tack. 'Tell me about that day, Katie, the day Gary left and didn't come home in the evening. Did he leave very early?'

Katie nodded. 'Just after eight it was. I was getting the kids their breakfast.'

'Had Gary eaten breakfast?'

'He had a bacon sandwich. He likes a bacon sandwich.'

'Did he say where he was going?'

'Totting,' said Katie simply.

'You mean cold-calling on householders? Knocking on doors and asking if they've anything to sell?'

Kate nodded, her long fair hair falling round her face. In contrast to her sister-in-law, she wore no make-up and no jewellery that Jess could see, apart from her wedding ring. The sweater sleeves came halfway down her hands, so perhaps beneath them Katie wore a wristwatch or a bracelet, but Jess doubted it. She wondered whether Katie had even dressed herself that morning, or whether Harmony had done the honours. Probably not, thought Jess. Harmony would've found some more jewellery.

'Did he go to many country houses? Or farmhouses?' Jess asked next.

Another nod.

'And did he drive long distances to visit new places, cold-calling?'

'He has to,' said Katie. 'He's done all the farms around here.'

Jess saw Trevor Barker's eyebrow twitch and was glad Harmony wasn't there to see it.

'What sort of things did Gary buy?'

'Furniture,' said Katie. 'A lot of old furniture. People are glad to get rid of it. Bits of china. Old picture frames. Anything old, really.'

The floor quivered to Harmony's heavy-footed tread as she returned with a tray and teacups. 'I told you,' she said to Jess as she set down the tray. 'You won't get nothing out of her.'

Jess wanted to snap, *Actually, I was doing quite well until you came back!* but that wouldn't have helped. 'Your sister-in-law is obviously in shock. I think a doctor ought to take a look at her.'

Harmony shook her mop of black hair. 'She won't see no doctor. She don't like doctors. She's worried they'll send social workers sniffing around. She's afraid they'll take the kids away from her.'

'Why should the authorities do that?'

Harmony gestured at Katie. 'You can see for yourself. She's a bit wanting.' There was no attempt to lower her voice. Katie herself didn't appear put out at being so described. 'But it don't matter!' continued Harmony fiercely. 'She's a very good mum! Those kids are her world. Gary's not here; but it will be all right for his little 'uns. We'll look after them all – me, Maria and Declan.'

Jess turned back to the silent Katie. 'Mrs Button, when Gary left that day, was it his intention, do you know, to visit farmhouses or isolated country properties, seeking unwanted old furniture?'

'Yes,' said Katie.

'But he gave no indication – he didn't tell you exactly where he was going?'

'No.' Katie looked up. 'Sometimes he don't know himself. Depends what he finds. When he gets back, you can ask him yourself.'

'Told you so,' said Harmony with grim satisfaction. 'She don't believe he's gone for good. You take sugar in your tea?'

They drank their tea in an awkward silence. Jess knew there ought to be more she should ask Katie Button. But, at the moment at least, there seemed little point in doing so. Harmony had handed her sister-in-law a mug of tea. But Katie simply sat immobile, with it cupped in her hands, until Harmony ordered, 'Drink up!'

The visit didn't last much longer. Clearly there was no point in trying to interview the widow until she came to terms with reality, if that ever happened. When they left, Harmony accompanied them to the car and stood, arms folded, before them. 'It's like I told you,' she said.

'She will have to face the fact of his death eventually, Harmony. It seems to me she accepts your authority. You will need to persuade her . . .' Jess paused. 'Or a doctor of some sort might have to be brought in.'

'She'll come round to it,' said Harmony.

Jess hoped she was right.

The old man and the dog watched them as they drove away from the house. There was now a wood pigeon on the pub roof, but Jess didn't know whether it was the same bird as she'd seen earlier. She glanced at Trevor Barker.

'The murder of the sister . . . Amber, did you say her name was?'

'That's right, Amber. She lodged with an old bat called Myrtle Clack and was, to some extent, estranged from the rest of the family. That may have been because there were things she didn't want them to know about her lifestyle. Or just because she was fed up with Harmony, bossing everyone about. I can't say I'd blame her, if so.'

'There has to be some connection, surely, between the two murders? How did Gary and the others take the news of Amber's death?'

'The old father was apparently distraught. But he's withdrawn into himself and there's no use trying to talk to him. The siblings have been thirsting for revenge, particularly the two brothers,

Declan and Gary. Declan runs a scrapyard. Michael, the third brother, is in prison, as I said.'

'So Gary – and Declan – might have been asking questions and caused someone to panic?'

They were coming up to a stone-walled pub, its thriving appearance underlining the dilapidation of the sorry ex-pub at Pitchett's Green. Barker swerved into the car park and drew up in a spray of gravel.

'Can't get on with discussing things while I'm driving,' he explained.

'Any use talking to Myrtle Clack?' asked Jess.

'There is no point at all in talking to Mrs Clack. It isn't just that she's a dragon. It's that she's a dragon with an uneasy conscience . . .' Barker paused and frowned. 'No, I shouldn't say *conscience*; because I don't think old Myrtle has much of that. More likely, she's scared.'

'Because she knows something?'

'She knows a lot, by my reckoning,' retorted Barker frankly. 'Hiding a lot, too. But you'll never get it out of her. The person we really would like to talk to again is Eva Florescu. Mrs Clack lets out two rooms as individual units. They are little more than the size of prison cells and about as comfortable. Amber Button rented one. Eva rented the other one. The wall between the two rooms, Eva's and the late Amber's, is thin. One way or another, Eva could probably tell us something useful. But after my unsuccessful original attempt to interview her, she scarpered. We're trying to find out where she is.'

'What about talking to Declan? If he's been asking around about his sister, he may have heard something relevant.'

'Oh, Declan,' said Barker. 'He'll be at his scrapyard.' He glanced at the pub. 'Care for a lunchtime sandwich? Then we can catch Declan as he finishes for the day. He won't like the police turning up while he's got customers there.'

Trevor Barker timed it right, thought Jess with some respect. The scrapyard was quiet, its machinery silent and the operators departed. The only creature was a large German shepherd dog in a pen. It had signalled their arrival with a bark of warning to a bulky figure of middle height, who stood at the top of a short flight of steps leading up to a prefabricated office. The man was clearly locking up and preparing to go home. He turned as the dog gave voice, and surveyed the new arrivals from the top of the steps. Face on, he confirmed Jess's first impression. Harmony's brother was a short but burly man, with a walrus moustache and heavily tattooed forearms. Without any of the flamboyance of his sister, there was something about him, nevertheless, that said he was a Button. 'Sit!' he ordered.

He meant the dog, of course, or at least, Jess presumed so. The dog crouched down obediently, anyway. That was always a relief.

'Declan Button,' Barker had explained to Jess on the way there, 'has gone into business, much as his brother Gary did. That is to say, it's about as legit as anything can be that Buttons get into. He was the usual sort of local ruffian in his teens and early twenties. Since his late twenties, he's had a fairly clean record. He's had penalty points on his driving licence, a few fines for being drunk and disorderly, and he's been charged with illegal dumping of building waste in the countryside. He can be an awkward customer, but there's no law against that. Scrap is a tough business to be in. Declan takes no prisoners.'

179

'No criminal charges?'

'Not since he was much younger, as I said. He is the eldest of the Button siblings. Must be middle-forties now. As far as we're concerned, his scrapyard has a clean sheet. I can't say we've never paid it a call. But we've never found anything.'

Declan had identified his visitors as soon as he saw them. Jess thought he'd probably learned to recognise cops, even plain clothes ones, when he was in infant school. For Barker to show his warrant card was an entirely superfluous, if necessary, courtesy.

Declan acknowledged it with a nod. Then he pointed at Jess. 'Who's she?'

'This is Inspector Campbell who is heading up the team investigating your brother Gary's death.'

'What, her?' asked Declan.

'Yes, me!' snapped Jess.

'We – Inspector Campbell and I – have just been to visit your sister-in-law!' interjected Barker hastily.

'Harmony there?' asked Declan.

'Yes, she was. Mrs Gary Button seems to be in shock.'

'Of course she's in ruddy shock,' retorted Declan. 'What do you expect? Her husband waves goodbye in the morning and drives off like he's done a hundred times before. Not only does he not come home, but your lot turn up and say he's dead. A motorway crash would be understandable – they happen. But my brother, according to you, was bashed over the head, tied up like a Christmas turkey, and done to a turn in his own van!'

'Perhaps, Mr Button,' suggested Jess, 'we could have a chat in your office.'

Declan eyed her again. 'Sure, darlin', come in and make

yourself at home. Excuse me if I don't offer you tea and biscuits.'

He turned and unlocked the office again. Declan went inside without waiting for them to climb the steps and by the time they joined him, he was seated behind his desk as if awaiting their business. 'Chair over there,' he said, pointing. 'And there's another one in the corner. You have to take those magazines off it.'

He then watched silently as they sorted themselves out. After that, it turned out to be not so much an interview conducted by the police as one conducted by Declan – into the police and their recent activities. Arms folded, and leaning back in a chair that appeared rather frail for his sturdy frame, Declan fixed them with a fierce gaze.

'So, what have you been doing, then? About finding out who killed my sister and who done for my brother?'

Cautiously, Barker began, 'Well, Mr Button, we are not at the moment treating the two events as necessarily connected . . .'

Declan gave him a look of disgust. 'Whatcha mean? Not connected? Of course they're bloody connected. One murder in a family is bad enough. We've got two, now! We ain't the Corleones, you know. We don't go around bumping people off, and, generally speaking, people don't bump us off. Of course they're connected. Stands to reason.'

'Mr Button,' Jess asked, 'I believe you made some enquiries of your own into your sister's murder? You and your brother both.'

Declan turned a distrustful eye on her. 'Natural, ain't it?'

'You must understand, Mr Button, that I am investigating your brother's death and, technically speaking, Inspector Barker is investigating your sister's.'

'Which,' pointed out Declan, 'is as good a way as any of saying one hand don't know what the other is doing.'

'We're trying to avoid that, Declan,' interposed Trevor Barker. 'That's why we're both talking to you, Inspector Campbell and I. Now, if the two murders are connected, we need to know. Also, importantly, we need to know if they aren't.' He held up a hand to block Declan's protest. 'Yes, I know you believe them to be connected. You may be right. But we have to proceed cautiously because, eventually, all this may end up in court. Well, it will end up in court if we get it right. That's why it's important not to get it wrong.'

'Fair enough,' agreed Declan, after a lengthy pause. He nodded. 'Right, then. Gary and I did try and find out what happened to Amber. We didn't have much luck.'

'You went to the house where Amber lodged, I believe?'

'S'right. We talked to old Myrtle Clack. Well, we tried to. You might as well accept that you *can't* talk to her, you understand. *She* talked to *us*. Non-stop. Bloody barmy, she is.'

Barker nodded sympathetically.

'She told us to clear Amber's belongings out of the room because she needed to let it again. There was my sister on a slab at the morgue, and all the old witch could worry about was the rent. Do you know?' Declan leaned forward. 'She actually wanted us, Gary and me, to pay the rent that Amber would've paid if she'd still been alive and living there! She said, Amber's stuff being there was the same as Amber being there! We told her to forget that! So she said we had to clear all her things out.'

Declan sat back and scowled at the memory. 'So, we went back the next day with Harmony and we collected up Amber's clothes

182

and bits and pieces and took them back to my house. Harmony wouldn't take them to her place because Dad might've seen them. He's very broken up about it all.'

'If you've still got them all,' said Barker, 'we would be interested in looking through them, in case there's anything that can tell us what Amber was about, who she was seeing, where she was going . . .'

'Clues, you mean?' asked Declan sarcastically.

'Yes, clues!' snapped Barker.

'Okay, Hercule Poirot, keep your hair on!'

This was a particularly tactless piece of advice to offer Barker, who scowled but managed, just, to avoid putting his hand on his head.

'What about the other lodger?' the inspector demanded.

'The foreign girl? Yes, we had a word with her.'

'Well, any luck there?' prompted Barker. 'I mean, did she have anything of interest to tell you?'

'Hardly said a word. Turned as good as deaf. Didn't speak much English, she reckoned.'

Barker sighed.

'Mr Button,' asked Jess, 'can you tell me, were you and your brother Gary on good terms with your sister Amber?'

'What's that supposed to mean?' snapped Declan.

'What I said. From what I've been told, Amber was estranged from her family.'

'Didn't get along with the rest of us? I don't see that it's any business of the police.' Declan scowled.

'Mr Button, you must understand that in a case of murder, everything comes under the spotlight. If something isn't relevant, we discard it. But, sometimes, the smallest fact can be of great help.' Jess gave him what she hoped was an encouraging smile.

'Come on, Declan!' urged Barker.

Button glanced at him and then turned back to Jess Campbell. 'All right,' he conceded. 'Since you say you need to know, we hadn't seen much of her for quite a while – coupla years at least. Family occasions, she might or might not turn up. If she did, she didn't stay long. She had a coupla blazing rows with Maria. As for Harmony, well, they very nearly came to a scrap a coupla times. Gary, now, she may have stayed a bit closer to him. I think she went over to his place occasionally. She didn't come to my place. My wife and her didn't get on. It upset my old dad, of course. She was the apple of his eye. He kept telling Gary and me to look after her. But you couldn't look after Amber. She went her own way.'

Declan folded his brawny tattooed forearms across his chest and drew a deep breath. Protective body language, interpreted Jess. But it was to Trevor Barker that Declan spoke next.

'You know my family, Mr Barker. One or two of them have been in a spot of trouble over the years. Even done a bit of time. But no Button woman had ever been on the game, not until Amber. We tried not to let Dad know about that. I reckon he guessed. Like I said, broke his heart. She was his pet, as a kid.'

'How did you feel about it, Mr Button?' asked Jess. 'Your sister's chosen lifestyle, I mean.'

'Me?' Declan glanced back to her. 'I washed my hands of the whole thing. She was always a bit – headstrong. That's the word, ain't it? Like I just told you, she always went her own way. You couldn't tell her anything. Comes of Dad spoiling her, maybe.

She thought she could do anything she liked. I saw the way it was, early on, and I thought, leave her to it. Just so long as she didn't hang around my wife and kids, and she didn't, like I told you.'

'And Gary? Is that how he felt?'

Declan shook his head. 'Gary, he worried a bit more about her. When we were all kids, Amber and Gary got on well. Acted as a twosome, up to all sorts of pranks. But once Gary got married, started up his antiques business, had his own kids, he didn't have time to worry about Amber. If you ask me . . .' Declan fell silent.

Jess prompted, 'Yes, Mr Button?'

Declan studied Jess from top to toe. 'Persistent, ain't you?'

'Yes, Mr Button, I am.'

'Married or got a partner or anything?'

'This isn't about me, Mr Button!' Jess snapped, losing her cool for a moment.

'Guess that means you haven't, not to speak of.'

Jess felt her face flame and struggled to keep silent.

If Declan was aware he'd insulted her, he didn't care. 'If you really want to know, I thought – when we heard what had happened to Amber – I thought, well, she'd got what was coming to her. But Gary, he went bananas, raged round the place, shouting and threatening whoever it was. Well, I want to know who killed her, of course I do. S'natural, ain't it? I want to see her killer in the dock and sent down for life. That's what I want. But Gary . . .'

'Yes,' prompted Jess as Declan fell silent. 'What did Gary want?'

Declan didn't answer immediately, and when he did, his voice was quiet and controlled. 'He wanted his guts. Whoever it was, Gary wanted to get his hands on him. I figured it was best to let him shout and wear himself out with threats. When he calmed down, it would be possible to talk sense to him. But right then and there, I couldn't. No one could've done.'

Jess leaned forward. 'Mr Button, this is very important. Do you think it's possible that, when Gary drove to Gloucestershire that morning, he was acting on some information he'd learned about Amber?'

'Acting on information received? That's what you coppers say, isn't it?' Declan gave a brief grin. 'Dunno, dear. That's the honest answer. Perhaps he was just in the area on the lookout for anything he could sell on. There was a bit of furniture in the van, wasn't there? So I heard.'

'A sofa bed,' said Jess.

'There you are, then – he was just there on business, most likely. I'll phone my missus and tell her you'll be over to collect Amber's gear, shall I?'

Declan and his guard dog, standing side by side, watched the police officers leave.

'I don't think,' said Jess to Barker, as they drove away, 'that he has a lot of confidence in us.'

'I warned you, he can be awkward. I'll send someone over to his home to collect the bags of Amber's belongings. He'll have been through them, mind, him and Gary. Probably, Mrs Declan will have had a good search, too, when her husband was away, even if she won't admit it. We'll be lucky to find anything.'

Chapter 12

'A sofa bed?' asked Ian Carter sharply.

It was earlier in the day, about the same time as Barker and Jess were arriving at Pitchett's Green to interview Gary Button's widow. Carter had managed to persuade the local radio station to appeal for information on the breakfast news. A lot of people listened to that, often in their cars on the way to work. They wanted to know about traffic problems affecting their journey. He hadn't expected such a quick response to his appeal.

A ray of sunlight moved as he spoke to spread itself across the top of his desk and the paperwork there. A portent?

'This lady reckons she sold someone a sofa bed?' he asked again.

'Yes, sir,' replied Nugent. 'She's a Mrs Williams. She lives at Long Weston. It's not a big place, Long Weston, just a few houses, a pub, and some livery stables. Well, you'll know it, sir. Her house is near the stables.'

'Oh yes, indeed! I remember Long Weston,' said Carter, with some feeling. 'And that pub.'

'She told me her son runs the livery business; and he also owns her house. But she has nothing to do with the business. She reckons a guy driving a white van called at her place, asking about any old furniture or pictures, china, anything of that sort.'

'Did he, indeed! How does the time line fit in with our enquiries about Gary Button?'

'It would be about midday on the morning of the day Gary Button would have been in the area. The fire occurred later during that night, nearer Weston St Ambrose. She's downstairs now, sir.'

'Does she give the impression of being credible? Not someone with a vivid imagination or an attention seeker?'

That was the trouble with appeals for information to the public. All manner of nutters might respond. At the very least, they wasted police time. At worst, they misled enquiries and put the investigation back days, if not longer.

'Very credible, sir.' Nugent grinned. 'No-nonsense sort.'

'I'll come down and speak to her!' said Carter, getting up from his desk. 'It certainly sounds as if she met our man!'

Mrs Williams was of indeterminate age, lean, weather-beaten and sunburnt, with fading, untidy fair hair, streaked with grey. She wore jeans, and a baggy sweater under a disreputable well-worn gilet.

County set! thought Carter immediately.

'Thank you for coming in, Mrs Williams,' he began. 'I'm Superintendent Carter. I hope they've offered you a cup of tea?'

'Yes, nice girl, didn't need the tea!' She treated him to a sharp, assessing once-over. 'Superintendent, eh?'

'Yes, for my sins.' He smiled at her.

'You reckon my old sofa bed is that important, eh?' There was a gleam of amusement in her eyes.

'Believe me, Mrs Williams, it could be very important.'

'Bless me. Well, there you go!' She gave a snort of laughter. 'Anyhow, I listen to local radio of a morning. Most of it just goes in one ear and out of the other, but then I heard the presenter of whatever show it was saying something about a sofa bed. So I pricked up my ears. Police were asking if anyone had sold or given an old sofa bed to a chance caller. Enquiry related to a burnt-out van found with a corpse and the frame of a sofa bed. Hello! I said to myself. Better get over there and tell someone about it.'

'We're very grateful. What time did he call?'

'It would be, oh, a little before eleven, because I was about to make myself a cup of coffee. Doorbell rang. Looked out of the window and saw a white van. Looked fairly new. And there was this chap at my door.'

'And can you describe the man?'

She frowned. 'Hard to tell. Late thirties, perhaps? Might even have been a bit younger. He looked a bit of a hard case and that adds age, doesn't it?'

So does any time spent in prison, thought Carter. He merely nodded.

'He was pleasant enough. I'm not saying he was in any way threatening. He said he had a reclamation and antiques business. That's what he called it. Any old furniture or unwanted china, artworks, anything like that. Or any unwanted fixtures and fittings, as he called 'em. Old iron grates. Victorian bootjacks or boot scrapers. I pointed out I lived next door to a livery stables, belonged to my son, and anything like a bootjack or scraper was still in daily use!

'But he wasn't put off. Kept insisting. He'd give me a fair price, he said. Well, normally, I wouldn't have bothered. I certainly wouldn't part with any antiques to a chance caller like that! But as it happened, I had this old sofa bed I wanted to get rid of. So I told him, he could have that and welcome to it.'

189

Mrs Williams snorted again. 'He gave me twenty quid for it. I'd have given him twenty quid to take it away, if he'd asked, truth to tell! I don't think for one minute he really wanted it, or thought it was worth paying money for. But he wanted to make a good impression on me.'

'Why?' asked Carter.

Her eyebrows shot up. 'Thought you coppers were sharp? Because then, at a later date, he could come back. I'd recognise him and trust him. Maybe offer him something a bit better – china, jewellery, or something like that? Actually, I have got an old Chinese bowl. I didn't offer him that, because I use it for the dog's water bowl. I reckon he spotted it, though. I was helping him carry out the sofa, through the kitchen. I saw him give the place a quick once-over. They're eagle-eyed, those fellows, don't miss a trick. I'd never have let him in but for needing to get rid of the old sofa bed.'

She put her hand in the pocket of the gilet and withdrew a piece of white card. 'Gave me his business card and told me, if I ever had anything, or heard of anyone wanting to get rid of anything, to give him a call.' She handed the card to Carter.

'G. Button. Antique furniture and reclamation yard,' read Carter aloud.

'That the feller?' asked Mrs Williams. 'The one you're interested in?'

'It may well be, Mrs Williams. Thank you for coming in. Thank you very much indeed.'

Mrs Williams rose to leave. 'Thing is,' she said thoughtfully, 'the old sofa ended up incinerated in that van, didn't it? Along with him?'

'There was certainly a burnt sofa bed in the van, only the frame left.'

'Do you know?' she replied. 'I'd have put a match to it myself, to get rid of it, if it hadn't been for the folding metal frame of the bed. That wouldn't burn.'

'It didn't,' said Carter, 'which allowed us to identify it. You have been very helpful to us, Mrs Williams.'

'Poor blighter,' said Mrs Williams. 'I quite liked him. If he'd come back another time, I might have sold him the dog bowl.' She gave Carter a dry look. 'Only not for twenty quid!'

Elsewhere, the Meadowlea Manor retirement home also had a visitor.

'I really, really want this job,' said Eva Florescu earnestly. She leaned forward, hands clasped, brown eyes pleading.

There was no denying, thought Deirdre Collins, mildly embarrassed, the kid was a dear little thing. She seemed to have all the necessary qualifications to work here, but well, she had left her previous employer rather suddenly. Deirdre's experience with young female staff had taught her that a sudden urge for relocation often meant a man was involved. That could be a problem. The last thing they needed was an agitated ex-boyfriend turning up – and creating merry hell.

'I still don't quite understand, Miss Florescu, why you left your previous job so suddenly. I have spoken on the phone with your former employer – that is, with the manager of the cleaning company – and he has expressed himself mystified as to why you suddenly left. He had thought you were happy enough. He was satisfied with your work. So I am just wondering . . .'

Deirdre paused and waited for the applicant to offer an explanation. But the kid just sat there, biting her lip, and gazing pleadingly at her. Deirdre grasped the nettle. 'Look, Eva, this isn't because of man trouble in your former place, is it?'

The girl looked stricken. 'I am not in trouble because of man.'

'No, of course, I didn't mean—' Deirdre floundered. Interviewing these foreign girls was always tricky. You never really knew how much they understood, or whether they'd interpreted something in a way it wasn't intended. Deirdre had an inspiration. 'Now then, my dear,' she encouraged, 'what I meant was, you didn't leave your previous job and the place – Bamford – because of an *affaire de coeur?*'

The girl brightened up. 'Ah! Because I have the broken heart? Oh, no, no. It is because I have the horrible old landlady. I couldn't find another place to live. So, I leave.'

'Ah, I see. Of course, the job here with us offers accommodation with it. We are rather remote, here at Meadowlea, so we can't always find staff who live locally. That's why we converted the old stable block into staff accommodation for single persons. However, Eva, we are a *retirement* home. That means you really need to be able to get along with *elderly people*. I can honestly say that all of our residents are very pleasant. But, occasionally, an old person can be a little difficult . . .'

'This I understand,' said Eva wisely. 'Often it is because they are deaf.'

'Oh?' gasped Deirdre, startled.

'Yes, yes, they are deaf. They do not hear, so they always say the other person does not speak clearly. My grandmother at home is like that. I am used to old persons, yes. It is not a problem for me.'

'Oh, well, so the – er – disagreement you had with your former elderly landlady, whom you described as "horrible", that was due to, well, what? If you don't mind me asking.'

'She drink!' declared Eva dramatically. 'Every day come from shop with bag. It make clink, clink . . . She sit every evening and drink. It is not nice. I do not like it. And she fall down on carpet.'

'Oh? I see . . . Well, in that case, of course you couldn't continue to live in that house. I do assure you, Eva, that none of our residents, here at Meadowlea, are given to drink. Well, one of them might invite two or three of the others for a little sherry party . . . but they're never, um, unwise in how much they drink. And certainly, no one has ever fallen down on the carpet inebriated! Of course, with the elderly, one has always to be alert for any unsteadiness, due to age. Falls on that account are not unknown. But never, ever have I known anyone here to fall over *drunk!*' declared Deirdre emphatically.

'It's all right,' soothed Eva. 'Little sherry party is all right. Whole bottle of wine, and sometimes whisky, is not all right.'

'Certainly not!' Deirdre realised she had become somewhat agitated herself. She made an effort to regain her poise. 'So, what have you been doing since you left your last job, in Bamford?'

'I stay with Romanian friends in Gloucester,' Eva told her. 'But there is not room for me. I sleep on floor. It is no good and I cannot get a job in Gloucester. Then my friend, she come home one night and tell me she has heard about your home for old people. She say, you always want cleaners and people to work here. I am very good cleaner. Also, you have rooms for staff to sleep. I need room.'

Poor kid, thought Deirdre. All she wants to do is work. 'Well, er, Eva. I hope you will be very happy here with us at Meadowlea.'

'Yes, yes,' agreed Eva. 'I shall be very happy. I shall be safe.'

Again Deirdre felt a twinge of unease. But it was so difficult to get domestic staff out here in the middle of nowhere. Her previous employer had insisted that Eva's work had been excellent and he was sorry to have lost her. Perhaps the girl's spoken English would improve.

Having brought some order to the garden centre's chaotic office system, Miff was taking a few quiet moments to work on his talk to the writers' circle. But it wasn't long before he became aware of a presence in the room behind him. His ear caught the sound of faint panting. He would not have been surprised to find a large dog had wandered in. But when he turned, it was to see Danny Garley, who stood watching him with his unsettling blank stare, and breathing through his open mouth.

'That your book, then?' asked Danny, nodding towards the computer screen.

It wasn't, it was his talk. But with Danny, it was advisable to agree. 'Yes,' replied Miff.

The confirmation caused Danny to press his lips, give a snort and nod, as if he had suspected from the first that Miff was weird.

Okay, thought Miff, I think *you* are pretty weird. It's a weird world.

'Going to be a long book, is it?' Danny jerked his bullet head towards the screen.

Probably the world's shortest, at the rate he was working on it, thought Miff. 'Not sure yet, Danny.'

'Uncle Bert's sent over some more traps,' said Danny next, abandoning his brief foray into literature. 'He reckons these will work.' He stooped and raised a long narrow cage for inspection. Its door appeared to work on the portcullis principle: propped up, to crash down as soon as the rat entered and made the cage shake. Or that was presumably the idea. It might even work. Miff wouldn't be surprised if it didn't.

'They're not the sort of thing that can slice a finger if anyone prodded the trap? They don't need poison bait? We can't leave poison round the place because of the visitors. Some of them come with dogs and would raise merry hell if we poisoned one of their pooches. And we can't risk a kid finding one and fiddling with it, chopping off a finger.'

What was more, Miff was thinking, if anything like that happened and it turned out we'd been using home-made traps, and not regular ones, it could screw up our insurance.

'Nah. They're straightforward. Uncle Bert don't make anything complicated. Anyway, you don't need to set them during the day, when the visitors are here. The rats don't come out then, probably because there are usually a couple of dogs about, like you said. Rats and dogs, well, they know one another. Best thing to catch a rat is a terrier.' Danny nodded decisively.

'I did think about a dog, but Sam is talking about a cat,' said Miff thoughtfully.

'Cat? Nah, a terrier, that's what you want. The rats come out mostly when it's quiet and dark and they can scurry around without anyone seeing 'em. You decide where you want to put the traps and, last thing before I go off home, you and I can put them out. We'll collect them in the morning, before we open for business.

You need some really smelly bait for best results. Auntie Glenys's cakes aren't enough. Cheese, or a coupla sausages . . . that's it.'

'Great. Thank Bert for me, will you?'

Danny grunted and, picking up an earlier conversation as though it hadn't been interrupted, asked, 'If you're not into motorcycles, how about cars? You know anything about cars?'

Miff wanted to say, *Yes, actually, I do. I owned a couple of really great cars, back in the old days when I was part of the financial world.* But that would have led to further explanations, none of which would have made any sense to Danny. So he opened his mouth to reply, *not really,* when a thought struck him.

'You wouldn't happen to know, Danny, if anyone in Weston St Ambrose owns a flash motor?'

'One or two,' replied Danny. 'There's a couple of guys with plenty of dosh got houses in the village.'

'Either of them own a black BMW?'

A gleam of interest entered Danny's gaze. 'Don't know of one. Why?'

'I saw one, late one night. I was down by the entrance, having a quiet beer. It drove past, out of the village. I hadn't seen one like it before around Weston, and I was curious, you know.'

'Want me to ask around?' asked Danny, apparently waking up. His gaze had become quite sharp.

'I'd appreciate it. Only, you know, quietly, not to get anyone asking questions back.'

Danny nodded. 'Let you know,' he said, before turning and ambling out.

Right, back to the talk. Where was he? Miff began to read aloud from the screen. He was learning that doing that was very useful. It was odd how things sounded different when you listened to them – to yourself. Or perhaps, it was simply that talking to oneself was what writers ended up doing. It was a lonely occupation, after all.

Or not. There was another loud crash from behind him. Miff spun round. The door had flown open. An alarming, wild figure stood there clasping a cardboard box. It was male, of indeterminate age. It wore grubby jeans and a stained leather jerkin. Its hair was long, tangled and greying. Its eyes glittered wildly. The Ancient Mariner had come to call. Either that, or one of his old acquaintances, from sleeping rough days, had tracked him down.

'Bloody hell!' said Miff – quite mildly, in the circumstances. 'Who are you?'

'Morgan Jay!' announced the visitor. 'I'm the potter. Sam tells me you want a dozen garden gnomes.'

'*She* wants them,' Miff told him. 'It's her idea.' He eyed the box suspiciously. 'You haven't got them in that, have you?'

'Course not!' roared the wild man. 'I haven't had time to make a dozen of the little blighters! I've brought one I made earlier.'

'Oh? Like in the cookery shows on TV?' This was not only tactless, Miff realised, even as the words left his lips. It also indicated he spent his spare time watching other people make sponge cakes.

'Don't watch 'em!' said Morgan. 'You want to see this or not?'

'Sure, bring it in,' said Miff resignedly. 'Sam will be coming in soon for a coffee break. Care to join us?'

'Brought my own!' said Morgan. He clomped over to the window seat, set his cardboard box on the floor and sat down. He took a hip flask from his pocket and drank a swig. He then

197

stooped, searched through the crumpled newspaper in the box, and took out a clay statuette.

'Oh,' said Miff in surprise. 'That isn't what I was expecting!'

'What were you expecting?' asked Morgan, taking another swig from the flask.

'Well, you know, little fat guy with a fishing rod and beard, wearing a nightcap. Yours is slimmer and not so jolly, more . . .' Miff sought for a word and failed to find one that wouldn't offend the potter. He wanted to say 'sinister'.

Morgan glowered at him. 'I don't make comic figures.'

'No, of course you don't. Apologies.'

'The gnome,' said Morgan, 'is an ancient traditional figure in folklore. Turns up a lot in Central Europe – Germany, mostly. People believed in them. They guarded the earth, particularly where there were mines. That associated them with buried treasure, so you didn't want to offend them. They were good things to have around the place. You know, sort of good-luck figures, like leprechauns.'

'He's, um, quite realistic, your gnome.'

'You don't like it?' asked Morgan.

'Actually, I do. I like it much better than the cartoonish ones. It's up to Sam to decide.'

Sam chose that moment to arrive, carrying a tray with three mugs of coffee on it. 'I heard you were here, Morgan. I brought you coffee.'

Morgan sighed and put the hip flask back in his pocket, accepting a mug of coffee.

'Is that the gnome?' Sam picked up the figure and beamed at it. 'It's really good, Morgan.' She turned to Miff. 'Don't you think so, Miff?'

'Great,' said Miff.

'Not bad,' agreed Morgan graciously.

'And you can make a dozen of these by Christmas? I mean, by mid-November? We'd need them to be in stock before people finish their Christmas shopping.'

'Should think so,' said Morgan.

'Then we should discuss price.' Sam indicated Miff, much to his alarm. 'Miff here is our financial director.'

Things were getting worse. He'd only come to Weston St Ambrose in the first place to escape BMW man. He'd found himself writing a book and all set to address a literary gathering. Subsequently, he'd only come to Minglebury Garden Centre to sort out the filing system, and carry a few flowerpots from here to there. Now he was its financial director.

Miff gazed at the gnome. It leered at him conspiratorially. Miff drew a deep breath. 'What sort of price had you in mind, Morgan?'

It had been a long day and not a particularly productive one. Jess was tired. Eventually, someone would persuade poor Katie Button that she was a widow. It would not be Jess. Katie was in deep denial. Most likely, it would be Harmony who'd get the sad message through to her. What would happen then, Jess could not imagine. Katie might lose it completely, trash the house, or do something desperate like swallow pills and booze. On the other hand, she might just sink into apathy. Harmony was going to have her work cut out. So have I, thought Jess. I'll have to try and interview her again.

Jess had received invitations to eat that evening from the Markbys and from Sally Barker via her husband. She had expressed thanks and declined both. Working with Trevor Barker all day, she needed a break – and so did he. The Markbys would want to know how she was getting on. It would be less a supper conversation than a debriefing. Better, by far, to go back to The Crown.

The hotel was not yet busy. But when she walked through its late-Georgian entrance portico, and into reception, it was to see a guest at reception, checking out. It was the pink-faced man. Now, thought Jess, why am I not surprised?

'Thank you, Mr Robinson!' said the receptionist cheerily. 'See you next week!'

Robinson threw Jess a hunted look, grabbed the handle of his small, wheeled case, and bolted towards the rear exit from the hotel. Jess walked into the nearly deserted lounge and went to the far end, where the windows gave a view of the car park. Here he came, dragging his wheeled case, and stuffing his credit-card receipt into his pocket. Suddenly, perhaps alerted by a sixth sense that he was being watched, he glanced back and spotted her. He didn't break into a run. He was more quick-witted than that. He walked with exaggerated casualness towards one of the parked cars. There was a faint but audible scraping sound made by the case wheels as it bounced across the tarmac. Robinson deposited his luggage in the boot with exaggerated care, before driving off, still avoiding catching Jess's eye. She smiled. His wife would be surprised to see him coming home a day earlier than expected. She was fairly sure of that. The car, a BMW, disappeared. She dismissed it from her mind and phoned Mike Foley.

'Hi, Mike, sorry to disturb you so late. I need a quick word of advice from you as a doctor. I have to pay a second visit to the widow of the man whose corpse was in that burnt-out van.'

'Grim,' said Mike. 'How is the poor woman?'

'Actually, presenting a problem. She's quite young, has several children, and she's in shock and deep denial. It's also difficult to get through to her. I don't mean she has serious learning difficulties. Just, well, she's not quick to process new information. But she is obstinate. I mean to go back in the morning and speak to her again. Any tips?'

'Don't press her,' Mike's voice said in her ear. 'Just try and get her talking about anything. On one level she's in denial, but it doesn't mean that she isn't aware, deep down, of what's happened. If she relaxes, she may just bring up the subject herself. If that doesn't happen, you may have to call in someone with special training. Main thing is not to frighten her or make her feel she's being bullied . . .' He paused and added, 'But I know you wouldn't do that, bully her.'

'Thanks, I'll bear all that in mind. It's really helpful.'

Mike's voice said casually, 'I've got a visit to make tomorrow. I'm going up to London to the head office. They've at last agreed to meet me and discuss when I can go back to work.'

This wasn't what she had rung about, and it threw her. She managed to say, 'Oh, good luck with that, then.'

The casual tone hadn't fooled Mike. He had the grace to sound discomfited. 'I won't lie, Jess. I just feel – I feel I left a job half done. But, in the end, well, it's up to the charity, if they have enough confidence in me to send me back. I'll miss you, of course I will. I hope we'll stay in touch. Can you understand, or does it sound hopelessly selfish?'

'No, not selfish,' she said crisply. 'My brother is the same. I suppose you have a calling, like someone who enters the Church.'

'I'm not a missionary!' Mike said a little sharply. 'Sorry, didn't mean to snap. But I'm not driven by faith. Perhaps it would be easier for everyone to understand if I was. I just want to finish the job I started.'

Meredith had said something like that, Jess thought. Being on a murder case can be a little like that. I want to find out who killed Gary Button and left poor Katie and her children to manage somehow, with Harmony's help. The trouble is, when you get your teeth into something like that, when the job becomes all-important, time can slip by. Mike and I are probably destined to be ships that pass in the night, all blazing lights and sounds of distant music and life. Then gone, swallowed up in the darkness, and each set of passengers on their own again on a vast empty ocean.

'Okay. Thanks for the advice,' Jess told him. 'I hope it all goes well in London.'

Harmony's car wasn't outside the house, thank goodness, when Jess arrived. The old man had not yet taken his seat outside the pub, but the wood pigeons were clattering about in the branches of the oak tree, and someone was singing. The tune sounded familiar, a nursery rhyme, thought Jess. The early morning dew was still on the grass, but Katie Button was outside in the garden, sitting on a child's swing and gently rocking to and fro. She watched Jess approach incuriously. That blankness in her large blue eyes was unsettling.

'You remember me, Katie?' Jess asked. 'I came yesterday to see you. Inspector Jessica Campbell.'

To herself, she was thinking how young Katie looked, far too young to be the mother of several children. Particularly now, sitting on that swing pushing herself back and forth, gaining the necessary impetus by kicking one foot against the ground. She wore red canvas shoes today, not the Ugg boots. Otherwise she was dressed, as on the occasion of Jess's previous visit, in jeans and an over-large sweater. She'd stopped singing the words of the song but continued to hum the tune. There was a moment, just a very brief one, when Jess felt a prickle of unease. Then Katie spoke.

'You're the detective,' she said. She sounded pleased at having remembered.

'Yes, I'm the detective.'

'You're looking for whoever killed my Gary.'

Jess was so taken aback by this complete volte-face on the interviewee's part that she struggled for a reply. Somehow, Katie had accepted the news of Gary's death. Had Harmony persuaded her?

'Can we go indoors and talk, Katie?'

Katie ignored the question and started pushing her red canvas shoe against the ground again to restart the swinging movement. '*Half a pound of tuppenny rice . . .*' she sang very softly.

'Katie?' Jess was beginning to feel alarmed. Had Katie's mind given way completely under the shock of Gary's death?

'*Half a pound of treacle . . .*'

'Mrs Button!'

This time Katie took notice and stopped the rocking motion. She still said nothing, but slipped off the swing and walked towards the open door. Jess followed her.

'Harmony's coming later,' said Katie, over her shoulder. 'She's going to take me to see the kids. Maria's got them.'

Jess breathed a sigh of relief. Katie hadn't retreated into a half-world, as she'd feared for a moment or two, back there in the garden. 'I'm glad you've got such good family support, Katie.'

'Declan came last night,' Katie told her.

Ah, so perhaps Declan had persuaded Katie of the tragedy. Yes, thought Jess, she'd accept it, if Declan told her. Declan was a man who dealt in day-to-day life and didn't have time for stories. He was a businessman, like the late Gary. He dealt in solid facts.

Katie sat down again on the same sofa she had occupied on Jess's previous visit. Jess took the armchair opposite her.

'I know it's very hard for you to talk about any of this, Katie. I only ask questions because we want to find out what happened.'

'Yeah, I know,' responded Katie in a lacklustre way.

Jess wondered if she had ever been animated, or whether this lack of animation showed Katie's natural personality, or lack of it. She tried a different approach. 'How about your own family, Katie? Are they being supportive?'

A faint furrow of the brow signified that Katie was adapting to a new line of thought. 'Haven't got one,' she said at last.

'Who brought you up?'

'I was in care, wasn't I?'

'But when you were a baby? Were you fostered out?'

Katie was silent and seemed to be thinking. At last she said, 'Some people looked after me. You know, like when I was a little kid. But they gave me back, when I got older.'

They gave you back, thought Jess sadly, when they realised the baby they had been so keen to take into their lives wasn't the brightest kid in the class. They wanted a perfect little girl. Well, they'd had one, in every way but one. Grown-up Katie is well able to raise her own children, run her own home. What had the couple wanted? Those who had 'given her back'? A rocket scientist?

Jess began again. 'Things have been very difficult for the Button family recently. I mean, before this latest tragedy, they – and you – had already lost Gary's sister, Amber.'

'Gary liked Amber a lot,' said Katie in a matter-of-fact way.

'Did you like Amber?'

This time Katie was silent for longer. At last she said simply, 'Not much.'

'Why was that?'

'She wasn't very nice.'

'Because she had a lot of men friends?'

Katie stared at her. 'Don't know about that.'

'So, why do you say she wasn't very nice?'

'Bad-tempered. Shouted at my kids. Shouted at me, sometimes.' A faint smile touched Katie's lips. 'But not when Gary was here. She was always very nice when Gary was around.' Katie leaned forward and, with the most passion in her voice Jess had ever heard from her, said, '*She tried to kill me!*'

'What?' gasped Jess.

Katie sat back and looked pleased at the result of her astonishing claim. 'That's right, she tried to get rid of me. I never told Gary. Harmony said I wasn't ever to tell Gary! No one must tell Gary. Gary liked Amber, you see. They were pals, always had been, as kids, too.'

'What did Amber do, Katie, to . . . to get rid of you, as you say?'

'I was on my own here. The kids were with Maria and her

husband, because he was driving them all, his kids and mine, to see some animals, zoo sort of animals, somewhere, in a special park.'

'A safari park?'

'Yeah, that's it. Gary had gone over to France to the – what do you call 'em?'

'Flea markets?' suggested Jess.

'That's it. Funny name. Nothing Gary ever brought back had any fleas on it. Anyway, I was on my own here. Amber turned up and said she'd come to keep me company. She'd never done that before!' A sudden and unexpected intelligence showed in Katie's dull gaze. 'She'd been over to Spain and she'd brought back some wine and some brandy. She said she was going to make me a sort of Spanish drink, with chopped-up fruit in it.'

'Sangria?' asked Jess.

Katie hunched her shoulders. 'Something like that. I didn't want it really. But she went out into the kitchen and started chopping up the fruit and messing about making the stuff. I thought I'd go out there and watch. I suppose she didn't know I'd come. I was by the door, just watching. She made two really big glasses of the stuff. It looked very pretty with the fruit and that. And then she took a little bottle out of her pocket.' Katie held up her hand with her thumb straight and her index finger crooked above it. 'About so big, you know? It had pills in it.'

'Go on,' said Jess, because Katie had paused and was looking at her enquiringly, to check whether Jess was following her story. 'What did Amber do with the pills in the bottle?'

'She squashed them all with a rolling pin, so they were just

206

dust, and she swept it all into her palm and tipped it into one of the drinks. Stirred it all up.'

There was a silence. Mindful of Mike's advice, Jess resisted urging her to go on.

'I came back to this room and sat down, and she brought in the two glasses. She gave me one. She raised hers and said, "Cheers!"' Katie gave Jess a sideways glance that was unexpectedly sly. 'I was never any good at school,' she said. 'I know I'm not very quick. I can't understand all the stuff they talk about on some of the telly programmes, discussions and that. But I'm not stupid. I knew she'd given me the glass with the squashed pills in it.'

'Go on,' Jess whispered. 'How did you avoid drinking it?'

Katie looked smug. 'I took a sip, and I said I didn't like it. I made like I was going to put it down on that little table there, and I dropped it, on purpose, but I made it look like it just slipped out of my hand. The sang-y drink went all over the carpet, bits of fruit everywhere. Gosh, she was really angry then, was Amber. I thought she was going to hit me. She called me all sorts of names, said I was a thicko – I ought to be in an institution. She said she didn't understand what Gary saw in me. Then she went running out and drove away. She left me to clear up all the mess!' concluded Katie resentfully. 'And the glass was broken. It was one of a set Gary brought back from one of his French trips.'

'But you told Harmony about this?'

'Harmony came later on, early evening. She'd brought the kids back with her. They were really excited. They had a great day with Maria's family. Well, Harmony helped me put them to bed, and then, while we were sitting here, having a cup of tea, Harmony asked why the carpet had a big damp patch on it. So I told her.

I took her out to the kitchen and showed her the broken wine glass in the bin, with all the bits of fruit. She said she'd take care of it. I must never, ever tell Gary, nor anyone else.' Katie looked doubtfully at Jess. 'But I've told you.'

'You were quite right to do that. Besides, Amber can't try to harm you again.'

'No, she's gone.' Tears began to roll down Katie's pale cheeks. 'And so has my Gary.'

'I'll fetch Harmony!' promised Jess. 'Get her to come over earlier than she arranged. She can take you to your children later.'

She realised, as she spoke, that it was what the Button clan did in any emergency. Someone fetched Harmony.

Chapter 13

'It's like an old western film,' Jess said later that evening on the phone to Mike in the privacy of her hotel room. 'Send for the cavalry! And they all come galloping across the screen. I waited until she arrived, made Katie some tea. When I saw Harmony's car draw up, I went out and told her quickly what Katie had said, about Amber trying to drug or poison her drink, asked if it was true.'

'Harmony admitted it?'

'Oh, yes, straight way. "Amber was always jealous of any girl Gary showed an interest in!" was what Harmony said. "They were always so close as kids. But Dad must never, ever know! So don't tell Maria, because she might let it slip."'

'What about the other brother, Declan?'

'He knows, according to Harmony. She told him. But he's always said he wasn't certain Katie hadn't imagined it. Harmony says she told him that Katie didn't have any imagination. If she said it, it was because she saw it. I think that's logical.'

'What does Trevor Barker think of it all?'

'It doesn't make his investigation into Amber's death any easier. Amber sounds a real piece of work, and she probably made numerous enemies.'

'You know what?' Mike's voice held something like awe. 'That

Button family sound like the cast members of something by Shakespeare. Creeping around with . . . well, probably not poison exactly. Not as most people think of it. But then, most people don't always consider that anything can be fatal if wrongly administered, and in sufficient quantities. Salt, for example.'

'Salt tablets wouldn't have worked for Amber's purpose, would they?' Jess countered. 'They need to be taken over a long time and, in any case, they're hardly a murderer's poison of choice – too difficult to administer. They'd have tasted in any drink or food, and probably made her vomit.'

'Sleeping tablets,' suggested Mike. 'Amber had just got home from a Spanish holiday, Katie told you. She could have obtained the tablets anywhere. They could've been anything, and might not have killed Katie. They would probably have made her very ill. Amber could still have *thought* she was administering a fatal cocktail. The intent was there.' He paused. 'It happens more often than a lot of people like to think . . .'

'Really? I'm a copper. I suppose I only get to hear about the cases in which the pills have done their work sufficiently, either for the illness to be suspicious or, in the worst cases, fatal.'

'Believe me,' Mike said. 'Go into a local bazaar in a lot of countries and you'll see all manner of herbs for sale. Some of them are very dangerous in sufficient quantity.'

'I was going to order the curry tonight, if they've got any left,' said Jess. 'But I've changed my mind. How did your visit to London go?'

Mike's voice became cautious. 'I think it went quite well. They want me to have a thorough check-up. That's progress. Before, they were digging in their heels and saying, no way! They're at least considering the possibility of my return. They need doctors, and I'm keen to go.'

Yes, you are, thought Jess. And in all fairness, he'd never pretended otherwise. This is a situation in which I'll always be in second place, whatever happens. 'Fingers crossed, then,' she said.

Miff and Danny were setting the mice/rat traps in the storage shed, watched anxiously by Sam. 'You won't kill them afterwards, will you? If the traps catch anything? I don't like to think we would actually kill a living creature.'

Miff and Danny, for once united, stared at her. 'What do you want to do with them, then?' asked Danny.

'I thought you and Miff could take them about a mile away and let them go free.'

'They'll likely come back,' said Danny. 'And where there's one, there's bound to be others. I told Miff here, you want a terrier.'

It was quite dark now and Sam stood by with a torch so that the men could see what they were doing. Without warning, as she moved the beam across the floor of the store, two bright points of light, close together, and at floor level, glittered back in response.

'The bugger's in here!' shouted Danny.

As he spoke, a furry shape, far too big for a mouse, shot out from the sacks of seed and peanuts. It scurried between their feet, making for the open doorway.

Danny grabbed a shovel and raced off in pursuit. There was a distant clang. Then they heard the crunch of Danny's boots returning.

'Got him!' called Danny.

211

Sam reached out and gripped Miff's hand. 'He's not bringing it back inside here, is he?' she whispered. 'I'll be sick . . .'

But Danny, as proud as any terrier with his kill, wanted to show it off. 'Here, see?' he said triumphantly. He held out the shovel, the blade flat. On it lay the still form of the rat, its tail dangling over the edge, and the light in its black eyes extinct.

Sam made a choking sound and then threw up on the floor.

'Sam! For crying out loud! Did you have to?' Miff leapt aside.

'I told you I'd do that!' she gurgled, pressing a tissue to her mouth.

'Well, another time, go and do it outside!' ordered Miff unfeelingly. He knew he'd have to be the one to clear the mess up.

'Big old blighter, ain't he?' said Danny, still flushed with success. 'Here, pass me that empty cardboard box. I'll take it over to Uncle Bert to show him.'

'It was awful,' moaned Sam, later that evening.

'Danny killing the rat? No, it wasn't. You vomiting? Yes, that was. Eat your supper!' ordered Miff unsympathetically.

'How can I?' Sam gazed at him in dismay. 'He just hit it with a spade!'

'What did you expect him to do?'

'Let it run away and hope that, well, later it went into one of Uncle Bert's traps.'

'And what is Uncle Bert going to do with it? Or any of its friends, if one does go into the trap? And don't, please, say he should take it out into the field and give it its freedom! We're not like those organisations that rescue orangutans and bears, and so on, from cages. Rats certainly aren't an endangered species. There are millions of the wretched beasts.'

'It's so awful!'

'Awful was what I had to do, clearing up that abominable mess you made, throwing up.' Miff spoke with deep feeling.

'Sorry, but it was . . .'

'If you say the word "awful" again, Sam,' threatened Miff, 'I swear, I'll walk out.'

'I don't want you to – to go . . .' Her voice began to break up.

Miff got up and went to put a consoling arm around her shoulder. 'Look, I won't walk out, I promise!'

'You just said—'

'Well, you kept going on about it. I didn't mean it. Danny ought not to have shown you the – shown you *it*, afterwards, on the spade. Now then, we're not going to talk about it any more, right?'

Sam nodded, gazing up at him. There was an awkward silence.

'We'll have to get a dog of some sort!' said Miff briskly.

It was after midnight when Miff awoke, suddenly and completely, senses tingling, alarm bells ringing in his mind. He had not been sleeping all that well. He kept thinking about Sam, and knew that too much concentration on her wasn't a good idea. After all, he was only here to write a book . . . Also, Sam had been deserted by the useless Stuart and was vulnerable, and lonely. It would be too easy to take advantage of that. Nice thought, though . . .

He drifted off into slumber eventually, until danger shook him by the shoulder and ordered him to get up and see what was wrong. Something you soon learned, when sleeping rough, was to respond quickly to a change in the situation. He didn't know what had changed. Though he listened hard, he couldn't hear anything except a patter of rain. It hadn't been raining earlier, and he didn't think that was what had awoken him now. He swung his legs over the side of the bed, and padded to the window. He looked out. Instead of the Stygian darkness usually enveloping the world at night hereabouts, the open area before the cottage was bathed in the pale glow of the security lights. Something had triggered them; and their springing into feeble life was what had awoken him.

It wasn't unusual for the lights to come on. A fox trotting across between the tables of plants could trigger them. Even another large rat might have done it; although the presence of another rat on the loose would have to be concealed from Sam. There was no sign of life down there. If Reynard it had been, he'd gone. And yet . . . That prickle of unease remained at the nape of Miff's neck. He ought to go down and check it out.

Ah yes, well, a bold decision but not that easy to carry out. He couldn't wake Sam and drag her out there with him, because if there were danger, she'd be safer in the cottage. So he'd be on his own and armed with a mobile phone and a frying pan picked up in the kitchen on the way out. Stupid or what?

Definitely stupid. But Miff pulled on his jeans and a sweater and, carrying his boots in his hand, because he didn't want to clomp downstairs noisily, crept out of his room and along the corridor. It had crossed his mind that, perhaps, for some reason he couldn't guess at, Sam had got up and gone outside. But as he passed her door, he could hear faint rhythmic snores. Not Sam, then.

In the kitchen, using his mobile as a torch, he swept the area, seeking some weapon. Aha! He'd forgotten the walking stick hanging from a peg near the back door. It was an old-fashioned sturdy countryman's stick, not one of those slender elegant jobs. This one had been hand-fashioned by someone long ago from a branch. It had a solid serviceable knobby handle and made an excellent club, if you gripped it in the middle of the shaft. Arming himself, Miff felt rather better, certainly a bit braver. He unlocked the kitchen door and switched off the mobile torch. The small beam it emitted would be pretty useless and only pinpoint his position, if anyone were out there.

At the last minute, before stepping outside, Miff hesitated. This was what he'd done before, wasn't it? Walked into a dark place to find someone there ahead of him, bent on attacking him? After one such bad experience, to repeat it now was the height of madness.

All I have to do, Miff told himself, is walk round the cottage and if there is anyone hanging about they'll clear off, because I have a right to be here, and they don't. I am the occupier of the premises. Confident body language, that's what was needed. Don't make yourself look like a target. Last time in the warehouse, he'd been apologetic, appeasing, a victim waiting to be attacked. Not so, this time.

Slowly he set off. The sheen of the security lights was cold and unfriendly. It made stark distinctions between objects, pinpointing their location, without actually illuminating them well enough to make identifying them entirely reliable. The rain made things worse. Puddles were forming and surfaces glittered. A wind had sprung up and blew the rain into his face, trickling into his eyes. He had to keep wiping the water away. That was a bay tree in a tub, wasn't it? Not a short, top-heavy figure, wearing big boots?

Pull yourself together! Miff ordered himself. It was a bay tree. He passed it several times a day.

The security lighting fell on the door to Glenys's coffee shop. Better check it out. Miff marched across with all the confidence he could muster and pushed it. It rattled but stayed firmly shut. That was okay, then.

He turned and set off back towards the cottage. He'd checked the area out. No one here. Go back inside, where it was warm and safe. Miff felt quite pleased with himself.

There was only one snag, and he became aware of it at that moment.

Out here it wasn't warm, and it certainly wasn't safe, because every atavistic instinct was awake now. You are either the hunter or you are the hunted. He'd kidded himself he was the hunter. But he wasn't. He was the prey.

The hunter was over there, in the darkness beyond the store shed, where the security lights didn't shed their glow. There was that ripple in the darkness that Miff remembered so well. It made him feel physically sick to the stomach. The hunter had watched, as Miff made his patrol of the area. He must have looked like a perishing battery-operated toy soldier, marching around like that with his walking-stick weapon resting on his shoulder. The hunter had been waiting for him to return to the cottage. That was the moment he'd spring out of the darkness and—

Above Miff's head there was an unexpected crash that made him jump out of his skin. He was suddenly bathed in bright light. Sam had opened a bedroom window and was leaning out.

'Is that you, Miff? What on earth are you doing?'

Miff's ear caught the thud of retreating running feet. The hunter had taken off.

'The security lights came on!' he called up. 'Just taking a look around.'

'They do that sometimes,' called down Sam. 'I expect it was the owl.'

'What owl?'

'It lives in the old stable where Danny puts his bike. Danny regards it as a sort of pet.'

We've got rats or mice, thought Miff. Stands to reason, an owl has sussed out the garden centre as a hunting ground.

'Come on indoors!' ordered Sam above his head. 'It's raining! You'll catch a chill.'

Faintly, in the distance, Miff's ear caught the diminishing growl of a car's engine. The hunter had made good his escape.

'Okay,' said Miff. 'I'll come in.'

Jess Campbell stood with Trevor Barker and Emma Johnson and gazed down at the heap of assorted clothes and personal items tipped out on a table. Amber Button's belongings had been brought from her brother Declan's house and were now in the keeping of the police investigating her murder.

'We should have had these from the first,' grumbled Barker. 'We would have done, if that old dragon hadn't insisted the family clear the room Amber was renting from her. They've probably gone through them, either Declan or Harmony, and taken out anything of interest.'

'We did ask Declan Button about that,' Emma assured him. 'He said they hadn't. He had a bit of trouble with his own wife, apparently, when he took the two bags into his house. She made him put them out in his garage, and they've been there ever since, until we picked them up this morning. She didn't like Amber and she said she never wanted any of Amber's things near her home, and she wasn't going to touch them. Declan was pretty fed up with the whole scenario and he didn't open the bags. They were "cluttering up" the garage, in the words of Mrs Declan. She was more than delighted when we picked them up. Oh, and she also said Harmony didn't go through the bags. Harmony did search Amber's room before it was cleared, so she would have already known what the bags contained.'

'And you can bet your bottom dollar,' said Barker, 'that old Myrtle Clack went through Amber's room again, after Harmony left, and before the Buttons returned to clear the room. She'd have taken out anything she didn't want us to see, or she herself took a fancy to.' He turned to Jess. 'There's unlikely to be anything to help you with the investigation into Gary's death, I'm afraid.'

Emma had begun to sort through the heap, putting different categories of garment into separate heaps, cosmetics in another little pile, and the box of Amber's trinkets on its own.

'Now wouldn't you think,' asked Jess, pointing at the little wooden box, 'that Harmony, with her liking for anything that glitters, would have taken Amber's jewellery?'

'Not if she was afraid the old father might see it and recognise it,' suggested Emma. She opened the box and tipped it all out. 'Nothing gold,' she observed. 'Perhaps there was, and Mrs Clack filched it.'

'Or the other girl, Eva Florescu?' suggested Jess. The two Bamford officers were staring at her, so she went on, 'She cleared out in a hurry, you said. One reason for that could have been that she'd taken something from Amber's room, when she heard Amber was dead. Just a suggestion.'

Trevor Barker had turned rather red in the face. He might well do, thought Jess uncharitably. They've pretty well messed up the investigation into Amber's death, one way or another. Okay, they couldn't have secured Amber's room or her belongings before her body was identified. That gave either Myrtle Clack or Eva Florescu ample time to rummage around in there. It gave Myrtle time to scrub out the room thoroughly. But once they knew the identity of the murder victim, the Bamford team should have collected the bags of Amber's belongings from Declan immediately. What's more, they shouldn't have let Eva, who rented the adjacent room – and must, whatever she told Barker, have known something – slip through their fingers. Where was Eva Florescu now? she wondered.

Aloud, she said, 'I plan to return to Gloucestershire this afternoon. I think I've done all I can here for the time being. I've left my suitcase at the hotel, all packed up. I just have to go and pick it up.'

Barker looked relieved. 'I hope you've been okay at The Crown?'

'Yes, thanks.'

'Good. Give my very best regards to Ian Carter.'

'It's been really nice to see you again,' Meredith told Jess Campbell. 'And I hope your trip to Bamford has paid off, workwise.'

'I think it will pay off,' Jess told the Markbys. 'I've got to justify the expense, anyway – staying at The Crown, and travel expenses. I've learned a lot about Gary Button's background. It's probably been worth it, just to meet Harmony.'

'It's a pity you couldn't stay longer, Jess,' Alan Markby said.

He sounded a touch wistful, and his wife glanced at him.

She's right, thought Jess. He does miss the job. Even being on the fringes of it has made him feel alive. Trevor wonders why the Markbys bothered to take time and help out Harmony. It's because when she came to them, and asked for help, it was, for Alan, like a distant bugle call to a retired cavalry horse. He's young again, just for the moment, and pawing the ground, eager to be off.

Perhaps not a very polite comparison. But true, Jess thought, as she drove away from the former vicarage.

Chapter 14

Extensive door-to-door enquiries at country houses and isolated farms turned up only one other sighting of Gary Button on the day of his death. He had called at the home of a retired military man, and made his usual enquiries about unwanted bric-à-brac, antiques and old furniture.

'Didn't trust the fellow!' declared the retired soldier, with a warlike glint in his eye. He had leaned forward and raised his walking stick in a gesture of defiance. 'You learn to judge a man when your own life may depend on his reliability! Can't face the enemy with a fellow behind you who's going to cut and run!'

'Yes, sir,' agreed Nugent. 'Did he say where he'd come from or where he was going?'

'He left a card! You know, a business card! Damn cheek. I threw it away. He wanted a painting I've got in the hall. Here, you can see it yourself. This is it!'

Nugent found himself looking up at a very large portrait in oils, depicting a dashing gentleman with magnificent whiskers, tight breeches and shiny topboots, who was surveying the watcher with an air of effortless superiority. He was standing by a horse, and holding the animal's bridle. The horse's head was turned towards the man, but it was rolling an eye at the observer, as if trying to convey some message. Probably, thought Nugent, something along the lines of: *this guy thinks he's the bee's knees but I think he's a prat.*

'That,' said the house owner with pride, 'is my great-grandfather. As if I'd sell it to a chap who rolled up here in a white van! What's more, do you know what the cheeky blighter said?'

'No, sir,' Nugent mumbled.

'He said family portraits didn't fetch much money in the sale-room, but equestrian paintings did. The horse, if you please, was of more interest than my great-grandfather!'

'I can see that would be annoying, sir,' said Nugent.

The military man turned a bloodshot eye on him. 'What did you say your rank was? Sergeant? Well, sergeant! It was more than annoying. It was impertinent! I told the wretched fellow to clear off!'

'I think,' said Jess Campbell to Ian Carter, 'that if I had to sum up what I've learned in Bamford about Gary Button's murder, it's that, whatever led to his turning up as a charred corpse here, the trail starts back there. Somehow or other, this has everything to do with the murder of Amber Button. We need to know *why* Amber was murdered. Now, technically, that's Trevor Barker's case, not ours, but the two are linked.'

It was a chilly evening. The clocks had just gone back, and the sun had set a while ago. The pub was by the river, and inside a roaring log fire was ablaze. Originally the three of them, Ian and Jess and Mike Foley, had been seated at a table. But Mike, after fidgeting about for a while, said, 'Don't mind me, will you?' He'd then risen from the table and settled down, on his back, on a sofa beside the fire. He wasn't asleep, because every so often he plumped one of the cushions.

This fellow, thought Carter, glancing down at him, and trying not to make it too obvious, is, let's say, eccentric. Jess didn't seem to find it strange to have Foley lying there with his eyes closed. But it added to Carter's feeling of having been roped into playing a role in an amateur theatre production, without prior sight of the script. As he'd been leaving work that day, Jess had found him in the car park and asked if he'd like to join her and Mike that evening. They were going for a meal at The Fisherman's Rest at Long Weston.

'It's been closed for ages since it was flooded out,' said Jess. 'But it's been reopened under new ownership and I thought it would be nice to try it. Mike's interested to see it, and then I thought, well, you might be, too. Because of . . . of what happened there.'

Okay, thought Carter, he could hardly forget what had happened there. The night of the flood had also been the night of a police operation, and chaos had been complete. He wasn't sure about going back there. Certainly, he wasn't sure about going there with Jess and Foley. But he'd found himself agreeing, and now here they were. Or rather, he and Jess were still facing each other across the table, and Foley was spread out on the sofa. Carter had been speculating on Jess's true motive in inviting him along. Now it occurred to him that both Jess and Foley were in retreat from whatever tentative relationship they'd had. Carter was here to act as Jess's shield, to deter any difficult discussions. Foley had simply removed himself physically from the table. Had they quarrelled? wondered Carter. Or were they determined to keep things civilised?

'Have you thought any more about going to France at Christmas?' Jess asked him suddenly.

'Oh, I'm not going. It's out of the question.'

'Told Millie?'

'No, not yet. I thought I might drive up to the school this weekend and take her out to lunch somewhere. Then explain it all. If she understands.'

'She will. She might be disappointed at the failure of her plan. But she will understand.'

Perhaps if you came with me to see Millie? Millie liked Jess and would listen to any comment she might volunteer. Carter wanted to say all this. But he couldn't. Not only because of that modern-day answer to Albert Schweitzer, lying down there as if he were on a beach. But because if he arrived with Jess, it would fuel Millie's other plan . . .

Carter had a moment of insight into his daughter's thinking. Poor kid. Her parents had separated. Her mother had a new husband and, now, a new baby. They lived in France. Millie was shuttled between France, brief stays with her father in his cheer-less flat, and school. She wanted a family, a proper family, not one that had disintegrated. He wondered, for the first time, if the invitation to stay in France at Christmas and spend it with Sophie and Rodney, and their friends, had really come from them. It might simply have come from Millie, a cunning plan. If he agreed and turned up, they'd have the shock of their lives.

Jess said suddenly, 'For what it's worth, I think you're right not to go to France for Christmas with your ex and her new husband. It's, well, a bit weird.'

Carter glanced down again at the prone body of Mike Foley. *Talking of weird*, he wanted to say. But he didn't.

Originally the two detectives had been scrupulous about not

talking shop over Mike's recumbent form. But neither was there anything more to be said at the moment about Millie. With Mike having opted out like that, and not offering any contribution to the conversation, the topic inevitably moved to the case of Gary Button's gruesome demise.

'Amber's death has been Barker's case from the outset,' Carter pointed out now. 'He's currently trying to track Gary's movements in Bamford – any contacts he had, the usual thing.'

'I'm grateful for anything Trevor can turn up,' Jess replied. 'But I'd rather he didn't muddy the water. Gary was Amber's brother, but his murder took place on our patch.'

'Take it easy,' Ian advised. 'Or Trevor and I will end up jostling for advantage like Nugent and Paget. I think they're getting on a little better. I did have a word with Dave.'

Jess gazed round at the peaceful scene. 'The last known sighting of Gary Button alive was right here, in Long Weston, at the livery stables.' Her forehead crinkled in thought. 'Those livery stables used to belong to someone else, didn't they? Penny Gower, yes?'

'Yes, that's right,' Carter agreed.

That had been the first case he and Jess had worked on when he arrived as the new man here. He didn't want to think that other cases, and much time, had elapsed since then. It wasn't as if he needed reminding that his personal relationship with Jess had moved on little since then. Professional, sure. A building of mutual respect? Yes. But otherwise? He glanced down again at Mike, and had to resist a strong urge to prod the fellow. When it comes down to it, he thought ruefully, we're all tempted to behave like children. Nugent and Paget, or me with this chap here. Perhaps we never entirely grow up.

'Beware of making assumptions,' he said aloud, draining his glass and setting it down again carefully. 'That's what I was taught when I was a young detective. Amber was a candidate for a central role in a bad event. She was a good-time girl, as far as anyone knows, and it is a high-risk lifestyle, especially if working casually, as Amber was. The girls get beaten up. They get killed sometimes, even in small towns. Amber should have been aware of the risks. Anyway, I repeat, her death is being investigated by Trevor and his team in Bamford.'

'Yes, but we've got Gary Button's death to sort out here and there *has* to be a connection, whatever you say!' Jess leaned forward to emphasise her argument. 'I can't forget Katie's claim that Amber tried to poison her. It was a clumsy attempt and didn't work. But I absolutely believe that she tried to do it. Katie hasn't got any imagination. In that way, she's a perfect witness. She just tells you what she saw. It tells *us* – or rather, the Bamford investigation team – a lot about Amber. She was selfish, unscrupulous, and a dangerous loose cannon. Maybe somebody decided she was altogether too much of a nuisance and needed to be dealt with, once and for all.'

'Who?' asked Carter simply.

'Katie says she didn't tell Gary about the pills and the sangria, because Harmony ordered her to keep shtum. But perhaps she did tell him . . .' She paused. 'Or possibly either Declan, or Harmony herself, told Gary what had happened. He might have gone out looking for Amber, intending to make it clear to her she was to stay away from his wife!'

Carter thought that over. 'So, you're suggesting it's a family crime and Gary killed Amber? Perhaps he didn't intend to kill her, only scare her, but that scenario's gone fatally wrong before now. But who killed Gary? And why *here*, not in Bamford? As far as we know, he was in this area looking for bric-à-brac and junk for his business. He left Mrs Williams's house fit and well, with her unwanted sofa bed in his van. How on earth did he subsequently meet someone who beat him over the head, trussed him up, and barbecued him? For any reason?'

'He went somewhere and saw something he shouldn't have seen,' suggested Jess, after a moment's thought.

'Okay, but what has that to do with Amber? The pieces don't fit together,' argued Ian. 'I wish we could find that girl, Eva. I am sure she knows something. But she's keeping her head down for the time being. Until she breaks cover, we're stuck.'

'She's got to break cover, as you put it!' Jess insisted. 'Look, she's young and alone and in a foreign country. She came here to work – and she has to work, or she has no money. Compatriots working in this country might shelter her for a while, but they wouldn't be able to support her indefinitely.'

'She could have slipped out of the country and gone back to Romania. Or just slipped across the Channel to any of the EU countries.'

From his prone position on the sofa, Mike spoke. 'Anyone asked questions of Amber's clientele?'

They'd both forgotten him and looked down at him, startled.

'Trevor told me that they're having trouble finding anyone who admits ever having been in receipt of Amber's favours,' said Jess.

'It's not that big a town, surely?' objected Mike. 'It doesn't offer the anonymity of large cities. If Amber was making the rounds of the pubs picking up punters, it would be noticed.'

'And it was! The waitress in the lounge bar at The Crown told me that Amber dropped in regularly. The manager didn't like it, tried to chivvy her away. But she found customers there, I'm sure of it. I think I even rattled one of them into packing up and leaving early.'

'Then surely you can find others?' persisted Mike. 'Or that chap, Barker, should be able to!'

Jess expressed her doubt. 'Passers-through, like the guy I spotted, may betray themselves by panicking. But anyone living locally, who'd have more to risk if he was found to have been Amber's customer, might be very difficult to find. Amber was a local girl. Trevor Barker keeps making that point. People in small communities don't wash their dirty linen in public. Even if anyone could give Barker's team a name or two, they won't. They either don't want to get on the wrong side of someone they know and drink with, or they don't want to get on the wrong side of the Buttons. Trevor reckons that Michael, the one currently in the nick, is a tough customer, if his record is anything to go by, and he's due out soon. Declan must be handy. And there's Maria's husband. He's been in a few punch-ups in pubs, Trevor told me.'

'Oh, well, sort it all out tomorrow,' said Carter with a sigh. He picked up his empty glass again and peered into it. 'There's a moth in my glass.'

Mike sat up and reached up his hand. 'Give it here. If you try and get it out using your fingers you'll damage it.' Ian handed him the glass, with its prisoner. 'I've eaten these fried,' said Mike conversationally. 'Where I was working, the locals sit outside of an evening in the dark, and the air gradually fills up with these

228

things flying around, quite big ones. Then, suddenly, they light a lamp. All the insects, particularly the really big moths, come to the light and they trap them. They're a delicacy.'

'You don't propose to take it home and fry it, I hope?' Jess asked.

'Just one wouldn't make much of a meal. I'll fish it out with my finger, if you don't mind, and leave it on the table to dry off.'

I am sitting here, thought Carter, with a woman I would rather be sitting with alone, having a nice, quiet, intimate dinner date. Only I am too awkward and slow off the mark to make that happen. As a result, I am watching her current boyfriend – if that's what he is, or was – manoeuvre a moth out of my glass with his finger, and the conversation is about fried insects being a delicacy.

'And this,' said Lucy Prescott, 'is my grandmother, so she'd be your great-aunt, once removed, Ben. I think that's right. Her name was Priscilla, anyway.'

While Jess, Carter and Mike had been making stilted conversation during a dinner at Long Weston, Ben Paget had not been so very far away. The conversation had also been conducted, on his side, with a certain amount of controlled impatience. He had shared the Prescotts' evening meal, and a very good meal it had been. But as they had been such good hosts, Ben was now required to be a properly attentive guest. This was why he was here, so that Lucy could tell him all he wanted to know – or didn't – about distant and very long-lost relatives.

'Oh, yes, I see!' He obediently studied the faded photograph. 'Who's the kid?'

'Oh, that will be Doris, her youngest daughter, who was my aunt. She married a soldier and went to live in Hampshire, in Aldershot. We lost touch.'

Paget offered up silent thanks.

'And this,' announced Lucy in triumph, producing a creased snapshot. 'This is your Uncle Jim!'

'Are you sure? I don't remember him like that!' protested Paget, peering at the black and white image, showing a dapper young fellow, obviously in his Sunday suit. 'He always wore baggy trousers, an old jacket and cap, when I was a kid.'

'Well, he was a young man when that was taken! You only knew him a bit later, and when he was in his work clothes. And this . . .'

Paget surreptitiously looked at the long-case clock in the corner, because to consult his own wristwatch would be too obvious. Reg had fallen asleep in a chair by the fire. But his wife was on a mission to trace every family connection she could find. She produced yet another old biscuit tin with a picture of Winston Churchill on it.

'And these might be interesting, too . . .'

'The tin might be worth something,' said Paget. 'People collect those old biscuit tins.'

'Fancy!' said Lucy. But she wasn't deflected from her purpose. She opened the tin and tipped the contents out on the table. 'Now, let's see . . .'

'Lucy?' Paget put out a hand to forestall her as she began to shuffle the yellowing snapshots. 'Perhaps I could look at those another time? It is getting late, and we – I mean, the police – we do have a murder case on our hands.'

'Oh, yes, of course!' Lucy sat back and shook her head. 'That poor fellow. And on our land, too. Reg!'

This only received a mumble by reply, so Lucy got up from the table and went to shake him awake. 'Cousin Ben is about to go!'

Prescott grunted and sat up. 'Off home, are you, then, lad?'

'But perhaps you'll come to lunch on Sunday, Ben?' Lucy asked. 'I'll be doing a really good roast with all the trimmings!'

'Well, I . . .'

'Good, that's settled, then! Now you'll drive carefully, won't you? Because the roads are all narrow around here. And we'll see you again on Sunday, around twelve, all right?'

Chapter 15

'So, what do you think we should do?' asked Edward Billings of his partner, Sergio.

'Do about what?' asked Sergio, pouring out wine for them both.

'Eva. I can't get her out of my mind.'

Sergio gave him a suspicious look. 'You can't get that girl out of your mind?'

'Oh, not like *that*, Sergio, don't be daft. I mean, I should have been more frank when that woman rang me up, checking Eva's employment history. I didn't say anything to her about the police being here earlier, asking for the girl, wanting to know where she'd gone. Perhaps I really should have done, you know, just mentioned it casually!'

Sergio made a gesture as of someone playing a five-finger exercise for the piano with his left hand. He held a glass of wine in his right. 'Police?' he said. 'I don't know. With the police, you never know. Maybe we should just keep out of it.'

'Look,' urged Edward, leaning across the kitchen table, littered with the empty dishes of what had been an excellent meal, and trying to avoid getting his sweater cuff stained with *ragù*, 'it's been five years since we started this business and, in that time, we've built it up into an operation with a first-class reputation. We're never short of new customers wanting to use our cleaning services. We're hard pushed to find suitable staff to deal with it all. That girl taking off, as she did, was a real nuisance. Having the police turn up here, asking if we knew where she'd gone, was another.'

'Exactly,' observed Sergio sagely. 'Why make a third problem, eh?'

'But the police!' insisted Edward. 'We can't afford to upset the police! It would be a bad move. They're looking for her. I've information. I should pass it on! They told me so. If I heard anything, call them and let them know.'

Sergio sighed and set down his wine glass. 'Why do the police want to find that girl, Eva?'

'Well, I don't know, do I?' muttered Edward. 'They didn't tell me! The cops never tell you anything! They just ask a damn lot of questions.'

'That,' declared Sergio in the manner of one who has solved the problem, 'is why we don't need to be involved. We don't know what is behind it all!'

'But in addition I had that woman, Deirdre Collins, on the phone! And I didn't tell her anything, either.'

Sergio sighed, shrugged, and poured another glass of wine. 'Does she matter?'

'Oh, for goodness' sake, Sergio! I've told you all this already. You never listen!'

'When I am cooking, of course I don't listen,' retorted Sergio serenely. 'I am busy. I am concentrating. A good sauce does not make itself!' He sighed. 'Why are you worrying about this woman Deirdre?'

'She's the general manager of an upmarket retirement home, out in the sticks. The old folk who live there are probably well-connected people. They are well-off people, at any rate! I looked up the place on the Internet. She had Eva wanting to work there. She wanted character and reliability assurances from us.'

'Eva worked okay for us. Just tell her that.'

'*I did!* I told her we'd employed Eva on a regular basis for six months and all the customers for whom she'd cleaned had been satisfied.'

'So, what is the problem?' Sergio made an expansive gesture, right hand still holding his glass of wine, left hand giving an elegant twirl.

'I think I shall go mad,' said Edward despondently. 'If I have to keep repeating myself, I shall definitely go mad. Because when Eva took off like that, the police were at the office *straight away*, as you know, wanting to know where she was!'

Sergio set his glass down with great care. 'You should not say anything about that to this woman whose name I can't remember . . .'

Edward opened his mouth to repeat Deirdre's name, but was silenced by a gesture from Sergio.

'I do not even want to know her name. And I will tell you why. If you go telling this woman, with the big house full of wealthy old people, that the police want to talk to Eva, then she will not engage Eva.'

'I think she had taken her on,' said Edward gloomily. 'They were very short-handed and keen to find someone. She told me she was checking up in retrospect.'

'So then, let us assume she did! If the home is still okay with Eva, then she will still be there and everyone is happy. But then you phone the manager again and start to say, "Oh, I am very sorry, perhaps I ought to have told you, the police want to speak to Eva and asked me if I know where they can find her." You put the cat among the pigeons, yes? That's the English phrase?'

'Yes,' agreed Edward dejectedly.

'Well, this is never wise, because after that, the manager sacks her, almost certainly. Of course, Eva will surely ask her why she is dismissed. The manager woman must give her some reason, yes? So, she says to her, "Oh, because your previous employer tells me the cops are after you!" And then,' concluded Sergio serenely, 'it can be that Eva sues us.'

'Sues us!'

'Yes, because we are the reason she loses the job. You just say to her that Eva worked very well: we have no complaints. Only that.'

'I did say that!'

Sergio nodded approvingly. 'And you were right. As to the other matter, we don't know why the police want to speak to her. Perhaps she parks on double yellow lines or something like that. It's as you yourself said. The cops never tell you anything. They only ask.'

Edward rattled his fingertips on the table. 'Mmm, all that's true, of course. But it doesn't pay to upset the police. Withholding evidence, they call it, when they ask you something and you don't tell them.'

'When they asked you if you knew where Eva had gone, you didn't know about the old people's home. So you told no lies. You concealed no knowledge at the time. You only knew Eva had suddenly left us, and that is what you told the police!'

'Well, when you put it like that . . .'

Sergio rose to his feet and smiled down at him. 'It is like that. Really, very simple. Now, I suggest a little glass of limoncello, just to finish.'

'I still think . . .' But Edward was talking to himself. Sergio had gone to fetch the limoncello.

And there it might have stayed, but for the fact that early influences during childhood tend to dog our existence throughout later life, whether we like it or not. In Edward's case it was having a grandmother who believed strongly in Fate. Some people have warm, kind memories of a dear old grandma, dishing out forbidden treats and telling entrancing yarns. Edward's grandmother had been a terrifying old bat. She believed sweets rotted the teeth, to complain about anything was a sign of weakness, and she always told him, 'Remember, Edward! What can't be cured must be endured! So, stop grumbling. We may not like what Life throws in our path, but we must Get On With It!' If he continued to protest, particularly as he grew older, she simply said, 'It's Fate, Edward. We cannot ignore the Hand of Fate!'

Edward had once told Sergio about this. Sergio, it turned out, had wonderful memories of a warm-hearted *nonna*, who cooked like a dream, and was an ever-present refuge in times of stress. Well, he would, wouldn't he?

So when, the next morning, Edward stepped out of the door of the office from which they ran their cleaning services, just as a police car drove past with a couple of burly coppers in it, he knew it was the Hand of Fate. It was pointing out his duty. He made sure Sergio wasn't around, returned to his office, closed the door, and took out his smartphone.

'Hello? I'd like to speak to Sergeant Emma Johnson, if she's there. It's about an enquiry she made earlier . . .'

After all, if he told Sergeant Johnson about Deirdre Collins checking Eva's employment history, with a view to giving her a job at Meadowlea Manor, he'd have done his duty, Edward told himself. It was up to the cops what they did with the information. There was no need for him to phone Deirdre Collins. She'd want to know why he hadn't told her everything in the first place. Far too complicated. He'd done enough to placate Fate – and Sergio.

Against all the odds, in Miff's opinion, a rat had entered one of Uncle Bert's traps and been unable to get out. From its cage prison, it surveyed them with its bright eyes, as it waited on their judgement.

'The traps do work, see?' said Danny. 'Uncle Bert will be over the moon.'

Sam, summoned to behold the living proof of Uncle Bert's creative talent, stood pressed back against the wall and gazed at the rat in dismay.

'It can't get out,' Miff told her. 'There's no need to stand right over there.'

'But it's another one,' said Sam in a small, depressed voice. 'We'll have to get the pest control people in. We'll have to close the centre until they've come and done whatever they do, and say we're clear of any infestation.'

'Don't be daft!' said Danny cheerfully. 'We're not *infested* with the little blighters. We'd have seen more of them than just a couple. Of course, there might be a nest somewhere . . .'

Miff scowled at him in warning. 'I'm sure there isn't. Not this time of year.'

Danny opened his mouth to argue that rats didn't care what time of year it was. But the look Miff was giving him was fierce enough to make him abandon anything he had been about to say about the breeding habits of rats.

'Listen,' said Miff. 'The reason the rats have turned up here is firstly, because the weather is getting colder and they like to be warm, same as us. Secondly, it's like a rat's restaurant in here, with all those sacks of seed: birdseed, grass seed, as well as peanuts, they're all breakfast cereal to a rat. So, what we have to do is find somewhere to store the food that is rat-proof.'

'Where?' asked Sam in a small voice.

'Well, in something like an old metal cistern, or metal bath. We'd have to find something to make a rat-proof cover. Wire mesh should do it. We can still store the seed and nuts in here, but if the rats, or mice, can't get at it, they'll shove off and find somewhere else. There's no need to contact pest control. We're out in the middle of the country, not living in a town. Pest control can come round and clear your house of any vermin, sure. But out here, well, the rats are all part of the country scene.'

'Ammonia,' said Danny. 'You know, bleach – rats don't like it. Keeps them away. My grandad sprinkles it all round his garden. He lives down by the river and the banks are full of rats. But they don't like ammonia. Or Grandad uses Jeyes Fluid a lot. That keeps them away . . .' He paused. 'Of course, his garden stinks of it for a while after he's put it down.'

From the wall, Sam demanded, 'If you know all these old tricks your grandad uses, why have we been putting down Bert's traps?'

'It's what they're for,' said Danny simply.

'Well, I'll get rid of this one, anyway,' said Miff, lifting the trap and studying the rat through the mesh. 'Unless you want to keep it for a pet? Hey! That's a joke! I don't mean it seriously.'

'How? You're not going to *kill* it, are you?' Sam left the wall and edged closer. 'Look, it's just an animal behaving naturally. You're right, we shouldn't have left food out.'

'I'll kill it!' offered Danny cheerfully.

'No, you won't!' Sam snapped at him. 'You killed the other one. It was horrid. Miff will take it out into the fields and release it.'

'Oh, all right,' said Miff resignedly. 'We'll put this in the old stable where you keep your bike, Danny, until this afternoon. I'm busy this morning. But later on I'll take the wretched brute out into the fields and turn it loose.'

'Not until then? It can't get out, can it?' asked Sam apprehensively.

'Not out of one of Uncle Bert's traps!' said Danny with family pride. 'He makes them strong. Getting the vermin to go in might be a bit tricky. But, once they're in there, no way are they going to get out!'

Trevor Barker was on the phone to Ian Carter. 'Yes, we've found her!'

'Found whom?' asked Carter, a tad shortly. He was getting pretty fed up with Barker on the phone every five minutes, and every time wanting something.

'Eva Florescu!'

'Eva? Oh, right, the cleaner who rented the room adjacent to Amber's. You mentioned her to Jess Campbell.'

'That's the one! She did a runner but now we know where she is. We haven't picked her up yet. That's why I'm calling you.'

'Me? What's it got to do with us here? Amber Button's murder is entirely your problem. I've got her brother Gary's death to sort out.'

Carter knew he sounded exasperated but couldn't help it. What's more, he didn't care. He had a right to be terse with Barker. So, Barker had a murderer to find. If he had got on with finding the culprit, and hadn't managed to frighten off a possible important source of information, there was a strong probability he'd have found out who killed Amber Button by now. That, in turn, might have prevented Gary Button's death – inconveniently, where Carter and his team had to investigate.

His lack of enthusiasm had got through to Trevor Barker.

'I'm informing you,' came Barker's voice in his ear, sounding affronted, 'because she's working at a residential home for the elderly called Meadowlea Manor. It's not far from Weston St Ambrose; and that's near the spot where Gary Button was incinerated in his van. I thought, in the circumstances, you'd want to know!'

'Hang on, Trevor!' urged Carter. 'How do you know this girl, Eva Florescu, is working at Meadowlea Manor?'

'We've had a tip-off from her previous employer. He's a chap by the name of Edward Billings and he runs an agency supplying contract cleaners. He'd had a phone call from this place, Meadowlea Manor, asking him to vouch for the girl. She applied to work there. Unfortunately, despite having been told we needed to find her with some urgency, Billings didn't see fit to inform us at once. His excuse for this is some rambling nonsense about data protection. Anyway, she has started working there now, I gather. They were short of staff and took her on without worrying too much about anything Billings said, or didn't say. Listen, I'll come down myself. Obviously, this could be connected with your investigation into Gary's death, and Meadowlea is in your part of the world, but you wouldn't object, I hope.'

Barker sounded so excited that Carter was visualising him jumping around his office. But it was one thing to cooperate with another force, and another to let Barker muddle up enquiries here. Time for a little nifty footwork.

'No, Trevor, I don't object!' said Carter heartily. 'You want to talk to the girl and I probably need to talk to the girl, too. You believe she may have information pertinent to your enquiries. There's an off chance she may know something helpful to our enquiries here. We need to tread carefully. The girl has already done a runner once, hasn't she? Why don't you come down here, and you and I will drive over to Meadowlea Manor together, and see what the girl has to say for herself.'

When he had put down the phone, he turned to Jess, who had been standing beside him, listening. He summed up Barker's call and then added, 'We need to get to that girl before Barker does. Eva has met Barker and she isn't keen to meet him again. She skipped out before, and she'll skip out again. She is not going to do that before *we* talk to her! After that, Barker can talk to her as much as he likes.'

'Do we need to talk to her? You really think she has something to do with Gary's death?' asked Jess doubtfully.

'I have no idea!' Carter told her frankly. 'But how is this as a scenario? Meadowlea is a mid-Victorian manor, a big place, in the Gothic style. It's been converted to an old people's home but someone like Gary might not realise that. He came down here looking for antiques; and big old houses in remote areas are one of his regular ports of call. He's driving along, he sees Meadowlea, and he thinks there might be something to be had there.'

'Not if it's a residential home,' objected Jess. 'And he would know it was that because there must be a board by the entrance saying so.'

'It's a pretty upmarket place, from what I understand. It might have a board or it might not have anything so crassly commercial. It might just have a discreet little plaque nailed to the gatepost reading "Meadowlea Manor". At any rate, Gary turns in, drives round to the tradesmen's entrance and . . .' Carter paused. 'I don't know. There's Eva shaking out a duster? We're wasting time. Barker is on his way. Come on!'

Jenny Porter had been riding the same bicycle for more years than she cared to remember. She'd ridden it to and from the school at which she'd taught for a good number of years, and, since retirement, had been riding it around Weston St Ambrose. But both the bike and Jenny were beginning to show their age. 'It creaks a bit!' she'd tell people cheerfully. 'But then, so do I!' It was creaking so badly, as she puffed along the narrow road, that it almost seemed to be crying out in pain. She'd have to get another bike. There was no denying it; the museum piece that had served her so faithfully would be consigned to the scrapyard. New bikes were so damn expensive. She wished that her dear old chum since college days, Elspeth, had not chosen to retire to a place miles from anywhere.

To be fair, Meadowlea Manor was a decent place and Elspeth seemed happy enough there. Nevertheless, Jenny Porter never went over there without telling herself that they could nail her down in a wooden box before she moved into any such establishment. She understood the fees were staggering. But you had to pay for decent care, that was a fact. Just had to face up to it.

Mrs Porter prided herself on being fair, as fair now as she had striven to be back in her teaching days. For some reason, this brought Debbie Garley into mind and that business of the furry tomatoes. Yes, it had been hard to be fair when dealing with some pupils. Debbie, Jenny remembered bitterly, had been a very difficult child: disrespectful, noisy and obdurate. Well, nothing had changed there! But she'd made it clear to Debbie that spoilt so-called 'fresh' fruit and veg should not be palmed off on unsuspecting customers!

Anyway, she couldn't compare Debbie Garley with Elspeth. Although Elspeth could be pretty obstinate, too. She and Elspeth had been great chums all their lives, and it was only when Elspeth had decided on Meadowlea, that they had really argued. She'd moved to Meadowlea, and Jenny Porter was obliged to ride her bicycle all this way, come rain or shine, to visit her. It had been suggested to Jenny that she buy a small second-hand car. Not just to visit Elspeth, of course, but for general use. Apart from the expense – and Jenny Porter was by nature thrifty – she had nowhere to garage such a vehicle. The bicycle had the advantage that it could be pushed down the narrow alley leading to Jenny's front door, and through the even narrower space at the side of her cottage, and be kept in safety and dry conditions in Jenny's tiny garden shed.

All this was passing through Mrs Porter's brain as her legs pumped steadily away and her heart beat faster and her breath grew more ragged. Perspiration gathered on her brow and trickled down her cheeks. Really, it was most inconsiderate of Elspeth to have chosen a retirement place so out of the way, not even on a regular bus route, given that bus routes nowadays were few and far between. There was some sort of country bus, operated by a local company, which rattled its way past Meadowlea's gate around breakfast time, heading for distant Gloucester, and then made the return journey around five in the afternoon. She'd seen it and its contingent of stout country folk, laden up with supermarket carrier bags. But that one round trip was the only one of the day. So it was of no use to Mrs Porter.

She rounded the bend in the road and saw, at long last, the gates to Meadowlea's drive. Relief swept over her as it might engulf a man dying of thirst in a desert. She turned in at the gates, the wheels now scattering the stones of the gravel. A cup of tea with Elspeth, with a slice of cake and, possibly, a few little sandwiches . . . Of course, later she'd have to make the return ride home but—

At that moment, a figure came flying down the drive and cannoned into her. The bike toppled, Jenny Porter fell off and landed painfully, grazing her elbow. She looked up from her seated position and saw a very young woman wearing the pastel uniform of the home's domestic staff. The child was staring down at her in horror.

'You are a very silly girl!' Jenny told her sternly from her position on the ground. 'Help me up at once! Well, come on, don't just stand there gaping like a goldfish!'

Jenny Porter had spent a working life issuing orders to young people, and she expected instant obedience. She hadn't lost the knack. The girl hurried to help her up, stammering profuse apologies in strongly accented English.

'Stop that!' ordered Jenny, as the girl was getting hysterical. 'Pull yourself together! Now then, what's all this about?'

'I didn't see you . . .' muttered the girl, her eyes staring wildly to the left, right and, with a twist of her head, behind her. 'I am sorry, very sorry. I am in very big hurry!'

You are in very big trouble of some sort, you mean, thought Jenny. That's the truth of it.

'Is someone chasing you?' Jenny peered behind the girl. She could see the entrance to the manor up ahead and, parked before it, a car. But there were no other people around. Very odd.

'What have you done?'

'Nothing!' muttered the girl. But she looked as guilty as hell.

'There's a bench over there!' Jenny pointed. 'Come and sit down and tell me all about it.'

'No, there is nothing . . . I can tell you nothing!' The kid had broken into a sweat.

'Don't be silly!' ordered Jenny, firmly but not unkindly. 'Come and tell me what the problem is. You will feel much better when you've explained it to me. Then we can see what we can do to sort it all out!'

'Cannot sort out!' mumbled the girl.

'Nonsense. What's your name?'

'Eva . . .'

'Well, Eva, I spent a lifetime as a teacher dealing with young people's problems. They are never, ever as bad as they seem.'

'Mine is,' said Eva obstinately.

'Don't be so dramatic! You youngsters always think you're the centre of the universe and everyone is against you.'

'They will be against me!' Eva rallied and met Jenny's eye. 'I know it!'

'Who are they? Your employers here, at Meadowlea?'

'No! It is the police. They are here!' Now Eva pointed at the car parked before the house. 'They have found me here. I thought I was safe here! It is such a quiet place and so beautiful, only fields and trees and no houses. Only one little bus in the morning to the big town and one in the evening to return . . .' Her voice tailed away.

'Why are the police looking for you?' asked Jenny sharply. It occurred to her that all the criticisms of Meadowlea's situation that had filled her own mind on the painful bike ride here were, apparently, its virtues in the eyes of young Eva. Even that rattling old bus.

'They want to talk to me, that is what Mrs Collins said. But I cannot talk to them!' was the sullen reply.

'What have you done?' asked Jenny simply. She knew Deirdre Collins was the office administrator here, so the girl must be running as much from Deirdre as from the police.

'I do nothing. But I – I know something . . .' Eva looked down at her hands and her voice died away to a mumble again.

'If you know something that's useful to the police, then you must tell them!' said Jenny sternly. She added, 'But tell me first. Then, if you like, I can tell them, on your behalf.'

Eva looked up hopefully. 'I must not see them myself?'

'Yes, of course they will need to see you and confirm anything I tell them!' Jenny clung to her patience. What the hell had the child done? 'But it may make it easier for you, if they know you are anxious to discuss with them any difficulty you find yourself in; and what the nature of the problem is. And I can come with you, if you feel you need someone at your side.'

Eva sat staring down at her hands and Jenny waited. This was the moment when they either confessed or stayed mulishly silent. Eva looked up.

'I tell you,' she said.

Aha! You haven't lost your touch, Jenny, old girl! Mrs Porter told herself. 'Good! Then start at the beginning. Where were you when all this happened?'

'I worked in Bamford. I worked for cleaning company and I have lodging in a house, one room only, and use of kitchen and bathroom. The landlady is nasty old woman, but it is hard to find a room, so I take it and I stay. She had another room and another tenant, a woman. The room is next to mine and the woman is older than me and she is not nice. She is prostitute—'

'What?' asked Jenny, startled. She hadn't meant to interrupt the narrative, now that Eva had finally got going, but this was really unexpected.

'Yes, yes, she is tart. Her name is Amber. She is big girl and flashy, yes? The word is flashy? I think probably she is the sort of woman men like – some men, anyway. I don't like her and I don't want to have anything to do with her.'

'Eva,' Jenny said warningly. 'Are you sure Amber was a prostitute? Perhaps she just had a lot of boyfriends. Just because she was flashy in style . . .'

'She bring the men to her room,' said Eva simply. 'It is next to my room and the wall is very thin. They pay. I know it.'

'Oh dear, did the landlady know it? Because if you had told the landlady, she would have turned Amber out, I'm sure. I mean, even if the landlady was a nasty old woman, as you describe her, I am certain—'

'She *know!*' interrupted Eva crossly. 'Yes, yes, she know! Of course she know! And when the man pay Amber, Amber she give a little of the money to Mrs Clack, so that she say nothing and let Amber stay.'

'Oh, I see. Eva, did either Amber or Mrs – Clack? Did either of them ever suggest that you could also earn some money like that and pay the landlady?'

'Yes, of course,' said Eva simply. 'Because I am younger than Amber and they think men will like me, too. But I tell them no, I have cleaning job, and I like it. Anyway, what Amber do is very stupid and dangerous. Then Amber was very angry and she don't like me.'

'So, what happened to make you run away?'

Eva leaned forward to impart a confidence. 'Although Amber see many men, there is one man she say is her boyfriend. He is different. She don't take money from him. She hope he will take her away and, maybe, even marry her. I told you, Amber is stupid. But it is the boyfriend who go away. And when he tell Amber he is going away, and he don't take her, they have terrible row! Shout, shout! And then they fight, yes, I hear it all. Then Amber, she made strange noise . . .' Eva made a gurgling sound and put a hand on her own throat. 'And she go quiet and there is big bump on ground. I think Amber fall down. She make no more noise.'

It was very quiet all around. A bird of some sort was in the tree behind them, fluttering around. Probably a pigeon, thought Jenny. 'What happened next?' she asked. Her own voice seemed to come from far away. She could only form the words with difficulty. She had expected something fairly dramatic, but not that it should be a matter of murder.

'He, the boyfriend, go and find Mrs Clack. Then I hear much noise, bump, bump, on stairs. I think they carry Amber downstairs. Then he leave. I hear his car. But Mrs Clack come back and she come upstairs and knock on my door. She call my name. But I did not reply and I hid in wardrobe. She came into the room and looked, then went away again. I stayed in wardrobe for a long time and then I left the house very quietly. Later I came back, made much noise, say "Good evening!" to old Mrs Clack, like I just came home. So they think I was not there and I know nothing.'

Eva drew a deep breath. 'Nothing happen for some days; but then police come, asking questions. So it is time for me to go, very quick, yes? He will kill me too, and Mrs Clack, she will help him, like she help him before!'

Jenny pulled herself together. 'But, Eva, my dear girl . . . This is really serious. You must tell the police! You should have gone to the police immediately, in Bamford, and told them all of it!'

Eva shook her head firmly. 'No, I cannot. It is not possible. They not believe!'

'But they were making enquiries about Amber! That's why they came to the house, asking questions. Of course they would have believed you! They would have investigated.'

'No! They would not believe me!' Eva clenched her fists and pummelled her knees. 'They would tell me to shut up!'

'But why on earth should they?' countered Jenny. 'That's nonsense, Eva, of course they would—'

Eva leaned towards her, her large dark eyes burning in her pale face. 'They not believe me, and they tell me to shut up or I shall be in much, much trouble, because Amber's boyfriend, he is also policeman!'

Chapter 16

'All right, Ratty!' Miff told his prisoner. 'You and I are going to take a walk. And don't worry. I don't mean that in the sense the Mafia use it. At the end of it, I shall be releasing you into the wild, as directed by Sam. She has your best interests at heart. But not mine. I have to hike out into the fields; far enough away from the garden centre to discourage you from hitting the trail back again. Don't mistake my promise to her for kindness of heart towards you. If you – or one of your mates – dare to show your whiskers again, I personally will clout you with a spade. So remember that! You won't just have Danny to deal with!'

'You're barmy, you are!' said Danny's voice behind him. 'Talking to a ruddy rat.'

Miff turned. Danny, all kitted up in his biker's leathers, and holding his helmet in one hand, was propped astride his steed and watching him.

'Just tell her you took it out and let it go! You don't have to really do it. Kill it.'

'I can't,' said Miff. 'She made me promise.'

'So, you promised. That's your mistake. Never make promises to women. I didn't make any daft promises to her. I'll kill it.'

'If I conspire with you to knock the wretched creature on the head, she'll say that's the same as me killing it.'

Danny thought for a moment and then his expression brightened. 'I'll feed it to the owl, out in the stable. That way, neither of us will have killed it. The owl will. She can't blame an owl. That will let you and me off the hook.' Danny squinted at him. 'You're scared of her or scared of the rat?'

'I am not scared of a rat!' snapped Miff. He added, 'But I am terrified of her.'

Danny grinned. 'Go on, no, you're not.'

'If I say I am,' Miff told him with dignity, 'I am. Well, no, of course not! But she'd be so upset if she found out the truth.' He added, 'It's a matter of trust. A good relationship is founded on trust. I read that in a book in the library I used to hang out in, when it was raining.'

Danny took the more worldly view. 'No, it's not. It's all about neither of you finding out what the other one is really doing. That way, nobody gets upset! Anyway, see you later! Enjoy your hike!' He jammed the helmet on his head, revved up the bike and roared off in a spray of gravel.

Miff set off towards the gate, carrying the trap with his prisoner. The rat crouched in the trap, bright eyes fixed on him. But before Miff got to the road, he had to jump aside, as a decrepit van rattled in. It drew up next to him, and Morgan Jay wound down the driver's window.

'I brought some more gnomes,' he said.

'Great, Morgan. Sam is in the office. She'll be pleased.'

'Where are you going with that?' Morgan nodded towards the rat trap.

'Sam wants me to release it in a field.'

Morgan chuckled but, to Miff's relief, didn't offer advice or attempt any jokes. He just rattled off towards the cottage. Miff heaved a sigh of relief. It had been a busy day, but now it was late afternoon and business was pretty well non-existent. The only visitors were a middle-aged couple, who were just going into Glenys Garley's coffee shop. They had their backs to Miff, which was just as well. The rat might have put them off. Actually, now that he was off the premises, Miff felt a lightening of the spirit. He walked away from the Minglebury Garden Centre, and from Weston St Ambrose beyond it, heading he was not sure whither, but happy to be going somewhere unplanned. It was ages since he'd done anything like this. It wasn't only the rat that was due for release. He, Miff, needed a break during which he was answerable to no man. He began to fantasise about regaining his liberty; real freedom such as he'd had when living rough. He hadn't to do Sam's accounts. He hadn't to worry about Morgan Jay's disturbing gnomes. He hadn't to write that book and, best of all, he could forget all about his talk to the writers' circle.

He couldn't forget the rat, however, so he kept an eye open for somewhere suitable to set it free, and at last came upon a large grassy field, with a roadside boundary of a drystone wall in which there was a five-barred gate. He leaned upon it and gazed at the peaceful, rolling landscape. It was all very calm and traditional, just like a picture on a calendar. Definitely, the rat would like it here. He propped the rat trap on the top of the wall, and picked up the one-sided conversation with its occupier.

'Ratty!' he told the creature. 'I have not felt this great since I arrived in this neck of the woods. Freedom, real freedom, you understand, got left behind with my beard in Bamford. Here, either I've been accountable to Henry and Prue, bless their hearts, or to Sam . . .'

He paused here to consider that he didn't want to be unfair to Sam. He ought not to list her with the drawbacks of his new life. She was definitely a welcome addition to it.

'I exclude Sam from the drawbacks,' he told the rat. 'She's definitely a plus. You ought to be grateful to her, too. But it's great not having to explain myself to everyone I meet, from Debbie at the supermarket to that terrifying Mrs Porter, and most of all to the rest of the writers' circle. I haven't tried to explain myself to Danny Garley, who wouldn't understand. No doubt he keeps his biker mates entertained with tales of how weird I am. I don't mind.

'Stay free, mate!' he told the rat. 'Human beings trap you in more ways than one!'

The rat didn't look appreciative. In fact, the wretched beast was beginning to look a bit travelsick, so Miff cheerily swung the cage over the gate and climbed after it. Across the sward they went, and then over another gate, and across another field. This spot should do. Miff set down the cage and cautiously raised the tiny portcullis, keeping his fingers well clear of the prisoner.

The rat hesitated, moved a millimetre, and then made a dash for freedom. It scuttled out of the trap, across the turf, and threw itself kamikaze-style into the nearest ditch.

Miff turned and began to stroll back home at a leisurely pace. He felt relaxed and happy and even started to whistle. He wondered if he could persuade Sam that there was enough money in the kitty to allow them an evening out at The Black Horse, with a pizza thrown in. He was pretty sure the Black Horse menu featured pizzas. The pub had no pretension to be a restaurant of any category, but was happy to offer various things that could be stuck in a microwave oven. They deserved a break from leftover sandwiches and dry cakes from the coffee shop.

Lost in the prospect of pizza and a beer, Miff's feet carried him automatically to the road and the first gate he'd climbed over. It was as he placed a hand on the top bar of the gate that his eye caught the sheen of early evening sunset on black-painted metal. There was a car parked in the road now, whereas there hadn't been before, when he'd come this way earlier. He couldn't see the entire car behind the drystone wall. But yes, it was a car roof. He hesitated, then decided to pull himself together. There were untold numbers of black cars in the country and he couldn't take fright at every one, even if it turned out to be a BMW, like the one that had passed by the garden centre gate recently. That had been in the evening, too. Someone who lived around here drove a black BMW and came home in it about the same time every working day: that was the explanation. Wasn't it?

He heard the door open and the driver clamber out. The car door shut again with a click. The driver came into view and stood on the other side of the gate, looking at Miff. No doubt about it. It was the killer from Bamford.

Miff felt sick. How the man had found him here, he had no idea. But he had found him, and any hope that shaving off the beard would be disguise enough to fool his enemy had been a forlorn and foolish expectation. The killer knew Miff, just as Miff knew him. The man's face wasn't twisted in murderous fury now, but the cold, calculating look in his eyes was enough to tell Miff that the killer's purpose had not changed.

Otherwise, now that Miff had a proper chance to take a look at him, the man looked surprisingly normal: a solidly built, fair-haired guy, ruddy-complexioned, as if he spent a lot of time in the open air, or played a lot of sport on muddy fields. He might look like a countryman, but he wasn't, Miff decided. He held himself like a townie. He looked very fit and sharp-eyed, yes, but that wasn't just down to being in good shape. To be frank, he looked like a man who'd been in a few tight corners, and got out of them. Miff, on the other hand, was now in the tightest corner of his life, and had no idea how he was going to get out of it. Or *if* he was going to get out of it. For the first time, Miff heard his enemy speak.

'It is you, isn't it?' the man asked, in a toneless voice.

Miff couldn't have answered, even if he had wanted to. He couldn't even nod.

'I wasn't sure,' continued the man. 'I noticed you a couple of times about the place as I was passing through. I was put off at first by the loss of the face fungus. Then I thought, yes, you'd have shaved all that off, first thing you did.'

Then he smiled, and it was the worst expression of all, because of the lack of any pleasantness about it. It was a smile of satisfaction; the smile of a man who had achieved a goal, and was now about to enjoy himself.

The old story about Death and Damascus was true, thought Miff. You couldn't avoid your fate. It was foolish to try. He had tried to run, but he'd have done better to stay in Bamford. In the end, it made no difference. His number was up – that was the old saying, wasn't it? He had been prepared to do anything to be safe. But there was nothing he could do.

255

The man reached out a hand and unlatched the gate. 'Out you come, sonny!'

It was the use of the term 'sonny' that unfroze Miff's mind. Bloody hell! The man was perhaps only five or six years older than Miff. What did he mean by calling him 'sonny'? But he accepted the invitation and walked through the gate to confront the man on the roadside verge. No point in antagonising him at the moment. Do as the guy said. Keep him happy. Lull him into thinking this was all going to be so easy for him. Gain time.

'I saw your car the other evening,' he heard himself say. Recovering the ability to speak brought him out of the unreal nightmare – and made him face the real one. But he did so no longer with that spineless surrendering to fate he'd just experienced. Sod fate! He had to *do* something. Anything but die, anything to get out of this. Just at this moment, he hadn't the foggiest idea what. Miff gripped the rat trap. It was the only weapon he had. *Keep your head*, he ordered himself.

The man was nodding. 'You were leaning on the gate of that garden centre place. I wasn't sure it was you. So I came back another time, and checked it out, on the quiet. I saw you, and the girl, and the yob who rides the motorbike. You all went into one of the sheds and then the biker came charging out, chasing something. He hit it with a spade. Must have been a rat?'

'Yes,' said Miff. 'We've had a couple round the place.'

The man gestured towards Uncle Bert's rat trap. 'Is that what you had in there?'

This whole conversation was surreal, but the longer it went on, the longer Miff stayed alive, and where there's life . . . Keep the guy talking, that's what he had to do, keep him talking. It leapt into Miff's mind that perhaps the man wasn't as sure of himself as he appeared. Or perhaps he had resolved to remove Miff permanently from the scene, but had not yet decided whether to do it here, or to force Miff into the car and drive him off somewhere. Somewhere where he could be murdered, and his body incinerated, like that guy in the van found on one of the local farms. In any case, the killer was taking his time because he had to be sure not to screw up, this time. The body in the warehouse had been found almost at once. Ditto the burnt-to-a-crisp remains in the van. Practice makes perfect. When it came to disposing of Miff, the killer would make no mistake. Third time lucky.

'I let it go, out in the fields,' Miff said, to explain why he carried an empty rat trap.

'That was a mistake,' said the man, shaking his head with every sign of regret. 'Never let a rat go free. Not the animal sort, and not the two-legged sort. Can't trust 'em, you see.'

You certainly couldn't. 'You came back to the garden centre, didn't you?' Miff asked. 'You came back more than once, right?'

'A couple of times,' admitted the man. 'I had to make sure you were the same fellow as the bearded guy I chased round the back gardens in Bamford.'

'And what made you decide that I was? That it wasn't a chance resemblance?' Miff asked, genuinely curious.

'I called into that little shop, they call it a supermarket, in Weston St Ambrose. I needed some mints to keep in the car. There was a noticeboard in there and I read it, just out of curiosity. Some writers' group was planning a meeting. The speaker at the forthcoming one was going to be some guy called Matthew Ferguson who had been living rough and was now going to write a book about it. It had to be you. Were you really planning to write a book?' Genuine curiosity touched the man's voice briefly.

Were, thought Miff. Not *are*. He wasn't going to get a chance to write the book. This burly thug was going to make sure of that.

'Well, it was an idea . . .' he said. 'You were prowling around the cottage the other evening, weren't you? The security lights were triggered. I took a look around outside. I heard you run off, and the sound of your car engine.'

'That was a very foolish thing to do, go outside on your own like that. In the middle of the night? And in an isolated, poorly lit spot, because you thought you had an intruder on the premises.' The man suddenly sounded censorious, very much like Miff's old headmaster. 'What you should have done was lock yourself indoors and call the police.'

Miff stared at him incredulously. 'Call the cops? What could I have told them? I didn't know straight away you were there waiting for me! A fox could've triggered the lights. Once I realised someone was there, I knew it was probably you, and you wanted to – eliminate me.'

The man nodded. 'I thought I had a good chance then. But your girlfriend threw open the window upstairs, started shouting at you, switched on all the lights. The cottage was shining like a beacon! I didn't need a witness. And I had no beef with her. It was only you I wanted to remove from the picture.'

'Gentlemanly of you!' snarled Miff.

'Oh, if I'd had to kill her too, I would have done so,' his opponent assured him. 'But I like to be fair.'

'Fair! You're a ruddy psychopath!' Miff burst out. 'I suppose you'd killed that girl you dumped in the old warehouse.' A thought occurred to him. 'Did you kill the other one, too? The body in the burnt-out van?' Of course he had. But Miff had a perverse determination to hear him admit it.

The faint frown of displeasure that had creased the man's brow, when Miff accused him of being a psychopath, deepened. 'I had to. That was a bit of bad luck. It was the girl's brother. He shouldn't have been around here at all. I'd been taking a trip down memory lane, because I used to visit this area a lot when I was a kid. I was driving home. The road was narrow. I met this white van coming the other way. We both stopped; we both looked through our windscreens. We recognised each other. Gary ruddy Button, of all the bad luck, for both of us, you understand. He got out. I got out . . . He started yelling at me about his sister. I used to date her a bit, you know. But she got to be a nuisance, could've ruined my career. He went for me, fists swinging like a maniac. I floored him and whacked him over the head a couple of times. That shut him up, permanently.'

'Then what did you do with him?' asked Miff, anything to prolong the nightmare conversation. The longer it went on . . .

'Oh, tied him up and put him in the back of his own van. I was pretty sure he was dead, but best to make sure. I parked his van, and him, in some trees. Later, I drove back there, moved his van to a field and fired it. Then I walked back to where I'd left my car and drove away. Pretty straightforward, really.'

The cold eyes swept over Miff appraisingly. 'Now, you,' he said. 'I'll have to dispose of you differently. I don't want anyone finding your body. Yes, get in the car.'

If he got into that car, he was done for, that much Miff knew for sure. He said simply, 'No!'

'Don't be silly, sunshine!' The man put a hand in his jacket pocket and drew out a revolver.

It sat snugly in his palm. Useful-looking thing, thought Miff. But what the hell was he doing out here in the middle of the countryside, tooled up like a gangster? In the countryside they had sporting guns. But, in the UK, normal-looking people – and but for the fact that this guy had a nasty look in his eye (and Miff had heard him confess to double murder) he looked like countless other men – simply didn't walk around with that kind of weapon about their person. Carrying a knife, now, that had become horribly common. Even school kids had taken to arming themselves with knives.

'Where did you get that?' he asked, genuinely curious.

The man glanced at it. 'This? I took it off a drug dealer. No, to be honest, I found it hidden in his house when we raided it one night. No one else had seen it. The dealer wasn't going to say he had a weapon. He was already in enough trouble, without being charged with possession of an unlicensed firearm. So I kept it.'

'You're a copper!' said Miff, light dawning. Bloody hell, he was in even more trouble than he'd realised.

At the same time, it was as if a mist cleared. Well, that explained why he'd been addressed as 'sonny' and even, heaven help us, 'sunshine'! Did they issue police recruits with booklets of useful phrases – like *Everything You Need in France*, etc., supposedly helpful to travellers? Or had this particular copper just decided for himself how to address small-time troublemakers like Miff? Perhaps he'd watched too many old episodes of *The Sweeney*, and wished he were on the force back in the good old days of the

Flying Squad, when an officer made his own rules. He hadn't been able to prevent himself turning back into a police officer when he gave Miff that lecture on calling the police, if the garden centre had an intruder. Split personality or what? A nutter, anyway, that's what he had in front of him. A genuine, twenty-four-carat loony. Walking around looking normal, but a real fruitcake.

British police officers were famously unarmed. The most Miff might have expected to see aimed at him ought to be a taser. But no, this officer broke all the rules.

Whatever the case, the snout of that neat little handgun was now pointing at Miff. A faint smile touched the impassive features of the gunman. The moment had come and he was looking forward to it.

At that moment, a distant engine roar filled the air, approaching rapidly. Miff recognised it and, as Danny Garley's bike appeared, Miff flung the rat trap at the gunman's head.

The man dodged it, but the movement jolted the revolver and it went off. There was a second of pure horror when Miff thought he'd been shot . . .

But then he realised he hadn't. He had no time to relax, because the gunman was clearly going to fire another shot at him and wouldn't miss a second time.

Or he would have done so, if Danny's bike hadn't scraped alongside him and caused him to stagger and fall forward on to his face. The weapon flew out of his hand and into the ditch, to be lost among the nettles and other weeds. The gunman swore, scrambled to his feet, and jumped down into the ditch to search for his weapon.

Miff wondered if he ought to dive in there too, and retrieve the revolver first, turning the tables. But Danny had a better grip on the situation. His bike screeched to a halt, the rider twisted in the saddle and his voice, muffled by the helmet, yelled some indistinct order. It had to be: 'Get on!'

Miff leapt on to the pillion behind Danny and clung on desperately as they raced away. He didn't know if the gunman was having any luck looking for his weapon. But when he found it, the process would have delayed him for a few minutes only, and then he'd be back in his car and pursuing them. But now they'd reached the garden centre gates. Danny roared through them and stopped.

Miff fell off the pillion and sprawled on the ground. Danny took off his helmet and looked down at him.

'Who the hell was that?' he asked, sounding, for the first time, genuinely curious, and not just baffled by Miff's antics. 'He was going to shoot you,' added Danny, and Miff hoped he was mistaken in thinking he heard a note of admiration in his voice.

'Of course he bloody was!' Miff snapped, scrambling to his feet. 'And he still will, if we hang around here in the open!' For good measure, he added, 'He'll shoot you, too!'

Chapter 17

Danny made no reply to that, and looked, if anything, faintly surprised. He dismounted and then, belatedly, asked, 'Whaffor?'

But this was no time to enter into a discussion. Miff glanced around. The car that had brought the middle-aged couple he'd seen earlier, entering the coffee shop, had gone. But Morgan Jay's rattletrap was still parked before the cottage.

'Fetch Glenys!' Miff ordered Danny crisply. 'And anyone else you see. Get yourself and the others into the cottage. We'll barricade ourselves in and I'll call the police!'

Do, in fact, just what his enemy had told him he should do. Good advice is never wasted.

'Go on, move! He knows I live at the garden centre and he'll be here any minute!'

Danny gulped and burst into a clumsy run, crashing his way through the plant tables in his biker gear, waving his arms and shouting, 'You gotta hide in the cottage, Auntie Glenys! There's a crazy bloke coming to shoot us all!'

Miff couldn't have put it better. He burst into the office, where his wild appearance caused both Sam and Morgan to jump up in alarm. They'd been drinking tea and, presumably, chewing the fat, watched by a row of pottery gnomes, delivered that afternoon by Morgan. Sam gazed at him, puzzled, with her mouth open, but speechless. The potter still gripped his whisky flask in his hand. He must have been lacing his tea. The crazed grins on the faces of the pottery gnome audience suggested they were enjoying the surprise.

'What's up, then, boyo?' asked Morgan, saluting him with the hip flask.

'No time to explain. Get into the hall!' ordered Miff, stabbing at his phone. 'Come on, get away from the window, any window! Sam, you and Morgan get under the stairs. No, I don't want the fire service or an ambulance, I want the police!' This last was addressed to the phone.

'What on earth for? Miff, are you okay? Hey, stop pushing!' argued Sam.

'Safest place! Hurry up!' He dragged her towards the stair cupboard. Morgan followed, more out of curiosity than with any haste or sense of danger.

'The cupboard's not big enough,' protested Sam. 'Why, anyway?'

'Because a maniac with a gun is about arrive, and is determined to shoot me. He'll shoot the rest of you, too, so don't start a conversation, just move! I need to tell the cops.' His phone had begun to squawk again.

At that moment Danny arrived, propelling a protesting Glenys Garley ahead of him.

'I haven't locked up, Danny! I can't just leave the till! Let go of my arm, you mutton-headed boy! Have you gone barmy, or what?' Her gaze swept around, taking in the other three. 'What's the matter with you lot?'

'Will explain later. Danny, get Glenys into the stair cupboard with the other two! You lie flat on the floor in the hall. I don't trust that rickety front door to stop a bullet. I haven't got time for this! Just do it!' Into the phone, he shouted, 'Is that the police? We've got an emergency! My name is Matthew Ferguson and we're at the Minglebury Garden Centre, just outside Weston St Ambrose—'

He broke off to demand, 'Have you locked that front door, Danny? Go and lock the back door, too!'

'We can't all get in there!' wailed Sam, as Morgan pushed her and Glenys into the dark cubbyhole of a stair cupboard. It already housed the electric and gas meters, a vacuum cleaner of considerable age, Miff's rucksack, a couple of pairs of wellington boots, and various other items not wanted on voyage.

'Then throw all that damn rubbish out! Go on, girl!' ordered Morgan, setting the example by dragging out the vacuum cleaner and sending it crashing to the floor.

The dreaded sound of a car engine was now audible, outside in the garden centre itself.

Miff was yelling into the phone again. 'Yes, I'm reporting an urgent incident!' He summed up the situation. 'He's outside now and he's armed!'

It had occurred to him that the police might not believe him. But, to his surprise, the recipient of his call reacted calmly, asking, 'What sort of weapon does he have?'

'A revolver, like a ruddy cowboy! And he's a murderer . . .'

'Hold on a minute, will you, sir?'

'*I haven't got a minute! We haven't got minutes. Get here!*'

Another voice came on the line. 'Do you know his identity, sir?'

'I don't know his name, no!' Miff drew a deep breath. 'But he's a copper – a police officer, plain clothes at a guess, one of yours!'

'Ah, yes,' replied the constabulary, 'we've had another report about him, and we're already looking for him. Just stay in the house. Keep away from windows. How many of you in there?'

'Five!'

'We'll be there shortly, sir.'

'The police are coming!' Miff told his companions, or the ones he could see. That meant Danny and half of Morgan, because with the two women in the stair cupboard, there wasn't room for his entire body. He looked oddly like half of one of his own gnomes, split vertically. 'But we've got to hang on somehow until they get here.'

From inside the cupboard, Glenys shouted, 'If he's out there, he could help himself to my till! I told you, it's not locked, nor the door of the coffee shop. Danny! This is your fault! You should have let me lock the till!'

'He's not interested in your till, Glenys!'

'What's he want, then?'

'He wants to kill me!' Miff shouted at her.

If they thought about it, they probably would all like to kill him right now.

From outside, a man's voice shouted, 'You in there! Ferguson! Come out!'

Miff and Danny were now both lying cosily, side by side, on the hall carpet. 'Not thinking of going, are you?' asked Danny, as if this were really an option. 'He's found his gun in that ditch, I reckon. I wouldn't go out there myself.'

'Of course I'm bloody not going out there! Keep your head down and don't talk! He'll hear you and know where we are!'

'He been after you all along, has he?' Danny had lowered his voice to a hoarse whisper.

'Yes! Shut up!'

'Always reckoned there was something odd about you!' retorted Danny, sounding satisfied.

From inside the cupboard Glenys's voice was audible, complaining, 'I've had a good day today, took a lot of money! It's all right you saying he won't look in the till. He's bound to, isn't he?'

'I'm only interested in the one of you!' shouted the voice outside. 'Send Ferguson out! The rest of you will be safe. I only want him!'

Now, at last, his companions decided to fall silent. Miff felt Danny and Morgan watching him.

'Come on, Ferguson,' called the gunman. 'You don't want to be responsible for anyone else being hurt, do you? Do the decent thing and come outside. We'll settle this, just you and me.'

Do the decent thing? The more Miff heard the gunman talk, the madder the guy sounded.

'He don't like you, do he?' whispered Danny. 'What're you going to do?'

'I don't fancy getting shot,' said the half of Morgan from the cupboard. 'Not part of my plans, you might say.'

Not part of Miff's either. 'What am I going to do?' he snarled at Danny. 'I'm not going out there for a start!'

Then he heard Sam's voice echoing from inside the cupboard. 'We *can't* send Miff out! He's going to shoot him! Anyway, I don't believe that man when he says he's only interested in Miff, not the rest of us! We'd be witnesses, if he shoots Miff! He's bound to shoot us, too!'

'She's got a point there, you know!' agreed Morgan who, despite all the pushing and shoving, had managed to hang on to his hip flask. He tipped it up with his visible arm and took a reassuring swig.

I'm shut up in a madhouse, thought Miff. There's a lunatic outside, armed and determined. Sam, two Garleys and a half-drunk potter in here, and only Sam seems to have any grip on what's going on!

Footsteps, crunching on the gravel, were audible outside. They seemed to be moving away from the front of the cottage.

'He's going round the back,' opined Danny.

'You did lock the back door?'

'Course I did! But he's only got to break the kitchen window and climb in, hasn't he?'

'I ran out of sausage rolls completely.' Glenys was in her own world and determined to stay there. Miff couldn't blame her. 'Both the Victoria sponges sold. All I've got left now are some sandwiches and fairy cakes.'

'Well done, Glenys!' said Sam's voice, playing along. Good girl, Sam! Got your wits about you!

'Oh, well,' continued Glenys, 'you and Miff can have the sandwiches for your supper, when that fellow out there has gone.'

The problem with 'that fellow out there' was that he was going nowhere right now and, quite probably, would soon find his way inside the cottage and join the rest of them.

Danny, despite Miff's instructions to the contrary, was on the move. He crawled from the hall refuge into the office and across the floor to the window, raising his head to peer out.

'Get back here, Danny!' ordered Miff. 'He'll blow your brains out!'

'Nah, he's gone round the back, like I said,' called Danny. 'Can't see him, anyway.'

Nevertheless, Danny crawled back to the hallway and, just as he reached Miff, they heard an explosion of breaking glass from the rear of the cottage. A bumping and rattling followed it. There was a crash of breaking crockery, and the sound of something heavy landing on the ground.

He's climbed in through the kitchen window, above the sink, and knocked the mugs off the draining board, thought Miff. Just as Danny said he would.

In the hall, they sat in silence, hardly breathing, and watched the rear of the passageway where it terminated in the door to the kitchen. The door handle moved, agonisingly slowly, and the door itself creaked open.

The gunman stood there, weapon in hand, and surveyed Miff, Danny and Morgan, who had given up trying to squeeze into the stair cupboard and had emerged into the hall, closing the cupboard door gently but firmly behind him, so that the two women were out of sight.

'Three of you, eh?' observed the gunman. 'I somehow thought there might be more.'

'Just us, mate,' said Danny.

To give the lie to his words, something fell down inside the stair cupboard.

'Oh, dear,' said the gunman. 'I think you've overlooked

someone. Open the door.' He gestured towards the stair cupboard with the barrel of the revolver.

Morgan scowled at him, but reluctantly opened the stair cupboard door.

'Come on out and join us!' invited the gunman.

There was a brief silence and then the sound of scrambling. First Sam, and then Glenys, emerged. They stood side by side, both red-faced and dishevelled.

'Who's he?' hissed Glenys, but no one answered.

'Now, isn't this nice?' observed the gunman. 'All together, nice little party. Right, into that room there, behind you.' He gestured with the gun towards the office. 'All except you, chum.' That meant Miff.

The others started to shuffle reluctantly into the office, but at that moment, there came the sound of a large number of vehicles approaching at speed. They screeched to a halt before the garden centre and there was much confused noise: running feet, shouted instructions.

Danny, who was already in the office and could see through the window what was happening, called out, 'It's really great! Just like the telly! There are armed officers out there, with bulletproof vests, guns, loudhailer and everything! Wow!'

Now even his Auntie Glenys ordered, 'Do come away from that window, Danny! Haven't you got any sense?'

The gunman was scowling. 'Nobody move!' he ordered. 'All of you, down on the floor! No, wait, not you, darling!'

To Miff's horror, the gunman reached into the office and grabbed Sam's arm. 'I need you!'

'Let go of her!' shouted Miff.

'Shut up!' he was told. 'Stay down there on the floor.'

They all waited in a tortured silence. Then, from outside, a voice echoed through the loudhailer.

'Ben Paget! We know you're in there and we know you're armed. Throw out your weapon and come out with your hands raised!'

So, thought Miff, that's his name: Ben Paget. Odd, somehow, to be learning his name at this late stage of their acquaintance.

Paget glanced his way. 'Had time to call them, did you? Told them I had a gun?'

'Yes,' croaked Miff from the carpet. Dust had entered his throat and he was unable to control an outbreak of coughing. When it stopped he found, to his mortification, that tears were running down his face.

'Right! Then this is what we're going to do.' Paget pulled Sam in front of him, raised the revolver and rested it gently at the side of her head. 'You lot are going to freeze, right where you are. You . . .' He glanced down at Miff. 'Don't try any heroics because if this gun goes off, you'll be scraping her brains off the walls.'

'What are you going to do?' Miff snarled up at him, still spluttering.

'I'm going out, just like they want. Only I'm taking her with me, in front of me. She's my hostage? My shield. Get it?'

'How far do you think you'll get?'

'As far as my car, or the nearest car, and then – she's coming with me.'

'You're nuts! You can't get away with that! They—' Miff said no more because Paget kicked him in the face. Pain shot through Miff's jaw and blood filled his mouth, together with something small and hard. One of his teeth had come out.

'Miff!' cried Sam. Still in Paget's grip, she could only berate him. 'You horrible man! You've hurt Miff!'

'Watch it, darling! No sudden moves, right? Off we go. Move! When we get to the door, you unlock it and we go outside, you in front of me. Don't get any silly ideas, because the slightest vibration could make this gun go off, right?'

Miff spat out his tooth and watched in horror as Paget propelled Sam ahead of him to the front door. He heard her fumbling with the lock, then watched helplessly as she pulled the door open.

'We're coming out!' shouted Paget to the team outside. 'I've got the girl in front of me, so don't fancy yourself as marksmen! You'll hit her! I've got my gun resting against her skull!' In a lower tone, he ordered Sam, 'Get going!'

Outside, someone shouted through the loudhailer, 'Don't be stupid, Paget! Let the girl go! You can't get away!'

'Watch me!' Paget shouted back.

No, he can't get away, thought Miff, through his pain. But he's going to try it, even so. He's crazy. He's killed twice and he's not bothered if Sam gets hit. He'll try it, and Sam will get hit . . .

But he couldn't do anything to prevent Paget. If he tackled him from behind, he couldn't move fast enough to get to him before Paget fired. If, against all the odds, he did get to him, Paget would still fire – he'd shoot Sam, or he'd shoot Miff himself – and Miff couldn't trust the marksmen out there to be sharp enough to take out Paget before that happened.

Paget, with Sam held before him, was outside the cottage now. Miff tried desperately to think of something but his brain might just as well have been set in cement.

Then, against the odds, something did happen.

Sam threw up. She did it neatly and copiously, just as she had when she'd seen the rat. The smell of vomit filled the air – and the ground, together with Paget's shoes and trouser legs, was liberally spattered.

Paget exclaimed, 'What the hell?' For a bare moment he reacted instinctively, pushing her away from him a little. Only for a moment, but it was enough. Two shots rang out. In a moment of despair, Miff thought Paget had shot Sam. But in pushing her aside, the revolver had moved off the target, Sam's temple, and Paget's shot went into the air. The second shot, following immediately on the first, came from a police marksman. Paget released Sam and staggered to one side, gripping his shoulder. He dropped his revolver and it went skidding across the ground.

And then it was all over. Miff was outside, with Sam clinging to him. Officers were leading Paget away, and Glenys was running towards the coffee shop, despite shouted orders to stay where she was.

'She's not armed!' yelled Miff, still spitting blood. 'She's only worried about the till!'

Danny emerged and stood beside him. 'That was great!' he said happily.

Miff looked down at Sam. 'Can you do that at will?'

'W-what?'

'Chuck up, like that.'

Sam shook her head. 'I do it when I'm frightened. I always have. I did it when I was a little kid. Still do.' She gazed at him in concern. 'Your face is covered in blood.'

'Well, the mad sod kicked out one of my teeth, didn't he?' Miff found it harder to speak than earlier. He realised his lips and the surrounding flesh were swelling and beginning to throb. He would have pointed out that Sam's own face was smeared with sick. But that would be both churlish and painful, so he didn't.

A man in a suit, but wearing a bulletproof vest, appeared in front of them. He was in his late forties, with greying hair and hazel eyes. He studied Miff for a moment and then asked politely, 'Matthew Ferguson?'

'Yesh . . .' mumbled Miff.

'I'm Superintendent Carter. Anyone hurt? Other than that injury to your mouth.'

'No – no, we're all okay. They won't shoot Glenysh, will they? She runsh the coffee shop, you shee, and she had to leave the till unlocked . . .' Oh, damn, he sounded drunker than Morgan Jay probably was, yet he, Miff, was sober. But his lips wouldn't move in the way he wanted them to.

'No one else is going to get shot,' said Carter. 'The only gunshot wound was sustained by the man under arrest. And he'll survive. You're the only civilian casualty.'

'He kicked Miff in the mouth!' said Sam, still furious. 'And he wanted to shoot him! He would have shot us all!'

'Fortunately, that didn't happen,' Carter soothed her. He turned back to Miff. 'Do you mind telling me, why was Paget after you?'

'I shaw him dishposhing of a body, in Bamford. I wash living rough at the time . . .' Pause to spit more blood. 'Oh, and he told me he killed that other one, the body in the van. Or he hit him over the head, put him in the van and set fire to it . . . shame thing.' Another gobbet of blood.

'Yes,' agreed Carter. 'Same thing.'

'He's a murderer!' stormed Sam.

'We have him under arrest, Miss French. I know you've had a pretty dramatic time, but let the law take care of things from now on. You will both have to testify in court, particularly you, Mr Ferguson. Until then, we'd appreciate it if you don't give interviews to the press. This has the makings of a lurid case, and they'll love it. So, just keep shtum, right?'

'Miff won't be able to talk, will he?' snapped Sam. 'Not for ages! Look at him!'

Morgan and Danny, who was still glowing with excitement, had joined them. Morgan peered at Miff's swelling jaw. 'Caught you a real good one there, boyo!'

Carter studied Miff and then Sam. 'Come on,' he said, 'we'll get both of you cleaned up!'

Chapter 18

The police took Miff to A&E, where they sent him along to X-ray to find out if his jaw was broken. It wasn't; he'd just lost a tooth.

'Looks worse than it is!' said the young doctor cheerfully. 'I had the same thing happen to me in a rugby match!'

Miff thought resentfully, I bet the guy who kicked you in the teeth wasn't also holding a revolver and planning to shoot you dead!

He didn't say this aloud, largely because his lips and the surrounding flesh of his face had now completely swollen up. He looked grotesque. The mirror had shown him a Halloween pumpkin of a phizog. He just couldn't speak. His lips wouldn't form sounds. His jaw and upper lip promised to develop some rainbow shades of bruises.

'Urrgh . . .' he mumbled.

'Cheer up, old chap,' said the rugger-hearty in a white coat. 'Be better in a week. You should see a dentist, though.'

A week? *Urrgh . . .*

'You'll have to eat liquidised food. Or you might try those diet mixes, everything you need stirred into a glass of milk.'

Grrgh . . . You know what you can do . . .

'Come along, Miff,' said Sam firmly, taking his arm. 'The doctor's busy. The waiting room is full. Thank you very much!' (This last bit to the medical man.)

The senior cop, Carter, then kindly informed Miff they needed a statement but it need not be that evening. Miff could either come to them the following morning, or they'd come to him.

Miff now had the opportunity to ask a question that had been worrying him. His injury meant that he had to make three attempts to ask it before Carter understood him.

'How did the officer who took your call know who Paget was, when you told him the gunman was a police officer?' Carter asked.

Gurgle, grunt, furious nodding on Miff's part.

'We found a witness, someone who had evidence Paget was a killer. The witness had left the location of Paget's previous crime and moved to work at a retirement home in this area, where she eventually told someone here about it. I think you know a woman called Mrs Porter?'

'It's not her, is it?' interrupted Sam, who was present at the exchange, hovering over Miff like a minder. 'Not Jenny Porter, she's not your witness?'

'No, but the witness admitted the facts to her. Mrs Porter then persuaded the witness to make a police statement.'

Sam considered this and appeared to file the information away for future action. Then she said firmly that they had a garden centre to tidy up, and the police were welcome to come and take a statement there. Right now, they needed to get home. The Blackwoods were waiting to drive them.

Miff had been given and had – gratefully – taken painkillers. He was starting to feel muzzy. He wondered how Henry and Prue had got there. But, in his confusion, he was forgetting how quickly word spread in Weston St Ambrose. It later transpired that Glenys had phoned her husband, Bert, who had phoned Debbie at the supermarket, as she was well positioned to spread the word. Debbie had then sent one of the younger Garleys to tell Henry and Prue. So, sure enough, when they left A&E, Henry and Prue fell upon him and Sam, and they were borne away with Prue fussing and Henry patting him on the shoulder and saying, 'Well done, my boy!' They wanted him to come back to their home to be cared for, but Sam was having none of that, so they were delivered to the garden centre.

There was another surprise on arrival at Minglebury, as the open plant area of the centre appeared to be full of bikers. Danny had also been busy sending out word of what had happened and was now conducting a guided tour for his mates.

Sam dealt with them in short order.

The following morning, as arranged, more visitors in the form of the police turned up. Miff was less muzzy now, and so found himself in the office with Sam and a red-haired woman inspector called Campbell, together with a sergeant called Nugent. The latter gazed around Sam's office, with its elderly computer, outdated general fixtures and fittings, and the row of pottery gnomes, in disbelief. You should have seen it before I sorted it all out, mate! Miff thought. Unfortunately, after a miserable sleepless night, and a breakfast drunk through a straw, he still couldn't speak a word. So they asked him to write it all out, in their presence, sign and date it.

How much do you want to know? Miff scrawled on a sheet of paper.

'All of it,' the redhead, Inspector Campbell, told him. 'From the very beginning, please. Tell us how you first encountered

278

Sergeant Paget, where, and why you left Bamford to come to Weston St Ambrose. Then how and where you met Paget again and what followed.'

So Miff switched on the computer and began, while they sat and watched him. He was still rattling the keys nearly an hour later, the script rolling steadily up the screen, and the printed version promising to cover several pages. He told them how he'd been living rough, and how that came about. Explained how and why he had been seeking a possible refuge for winter ahead. He explained how he chose to examine the disused warehouse, had obtained entry, stressing that he had not technically broken in, and found an unknown man already there, standing over what later proved to be a dead body. He described the chase through the back gardens, not forgetting the broken statue. He even explained his visit to the barber.

The more Miff wrote, the more he found he got into the swing of it. The words flowed. He'd got the hang of this writing lark. Sam fetched coffee from Glenys's coffee shop for herself and the officers. But not for Miff, for whom she brought a bottle of chocolate milk and a fresh straw. Miff wrote steadily on, pounding the keys with enthusiasm. Inspector Campbell watched him, fascinated, as did Sam. She had earlier made a separate statement to Sergeant Nugent. In her statement she described emotionally how Paget had kicked poor Miff in the mouth in a cowardly and unprovoked attack. She also described how she'd thrown up, and explained how this had been a nervous response since childhood. Nugent kept well clear of her, as he listened.

Back at the office, as Miff printed off each sheet, he handed it to Jess Campbell, who read it through. By the time he'd eventually finished, Campbell was holding what looked like the first draft of a novel. She asked him to elaborate on a couple of points, and Miff happily did so, adding to the pile of script in some cases, and scribbling a few words here and there, in pen, on the printout. Eventually the police officers seemed satisfied, so Miff signed it all off and dated it. The cops went off looking reasonably happy. Mind you, one could never tell with the police, thought Miff. They always played their cards close to the chest. He hoped they weren't going to charge him with anything, like, well, withholding information, back in Bamford. But staying alive had occupied his mind solely then.

While he'd been engaged on his masterpiece of total recall, Sergeant Nugent had set off to interview everyone else he could find who had been present during the siege of the cottage. Glenys Garley fed him cake and told him proudly how she had defended her till. Danny, though wary of all police officers on principle, related how he had heroically rescued Miff who was being held at gunpoint by 'that nutcase of a pig, I mean, a copper'.

Nugent, who normally would have objected to any police officer being so described, especially by a tearaway like the biker here, accepted the description of his erstwhile colleague without batting an eyelid. He, Nugent, had always suspected there was something fishy about Paget. 'Instinct!' he told his wife later that evening. 'I knew he was a wrong 'un!'

The only interview that could not be completed on the day was with one of the hostages, Morgan Jay. Nugent went to his cottage and found the potter 'drunk as a skunk!' So Morgan's contribution to the saga of the siege of the cottage had to wait.

* * *

Miff and Sam were alone at last at the garden centre, having waved off the visiting police officers. The sun was setting.

'Gosh, what an awful mess,' lamented Sam, looking around them. 'The police knocked over that whole table of plants. Then Danny's friends trampled on them. Most of them are damaged beyond rescue.'

Miff grunted and pointed at the cottage. So they went back indoors and into the office, where they began, between them, to tidy up in half-hearted fashion. Sam was by the desk where Miff had sat to write his statement. She picked up a pen, stared at it thoughtfully, then sat down, pulled a notepad towards her and wrote something on it. Miff came over to see what it was.

I suppose, wrote Sam, *that now Paget is under arrest and no one is looking for you, you'll be moving on again?*

Miff took the pen and wrote underneath: *I'll have to wait until the police say I can go. They'll want to be able to find me. They've warned me that, eventually, I'll have to testify at the trial. That won't be for quite a while. I need a permanent address. Anyway, I've got the talk to the writers' circle, and the Christmas Fayre to organise.*

'Thanks,' said Sam, aloud, but without enthusiasm.

Miff picked up the pen again and wrote another line. He handed her the sheet of paper.

Anyway, I like it here. With you.

Trevor Barker and Emma Johnson, informed of events, drove down the following day and were now sitting in Carter's office, with Jess Campbell. Ian and Jess watched as Barker read Miff's statement slowly, twice, before handing it to his sergeant. Emma settled back to read it herself, with a smile, as though she'd been handed a novel. Her boss had made a similar judgement, but he wasn't smiling.

'This chap, Ferguson,' said Trevor Barker, his voice and face marked by deep suspicion. 'He's a writer, I understand. A fantasy merchant, in other words.'

'Well,' Jess told him, 'he belongs to a writers' circle in the village, or his uncle and aunt do. He told them he came to Weston St Ambrose from Bamford to write a book. We now know, from that statement, that he came to avoid Paget, whom he'd surprised disposing of Amber Button's body in the warehouse.'

'Only, I've read some statements,' continued Barker, 'but this one rivals a novel by one of those nineteenth-century authors who churned it all out by the metre. There are pages and pages of it.'

'I understand,' said Carter, 'that Matthew Ferguson really is planning to write a book. It's not just something he told the family. Oh, not about all this!' he added hastily. 'His book is to be about homelessness. He's going to talk about it to the writers' circle in Weston St Ambrose, in a couple of weeks' time. If he's fit, presumably.'

Barker was still staring bemusedly at Miff's statement. 'Don't reckon he'll have any trouble writing his book,' he said. 'Ruddy thing will probably rival *War and Peace*.' He scowled. 'Look here, how much of this can we believe? Will it stand up in court? The guy's a writer. He makes things up. It's what they do, writers. It's what Paget's defence will claim, anyway.'

'Events do support what Ferguson says,' Carter pointed out. 'And Paget won't be able to claim he wasn't at the garden centre holding hostages and threatening to shoot at least one of them.'

Emma ventured to say: 'It's just a pity we didn't know all about this earlier, about the warehouse and Ferguson being chased by Paget, even if he didn't know at the time it was Paget.'

'It's more than a pity, it's outrageous!' exploded Barker. 'All Ferguson had to do, what he *should* have done after he escaped Paget's pursuit in Bamford, was come straight to us and report what he'd seen. If he'd done that, we might have got to Paget earlier. Gary Button would still be alive. He wouldn't have made a mass of work for two police forces. Matthew Ferguson has a lot of questions to answer! When he can speak again properly, I want a long chat with him!' He shook the statement. 'Never mind this! He's still got a lot to explain!'

'He was afraid the man he'd seen at the warehouse would find him,' offered Jess in mitigation for Miff's flight.

'All the more reason to go to the police immediately!'

'He had been living rough on the streets for almost two years. He now says you wouldn't have believed him.'

'We would have checked it out!' said Barker huffily. 'If we'd gone to the warehouse that day, we'd have found Amber's body hardly cold. We could probably have been able to trace the scene of the crime back to Mrs Clack's house. She might not have had a chance to clean up the place, and the Buttons would not have removed all Amber's belongings. There might have been something in them that would have given us a hint. Myrtle Clack will be charged with aiding and abetting. She's denying it furiously, of course. But we could have got her, there and then. We'd have been able to speak to Eva Florescu before she took off and did her own disappearing trick. Eva knew Amber's boyfriend was a police officer. She actually heard the murder as it took place, through the party wall. Did she come to us? No, she scarpered, too!'

He was silent for a few minutes and no one disturbed his thoughts. At last, Barker said in a low, angry voice, 'I hate it when a police officer goes wrong! It touches us all!'

Carter said quietly, 'We all hate it.'

'We'll have to talk to Ferguson ourselves, when he's able to speak,' said Carter to Jess, when the visitors had left and were on their way back to Bamford. 'There are points I'd like him to expand on. I can understand how rattled Trevor is about it all.'

'Ferguson will be able to speak well enough in a few days' time, so the doctors have told him,' Jess said. 'And his girlfriend, Sam French, is taking good care of him.'

'He could have got that girl killed!' said Carter fiercely.

'Together with several members of the Garley family!' Jess pointed out, with a smile. 'And that crazy potter. I noticed some pottery gnomes stored in the office. Sam told me they were gnomes. I wasn't sure. They've got minimal clothing – and it doesn't leave much to the imagination. Apparently, they're all to be painted and sold at a Christmas Fayre they're planning.'

'I thought gnomes had pointed hats and fishing rods or garden tools,' said Carter.

'Sam told me the potter, Morgan Jay, makes a more authentic, earlier type of gnome. More . . . pagan.' She added, 'You know that Ferguson is giving a talk the week after next to the Weston St Ambrose writers' circle?'

'Yes, but he's not going to tell them all about him and Paget, is he?' Carter growled. 'He can't! That matter is still subject to our enquiries!'

'No, no,' Jess soothed him. 'He does understand that. I've had a word with him about it. He's going to talk about the book he's planning – about homelessness. He'd written all the notes for his talk before Paget got him cornered in that cottage at the garden centre.'

'I still don't like it,' growled Carter. He was struck by a thought. 'We don't have to go along and listen to him, do we? Perhaps one of us should, in case he goes off script?'

'Honestly, it will be all right. He showed me his notes, for his speech. If that's what you'd call it. There's absolutely nothing about Paget or Amber Button's murder or what happened at the garden centre.'

'He might be asked questions about it, all the same, after his literary performance!' warned Carter. 'It's had press coverage. It's got to be a more interesting subject than this book of his, for the locals, I mean. It all happened right here, in their community.'

'We discussed that. I told him, he mustn't take any questions about the siege. He's a pretty clued-up sort of person. He isn't stupid. Before he took to living rough, he held down a highly responsible job. He seems to have had some kind of personal crisis and simply walked away.'

'I suspect,' Carter retorted, 'that walking away from situations he doesn't like is his speciality.' He heaved a sigh. 'We'll just have to keep an eye on him and make sure he doesn't disappear before Paget comes to trial – and that could be a while.'

There was a pause, during which the distant sound of cheery whistling could be heard.

'Someone is happy, anyway,' said Carter.

'It's Nugent,' Jess told him. 'He's cheered up considerably since Paget's arrest.'

'I thought he looked a lot happier when I saw him earlier,' Carter agreed. 'It's an ill wind, and so on. They would probably never have worked well together. I understand Paget has claimed that Amber Button attacked him first, and he reacted initially to defend himself.'

'Pity he trussed up Gary Button and incinerated him in his van, then,' Jess replied. 'He'll have a job to plead self-defence to that! But perhaps she did attack him. She was a woman scorned.'

There was an awkward silence, then Jess continued quietly, 'I don't consider myself scorned, in case you're wondering. Mike and I have talked it through and agreed, we want to go our different ways. It doesn't mean we can't stay good friends.'

It does, and you won't! thought Carter. Aloud, and before he could stop himself, he heard his voice asking, 'Do you love him?' Hastily, he added, 'Not that I've any right to put such a personal question!'

'Ask away. No, no, I don't. Not in the way you mean, or I think you mean. I like him a lot. I admire him. I respect him and what he wants to do. He's my brother Simon's friend. Simon wanted me to keep an eye on him, while he was convalescing, and I have done. So, the answer to your question is that, yes, there was a moment when I thought I might be falling in love with him. But I've come to my senses and I haven't. He probably feels much the same way about me. If anything, he's in love with his medical work. It's his life. No room for personal relationships.' Jess gave a wry smile.

'Bit like police work, then,' said Carter drily, 'although not for everyone, of course. Plenty of police officers are happily married with families. But a lot of police marriages also hit the rocks, like mine.'

'You haven't changed your mind about going to France, then?'

'No. No chance. Millie will be disappointed but she'll understand, I hope. I'm still planning on explaining it to her when I go and visit her this weekend.' Carter hesitated. 'You, er, you wouldn't care to come with me, to see Millie? I quite understand, if you don't.'

Jess considered it, and smiled. 'Yes, it would be nice to see Millie. I'll be pleased to come with you. I'd like to see how Millie is turning out.'

'Oh,' Carter made a wry face. 'As to that, she's turning out very much like her mother.' He glanced at Jess. 'It would do her good to talk to you!'

He wanted to add that it would be good just to have Jess come along with him. But the time wasn't right for that yet.

Chapter 19

'The thing about our Amber,' said Harmony with a sigh, 'was that she was always selfish. She never wanted to share her toys when she was a kid. When we got older, us sisters, Maria and I, would borrow one another's clothes. But Amber never would lend you anything; and if one of us borrowed without asking, she'd hit the roof. Hit us, too, whoever took the shirt, or whatever it was. And we didn't have a lot, you know. So it would have been nice if she'd been more willing to share a bit. But not Amber!'

She was seated at the Markby kitchen table again, in her regular seat. She had not rung the doorbell or knocked. She'd just marched round to the back of the house, in through the kitchen door, and taken her habitual place.

'Amber was possessive?' suggested Meredith. So was Harmony, she thought, in her own way. She'd got a good grip on all her family – and now, it seemed, she'd got a grip on her and Alan.

'Yeah, that's the word. It was the same with her and Gary when they were little. They were near in age and they played together all the time. They got up to all sorts of tricks. But, even then, I remember she never wanted Gary to play with any other kids. Of course, when they got older, Gary wanted to hang out with the lads. Play football . . .'

Harmony hesitated and cast Markby an unusually apprehensive

288

look. 'You'll know about the hooliganism at football matches and that business of duffing up visiting supporters?'

'Oh, yes,' said Alan. 'I do remember. Gary was a real tearaway and pretty violent, as I recall.'

'He wasn't really!' Harmony defended her brother's memory. 'He was just trying to prove himself, like young men do. Wanted to be thought tough. Actually, he wasn't – tough, I mean. He was a pushover.'

Markby thought, try telling that to Gary's bruised and bleeding victims.

'He did a spell in a young offenders' institution, didn't he?'

'Best thing that could've happened,' said Harmony. 'They taught him a bit of carpentry and he got interested in making furniture. Then, after he came out, he met Katie and she calmed him down. Then he got into the antiques business. He did really well.'

Well, that all made sense, thought Meredith. Katie would calm anyone down because she never contributed anything to a conversation, much less to any discussion. You couldn't argue with her. Aloud, she asked, 'What will Katie do now?'

Harmony brightened. 'She's had an offer for the business, and the house with it. Declan is handling that. He's good at doing deals. Katie will have plenty of money. She'll buy a house nearer the family. Declan will see to all that, as well. Somewhere near the kids' school would be best. We'll all keep an eye on her, help out. She's a bit lost without Gary, but she'll be all right with the family round. We Buttons look after our own.'

There was a pause during which Harmony finished her cup of tea and absent-mindedly helped herself to the last chocolate biscuit. 'Of course,' she continued, 'Amber couldn't accept Gary getting married.' Harmony bit off half the biscuit and chewed it thoughtfully. After swallowing, she went on, 'Being possessive, like you said, Meredith.' She waved the uneaten half of the biscuit in the air. 'She knew she couldn't interfere with Gary having mates, hanging out with the lads. But another woman, oh, no!'

'So,' Meredith ventured to ask, 'you believe it's true that Amber tried to poison Katie?'

'Oh, heard about that, did you?' Harmony raised her eyebrows, displaying a large area of mauve eye shadow. 'Sort of thing she'd do.' She leaned forward confidentially. 'She'd got no common sense, Amber. I told you that before. I mean, taking up with a police officer, a CID bloke, at that.' Harmony gave a snort of disgust. 'She kept that pretty quiet from all of us. And as for thinking she could hold on to him! I'm not surprised she went crazy when he told her he was leaving town, and her.' She contemplated the remains of the biscuit. 'I'm not excusing his killing her, mind you. They can lock him up and throw away the key, as far as we're all concerned. We had to tell Dad all the details.'

'How did Harry take it?' asked Markby.

'Very upset,' said Harmony. 'He said you never could trust a copper. No offence, Mr Markby.'

'None taken,' said Markby politely. 'And the law will throw the book at Paget. He'll have a bad time in stir, too.'

'Yes,' said Harmony simply. 'Michael is already passing the word around the other cons; and they're passing it on to mates they've got in other gaols. They'll all be waiting for him.'

She brightened. 'But we've had a nice headstone made for Amber, with her photograph on it. It's in the churchyard here, right at the back. You can walk down and take a look at it. Anyway, the headstone made Dad feel a bit better. He reckons, everyone makes mistakes; we all do something daft at some point in our lives. Some people get away with it. But Amber paid for her bad decisions. So, Dad's sure she's resting in peace.' She put the last scrap of biscuit into her mouth. 'Not so sure about that, myself!' she said indistinctly.

Epilogue

'Look at that!' said Glenys Garley to her husband, Bert. 'Call that nibbles? It's just nuts and green stuff in a bowl. It looks like pease pudding, but someone said it was called gwaky-something. I don't go for foreign food. That's a funny-looking cheese. I suppose that's what it is, that round flat thing. It's got white mould all over it! And what's that great big lump of bread?'

Glenys intended this to be a whisper but it was perfectly audible to anyone nearby. Bert agreed, making no attempt to whisper. 'Use that as a building block, I reckon!'

Peter Posset, realising his prized home-made bread was coming in for criticism, turned puce and considered requesting the critical couple to leave his house immediately. But, on the other hand, they'd never had such a large gathering for one of the writers' circle meetings. And village people, too! The real natives, not incomers like himself or the Blackwoods! It just went to show that a thirst for literature could be inspired in anyone, if you just went about it in the right way. He didn't doubt that, in due course, they would come to appreciate guacamole and his home-made bread. Patience, that was all that was needed.

Glenys hadn't finished. 'They should have asked me, Bert! I'd have made them some proper food. You know, some of my rocky road cakes. They would have been just the thing, and cheese scones.'

'I reckon,' said Bert.

The room was certainly crammed full. Sadly, it was not entirely a desire to know more about creative writing that had brought everyone. Peter Posset was kidding himself. The truth was that, following the siege of Minglebury Garden Centre – as the local paper had called the event – Miff and Sam were now celebrities. Well, the nearest thing to local celebrities that Weston St Ambrose had ever boasted among its residents. So, of course, everyone had turned out, with two exceptions. One was Morgan Jay, who had promised he'd come but failed to appear, and was presumed to be too 'squiffy'. The other absentee was Danny Garley. Danny had confided to Sam that he'd taken the opportunity to read some of Miff's on-screen notes while Miff was out of the office. 'Couldn't understand any of it,' said Danny.

'Tell you what, Bert!' declared Glenys now. 'The supermarket's not closed yet, got another five minutes to go. I'll call our Debbie and ask her to come over when it shuts up, and bring some bits and pieces, like some Swiss rolls. Them miniature pork pies, too, if they've got any left.'

Miff, trapped at one end of the room, the furthest from the door, with only Sam between himself and what seemed to be an ever increasing mob, fought back panic. They all looked at him so expectantly. They whispered to one another in clear excitement. Somehow, he was supposed to live up to all this. He was supposed to stand there and deliver his talk – his talk! He felt physically sick. What if they didn't like what he had to say? Would they turn on him?

Sam squeezed his hand encouragingly. 'Great support, Miff! Isn't it exciting?'

'No!' he muttered. 'It's terrifying. I should never have let myself in for this!'

'Don't be silly!' retorted Sam sternly. 'There's no need for stage fright! You know nearly everyone here!'

'That's makes it worse. Strangers would be okay. Then, if the talk is a disaster, they'd go home and I'd never see them again. But this lot, I'll be running into them every day!' He paused and added in a tone of wonder, 'I tell you, Sam, it's just like my old school Speech Day.'

And so it was. In the front row, standing in for his absent parents, were Uncle Henry and Auntie Prue, beaming with pride. Next to them sat Mrs Porter, giving him nods of encouragement whenever she caught his eye, just like his old headmaster. Next to her sat an elderly woman he'd never met before, but who had been introduced to him as Mrs Porter's old chum, Elspeth, from the Meadowlea Manor retirement home. She wasn't the only visiting resident of the home. Accompanied by their manager, Mrs Collins, they'd come en masse, in a specially hired minibus; all dressed up to the nines and chattering merrily like a lot of sparrows. There were Glenys and Bert; the latter crammed into a well-worn and old-fashioned suit, probably brought out for weddings and funerals. He had the look of a man who'd been coerced. Extra chairs had been brought in from neighbouring homes but all seats were taken. Now it was standing room only and, just when it seemed another person couldn't be squeezed in, Debbie Garley arrived, panting, with two plastic bags full of supermarket goodies. These she proceeded to unload on to Peter's dining table, swamping his guacamole, nuts and crisps with pork pies, sausage rolls and Mr Kipling cakes.

'That's a bit better!' said Glenys. 'Though not as good as my rocky road cakes would've been. It's a real shame.'

Even Peter Posset was forced to express gratitude because, he had to admit, his nibbles, bread and Brie wouldn't have been nearly enough. He hadn't realised he'd be feeding the five thousand.

'That's okay!' Debbie told him cheerily. 'I brought the bill. Here you are!' and she handed him a till receipt.

'Oh, well, yes . . .' gasped Peter, hoping the other regular members of the writers' circle would chip in.

Debbie had divested herself of her working overall and was revealed to be wearing a jumpsuit patterned all over, head to toe, with bright scarlet flowers.

'Hibiscus!' whispered Sam knowledgeably.

'You do realise,' Miff whispered back, 'that if she and those Garley kids paint Morgan's gnomes, they'll decorate them all over in outfits like that!'

'Be all right for Christmas,' returned Sam, her confidence unshaken.

Everyone was now provided with a picnic paper plate laden with food. Wine, red or white, had been donated by the Blackwoods because, after all, this was Matthew's special evening. The audience had begun to settle down. Even the Meadowlea brigade had fallen silent. All eyes were turned to the end of the room, where Miff stood, clutching his notes in perspiring fingers, with Peter Posset alongside him, holding the notes of his speech introducing their speaker for the evening. An expectant silence fell.

'A very warm welcome to you all!' boomed Peter. 'It is a very great pleasure to see so many familiar faces from our village, and our visitors, too!' He made a bow in the direction of the Meadowlea attendees, who beamed and blushed. 'We have a very special speaker this evening . . .'

He burbled on, but that was fine, in Miff's view, because as long as old Posset spoke, he, Miff, didn't have to start. But Peter had finished. Everyone was looking expectantly at Miff. Sam beamed. Mrs Porter's head was going like one of those nodding dogs. Henry and Prue were still smiling. Debbie Garley was taking photos on her phone. Miff had a foreboding that after the event, whether it went well or not, Debbie would swoop on him and demand he pose with her for a selfie. Sam prodded him in the ribs. Miff drew a deep breath.

'Good evening, everyone. It is very kind of you to invite me to talk to you tonight about my book . . .'